A Cold Morning

in MAINE

A Cold Morning in MAINE

Terry Boone

ISBN 978-0-9962397-0-7

Second printing: March 2015
10 9 8 7 6 5 4 3 2

Published by
THREE RIVERS GROUP

Cover photo by the author.

A Cold Morning in MAINE

Published by **THREE RIVERS GROUP**

Contact: threeriversgroupvt@gmail.com

For Margie, Rosalie, Linda and Randy.

And a long, long list of so many others who were gone far too soon.

One

It was a very cold Saturday morning in western Maine. Bright sun and mostly blue sky two days after Thanksgiving. I was out for a quick drive to charge up my cell phone and take in the rural landscape with a fresh cover of snow.

Sipping coffee while driving, I laughed at what a woman had said when I stopped at a country store 3 miles back. The coffee was self-serve and there was a glass tray with homemade muffins, scones, and pastries. I commented that it was a beautiful morning.

"We're in for a serious intercourse spell," she observed, as I paid for the coffee, a cranberry muffin and a copy of the *Portland Press Herald.*

"Sorry. How's that?" I said, uncertain of her meaning.

She handed me change for the 10 I gave her and leaned across the counter closer to me. Looking back at the young boy stocking the cooler twenty feet away, she lowered her voice.

"It's going to be really fucking cold this winter. Nine degrees at my house this morning! It's only November." She hugged herself and shivered.

Walking back to the car, I imagined that it was a might colder up near Presque Isle or Fort Kent along the Canadian border.

Ten minutes later, driving through the village center of Waterford, I nearly went off the road craning my neck. I saw a clump at the edge of the lake. The clump looked like a person – and it wasn't moving.

No cars behind me, I braked, drove on a short distance and pulled in front of a large white building that appeared to be an old church. A sign above the door told me this was The Waterford Historical Society.

Turning in a wide arc, I headed back in the direction I had just driven. The compass reading indicated NE with 7:46AM - 18°F glowing on the digital display of the dashboard. I pressed the button for my emergency flashers, slowed and pulled off the pavement.

There was no other traffic coming either way. Leaving the warm comfort of the car, I took another swallow of the coffee, put the cup back in the center console holder, zipped my sweater to the neck, and walked across the road toward the lake.

I was pretty sure I was looking at a body just over the bank. A skim of ice had formed across most of the water's surface.

Half on the rocky edge of the embankment and partially in the water, a dark blue, almost black coat covered the clump now in front of me. Not very large, it appeared to have been face down, arms under the torso. But the body was missing a head.

Legs extending from beneath the coat, both feet missing. Getting closer without actually stepping into the water, I saw no signs of fresh blood and no apparent footprints in the snow, on the bank or near the guardrail.

I stopped myself from turning the body over or dragging it clear of the water. This close, I was now certain there was no head. Bending at the waist to get a better look, I was just as certain there were no feet.

Glancing toward the village as I went back to the car, I saw a person running farther up the road, some 200 yards beyond the parking area of the Historical Society.

Two

My phone was now fully charged. Still no other cars anywhere in sight. Emergency flashers on, I backed onto the highway, slowly continuing in reverse until I could turn the car and again drive toward the village. The person I saw running was now out of sight. And my phone was still out of range, no bars showing.

No stores or businesses anywhere to be seen. No roadside pay phone. Nothing but a few houses on both sides of the road; a small triangle-shaped town common at the center of the village. Smoke rose from a chimney three houses ahead on the right.

Pulling into the driveway behind an old green Ford pickup truck full of firewood, engine running, I could see two people standing inside a door off the porch. The door opened as I got closer to the house, and a short, older man came out. He stopped when he saw me.

"Good morning," I said. "Could I use your phone?"

The man stared at me for a couple of seconds, looked at my car blocking him, shrugged, and with his left thumb gestured to the door he had just closed behind him. He continued to the cab of the idling truck. Standing holding its door open and looking at me with an expressionless stare, he said nothing.

I left my car idling and continued walking toward the house.

"Just one minute. I'll back out," I said, holding up the index finger of my left hand.

Not a word from the geezer in faded brown coveralls and old, worn Bean boots unlaced at the top. Stocky build, a little over 5 feet tall, curly gray hair under a black knit watch cap, a face darkened and wrinkled with age.

As soon as I knocked the door opened. Clutching the top of a flannel bathrobe, an older woman looked at me with bright blue eyes. Silver hair up in a bun, high cheekbones, and just a hint of a smile.

"Hello," she said.

"Good morning. I'm Michael Hanlon. May I use your phone? I need to call the police."

"Has there been an accident?" she asked, stepping onto the porch to look at the highway behind me.

"No. My cell phone can't get a signal and I want to check in with your police chief on something I saw down the road."

"Don't have a chief. Don't have any police, either.

Only 1,553 people year round, by the last census," she went on. "More in summer." Her voice was strong and clear, with precise diction.

"We use the county sheriff's office and the state police. They have a small sub-station in Bridgton, 10 miles south," she added, moving back inside and opening the door wider.

"Thank you." I stepped into the kitchen and was hit with the smell of coffee and breakfast. Oatmeal and maple syrup was my guess.

"Will the guy in the truck be OK for a couple minutes?" I asked, looking back at the driveway.

"Oh, Chauncey's never in a hurry. He'll be fine. He has wood for my stove." Turning from me, she continued talking.

"The phone is right here." She walked toward a room off to the right. No hesitation in her step; erect posture. I guessed her age at late 70s.

She pointed to an honest-to-goodness antique roll top desk. There was an ancient, beige princess-style phone on top of a new phone directory. I opened the phone book.

"All the important numbers are right there on that card," she said.

A yellowed with age 3" x 5" index card was taped to the inside of the desk. There were several numbers neatly printed in faded red felt-tip ink.

FIRE > 583-2200   STATE POLICE > 647-1450
DR. BOWER > 583-3095   MELBY'S > 583-4447

The phone had a rotary dial built into the handset receiver. Not having seen one of these in years, I listened for a dial tone; then, with my right index finger, turned the dial clockwise each time for 6,4,7,1,4,5 and 0.

After two rings a male voice answered, "State Police dispatch."

"Yes. My name's Michael Hanlon. I'm visiting from Vermont. Driving up in Waterford a few minutes ago I saw something by the road." I turned to be sure the woman had gone back to the kitchen.

"There's a body next to the lake here."

"Where are you, sir?" the dispatcher asked.

"I'm in the village center of Waterford. No cell service, I'm calling from a private home."

"Hold for a minute, please." Ten seconds later another male voice came on.

"Lieutenant Merchand." He pronounced it mur-SHAWN, a French Canadian name. Most people say MERCH-und. Again, I gave my name and repeated the information I'd just given to the dispatcher.

"Look, I've been around dead bodies before. Unless this is some sick joke, you have someone out there next to the lake who's not only dead, but decapitated and with no feet."

"Keoka Lake in Waterford?" he asked.

"I didn't see a sign. Lots of lakes and ponds. I was driving north on Route 35, just past the historical society building."

"We'll be there in 20 minutes. Please see that no one touches the body or goes near it." He clicked off. I put the princess phone back in its cradle.

"Would you like a cup of coffee?" the woman asked when I returned to the kitchen.

"Yes, thank you. I apologize, I didn't get your name."

"Helen MacRae," she answered, coming back over to shake my hand.

"One of the few Scots around here. Mostly French, Irish and Massachusetts transplants. You said your name is Hanson?"

"Hanlon. Michael. I'm from Vermont. Visiting friends down the road in Center Lovell."

"Oh. Do your friends live on the lake?"

Kezar Lake is a well-known small resort area, especially popular with those from down country. Summer people have been coming north for more than a century.

"Yes, in fact they do. On the eastern shore, a little below the narrows."

I watched her reach into a cupboard and pull out a heavy, ivory-colored china mug, the kind you used to see in diners before today's typical mugs – smaller and with advertising logos. She poured the coffee from a glass pot on the stove, turned, and brought it to a table in the center of the kitchen.

"Cream and sugar?" she asked, placing the mug opposite where she had been finishing breakfast.

"No thanks, black is fine." I took a sip. Not scalding, so I drank more. She took a seat at the table. I remained standing.

"So what did you see that made you call the police, if I may ask?"

"There's a body next to the lake about a half-mile back."

"Good lord," she exclaimed, putting her hand to her mouth and turning to look out the window. I didn't say anything for a few seconds.

"A state police lieutenant said he was coming right over. He asked me to see that no one disturbed the body." I took another swallow of coffee, placed the mug on the table and put my hand on the door to leave.

"I better go back. Thanks for letting me use your phone. And the coffee."

Helen MacRae slowly shook her head before reacting.

"Do you think it's a hunter? I believe today is the last day of deer season."

"Maybe," I lied. I was not about to mention a missing head, no feet and *no chance* this is a hunting accident.

When I stepped back to the driveway, the old guy was sitting in his truck, head tilted back against the window and eyes closed. I couldn't tell if he was snoring. I'd been in the house not more than 10 minutes.

My tapping on the window caused his head to come forward slowly. He blinked, then looked at me and rolled down his window. Up close, the darkened face now looked like maybe he hadn't had a serious bath for some time, added to a jumble of dark whiskers from his cheeks down over his neck. He was still giving me the wordless stare.

"Sorry. I had to make a call. Let me back up so you can get out," I said.

"Not goin' nowhere. Gotta' turn around 'n' unload," he answered, hooking his right thumb over his shoulder toward the back of the pickup.

The inside of my Honda CR-V was still warm. I got in, snapped the seatbelt and slowly backed out. No traffic at all. I looked at my watch; 8:17.

Three

Driving back to the lake, I pulled farther off the pavement and put on the emergency flashers. Reaching behind me, I got my wool jacket and gloves. From under the driver's seat, I pulled out a fleece hat, put it on, and pulled it over my ears. Normally I'm not a hat guy. But I like to think I'm not stupid, either, so the hat is always with me.

As I stepped over the guardrail on the opposite side of the road, a dark green Cooper MINI came from the village toward me. A woman was driving, no passengers; slowing down, she looked right at me. She was wearing aviator sunglasses and a bright orange down vest over a black turtleneck. She smiled, but kept going. I had a flash vision of Nicole Kidman as the woman drove on.

No change in the appearance of the body. I walked a few feet beyond where it lay, took out my phone. Maybe no signal, but the camera worked. I snapped three shots at slightly different angles from the bank. I wasn't wearing boots, so I avoided stepping onto the thin ice at the edge of the water. I walked in the opposite direction and took three more photos.

I put the phone back in its case and returned it to my right coat pocket. I put my gloves on, buttoned my coat, and waited.

I alternated stomping my feet to warm up and thinking that my leather sandals were really comfortable for driving, but not so great for standing outside at below-freezing temperatures, even wearing wool socks. I looked at my watch. Five minutes had gone by.

Sight before sound. Out of the corner of my eye, a rapidly approaching vehicle came on fast from my left. No siren, just a flashing blue light bar across the top. I saw the cruiser, then heard the hum of the tires on the pavement.

The slate-blue Maine State Police car pulled up next to me. Two troopers got out. The driver was a young guy with carrot-orange closely cropped hair and a scrubbed, shiny complexion. Maybe 6 feet tall and 175 pounds.

Rounding the front of the car, the other trooper was pulling on his jacket. Older, probably mid-40s, stocky build and about 5′ 10″, a little taller than me. He gave me a nod. His name tag read Lt. R. Merchand.

"Where's the body?" he asked.

Extending my left arm, I pointed across the highway.

"Over the bank." I walked in front of them, stopped at the guardrail, and we stood looking at the clump 10 feet below.

"Get your camera, Corporal Snyder," the older trooper said.

The other trooper did a quick pivot and went back to the car. Blue lights still flashing, the cruiser blocked one lane of the highway.

As I'd done earlier, Merchand lifted his right leg cowboy-style, then his left leg over the guardrail, and started down the bank. I stayed at the edge of the road above the body. Corporal Snyder came up behind me and followed Merchand to the water.

Both state policemen were wearing some special-issue rubber-bottom/leather-upper boots. Not the ubiquitous brown Bean boots and knockoffs you often see in this part of the world, but a military green rubber, something a fish and game warden might wear.

Merchand pulled latex gloves from his coat pocket, put them on, and stepped into the water next to the body. He squatted down. Snyder adjusted the lens on an expensive-looking camera. He stepped closer and began snapping photos.

Still in a crouched position, Merchand carefully duck-waddled his way around the body, his ass about 2 inches out of the water. After a minute, he stood, looked around, and then looked up at me.

"Your footprints?" he said, pointing at the bank.

"Yes."

"Tell me about how you found the body."

I started to step over the guardrail, and Merchand held up his hand for me to stop. A car slowed on the highway behind me, a man driving and looking over the bank. He moved on slowly but continued gawking back at us.

"You can stay up there," Merchand said.

"I had driven north earlier this morning and was on my way back. When I came around that curve, I saw it from the road."

"What time was that?"

"A little after 7:30. I got out of my car, thinking someone had fallen. When I got closer, it was obvious that it was a body. Then I saw the head was missing."

Merchand had not taken his eyes off me as I explained this. He nodded.

"I went back to the car to use my cell phone. No signal. The clock on my dash said 7:46."

The young trooper adjusted the zoom on his camera, then stopped taking photos and knelt down next to the body.

"Lieutenant. You wanna' take a look at this?" he said.

Merchand turned and stepped back toward the water. Snyder pointed underneath the body. Kneeling next to him, Merchand cocked his head at a right angle close to the body. He moved forward a step and got even lower, maintaining his balance with his left hand on his left knee and leaning out, his face nearly touching the water.

"The van'll be here pretty quick," he said, raising his head.

The senior officer stood-up, pulled the latex gloves off his hands and shoved them in his left coat pocket. Both men came back up the bank toward me.

I stomped my feet a couple more times to warm up. When I'd left my friends' house back at Kezar Lake a few minutes before 7, my plan was a short drive in a warm car and then come back in time for breakfast.

"Let's wait in the car," Merchand said, pointing to the cruiser.

Both of them got back in the front, Snyder again behind the wheel. I climbed in the back behind the driver's seat.

"Where's the house you called from?" Merchand asked, pulling his door closed.

"Back in the village," I turned my head and pointed. "Gray colonial on the right. The woman who lives there said her name is MacRae."

We talked for maybe 10 minutes. Merchand asked lots of questions, more about who I was, where I was staying, and had I visited this area before.

I gave him the personal summary: longtime radio news reporter, now sole proprietor of a very small – that would be one person – freelance media/public relations firm. I explained that friends invited me for Thanksgiving to their vacation home on Kezar Lake and that I was driving back to Vermont later today. Or, early tomorrow. And this was my first time north of Kezar.

"My cell phone battery was low and it was such a beautiful morning, I decided to go for a drive, get a newspaper and charge up the phone," I explained.

"Have you talked to anyone about finding the body?" he asked.

"Only the woman back at the house where I made the call. I didn't say anything about the missing head and feet. She asked if I thought it was a hunting accident."

"Did you see anyone else?"

"When I first stopped and went down to the lake to get a better look, as I was coming back to my car, someone was running farther up the road. Not like running away. More of a jogger's pace. I couldn't see if it was a man or a woman," I went on.

"And there was an old guy delivering firewood. He's still back there," I added, twisting around to look out the side window of the cruiser.

"Here they are," Corporal Snyder said, as a state police van came to a stop behind us.

Same slate blue color, also with the blue flashing light bar on the roof. Merchand put his hat back on. Both he and Snyder got out of the car and I followed.

A man and woman got out of the van, each wearing state police uniforms. Below the State of Maine insignia on the van's left front door were the words Forensics Crime Lab.

"Sgt. Domina. Thanks for coming out," Merchand said.

"Not a problem," the woman trooper replied. "This is Corporal Bramhall. Fresh out of the academy," she added. The male trooper gave a quick, crisp salute.

"Bramhall," Merchand nodded, returning the salute. "Glad to have you with us."

"Where's the body?" Domina asked.

"Over the bank." Merchand was walking back to the lake. He stopped and turned to look at me.

"This man found the body around 7:30," he said. I started to introduce myself, but Sgt. Domina continued walking and didn't look back.

The four of them climbed over the guardrail. The rookie trooper was carrying a black nylon duffel. I waited next to the highway.

Domina and Bramhall each put on latex gloves. After five minutes of examination, more photos, and no talking, Domina motioned for the young trooper to help her turn the body. The arms were crossed, tied together with electrical cord above the wrists. No hands, just bloody stumps.

I thought of all the dead people I'd seen in my lifetime. Nothing ever this horrific. Decapitated with blood at the neck, at the wrists, and above the ankles. This was flat-out grisly.

Four

Somewhere in the wilderness of western Maine, bear, moose, deer, coyote, fox, squirrels, pheasants, rabbits, fisher cats, and other creatures, all within a reasonable distance of sound travel, were being assaulted by blaring speakers pumping out Tim McGraw's *Two Lanes of Freedom* at full volume.

Butch Raley pissed into the snowbank, shook his dick, zipped up and got back into the cab of an oversized Dodge Ram pickup. He cranked the heater fan to max. Goddamn, it was cold! Especially for a Southern boy.

Lighting another cigarette, the 15th since he left Nashua, New Hampshire 4 hours ago, Raley twisted the cap on the Jack Daniels next to him and took a good swig. It was a new bottle that he'd save for his return trip. Checked his watch: 10:30 AM. He waited.

While the wild kingdom and innocent souls along the way might protest the decibel level of the music, Raley didn't give a rat's ass. He'd listened to this CD a hundred times and never tired of it. Taking a deep drag on his smoke, it dawned on him that maybe he should turn the volume down just a little. Marco had cautioned him that while his smarts and spunk were important, he was going to have to work on his social skills and attitude if he wanted to move up.

On the seat and the passenger floor next to him were two large boxes of MOPA auto supplies. At least the boxes had MOPA marked all over them. Spark plugs, fan belts, and other miscellaneous automotive parts. The "product" was hidden beneath the smaller blue and yellow parts boxes and fake invoices.

The GPS unit mounted on the dash showed his exact location. Middle of fuckin' nowhere, as far as he was concerned. This was his second run on the northern route. The bleakness of the small towns in winter reminded him of his native Georgia. At least they didn't have the fuckin' snow back home.

Under the seat, $5,000 in cash and a new Glock 19. In less than an hour, when he was ready to head south again, he'd have another $25,000. He fondled the gun like it was from a museum collection. Definitely the sweetest piece of firepower he'd owned in his 29 years on the planet.

The instructions Marco gave were almost identical to the run a month ago. Visit the truck stop on Route 2 west of Bethel. Check. Look for an older model gray Jeep Cherokee with Maine plates. Check. Be sure the guy driving that rig sees you leave. Check. Proceed another 6.4 miles to a loggers' staging area on an unmarked dirt road.

Check. It was the unmarked dirt road that was different from last time. In October, it had been a side cutoff from the access road to Sunday River ski area. Now Marco's instructions were for him to wait.

The guy in the Cherokee would be there 20 minutes after he saw Raley leave the truck stop. And the guy driving the Cherokee was *not* the same guy as on the previous trip. When Raley slowly drove past him in the parking lot, he saw the guy was fucking enormous. Had to go 300 pounds.

When Marco recruited him four months ago, he told Raley that he could do OK in the Northeast.

"Start out in the sticks for a while, then we'll get you down here," he'd said quietly. "Lot of market potential."

Raley was impressed with how calm and controlled his new employer seemed to be. He, what was the word his mother used, "aspired" to be like Marco. Sooner rather than later.

Five

Sgt. Domina opened the coat on the body. While Merchand and Snyder watched, she raised the inside garment, continued the examination for a minute, then stood up.

"This could be one of them," I heard her say to Merchand. No reply. He took a deep breath, nodded, and stepped back.

"I'll get on the radio to Augusta. You need anything, tell Corporal Snyder" he said.

Merchand came back up the bank. He climbed over the guardrail and motioned for me to follow him.

"We'll need all your contact info," he said.

Reaching inside his coat, he pulled a card from his shirt pocket and handed it to me. All official, nothing extra: Lt. R. Merchand, Maine State Police, division and barracks number, address, phone, and email.

"Please take a minute and write everything down. Give it to Corporal Snyder," said Merchand. "You need paper?"

"No. I have a pad in my car. And I'll give you one of my cards."

Inside the CR-V I started the engine. From the visor above my head, I retrieved one of my business cards. From the hiking backpack on the rear seat, I pulled out a spiral notebook and tore off a sheet of paper. I printed my name, home address, email, and both home and cell phone numbers, most of the same information from my card. Then I hit the contacts prompt on my phone and copied the number of Dave and Linda Walton, my friends in Maine. I got out of the car and walked to the police cruiser.

Down by the lake, Corporal Snyder was erecting a portable fabric barrier mounted on telescopic poles. It would block any view of the body from the highway. I saw a roll of yellow crime scene tape on the bank next to his feet. The other two continued their examination of the corpse.

Merchand was back in the cruiser talking on a two-way radio. When he noticed me approaching he held up his right hand. He continued speaking into the handset for a few seconds, then placed it on the seat and got out of the cruiser. I gave him my card and the sheet of paper. He looked at both.

"Thank you. This is going to be all over the media in short order. For the moment, please do *not* share the details of what you saw here."

I nodded in agreement and he continued.

"We have work to do. I'll call you later today. You said that you're headed back to Vermont?"

"Yeah. Probably this afternoon, but certainly by early tomorrow morning," I said. "Try the 207 number first, the friends I'm staying with down at Kezar."

"Safe travel," he said, turning and getting back into the cruiser. He picked up the radio handset and resumed talking.

Twenty minutes later – right at 10:05, as NPR news ended on Maine Public Radio – I pulled into the driveway of the Waltons' contemporary cedar-log home. Dave came out of the house as I backed my car next to his.

"We thought you got lost," he said with a laugh.

"Sorry. A bit of an incident up the road in Waterford," I replied. "I'll tell you inside."

There were other guests visiting. A couple from Bowndoinham, Jane and Gene McKinnon, old friends of Linda and Dave. And a very attractive woman, maybe early 40s, who arrived the previous evening.

Her name was Karen Genest, a CPA friend from New York whom Linda had known in college. It was obvious Linda thought I should get to know Ms. Genest. Linda had been hinting since Thanksgiving morning that I ought to stay over for dinner Saturday, when her friend arrived for the weekend.

I followed Dave to the living room, a spacious area with a spectacular stone fireplace, lots of glass doors, and a wide view out to the lake. Everyone was having coffee or tea and reading something. They all looked up as I entered.

"He didn't hit a moose and didn't drive off the road," Dave said. He then turned back to me. "So, what's the story, counselor?"

A successful lawyer with his own practice in Massachusetts, I'd often heard Dave refer to others as "counselor." He always did it with a mischievous challenge in his voice. Taking a chair from the adjacent dining area, I sat next to the fireplace.

"Pretty unpleasant, I'm afraid" I replied. After a brief hesitation, I continued.

"I stopped for coffee a few miles up the road and had just gone through Waterford, turning to head back. As I drove around the lake back to the village, I saw something over the bank."

Everyone stopped reading their books, newspapers, and magazines. They now gave me their full attention. I had to think about how to proceed.

"You're going hear about it soon enough. A mutilated body was dumped next to the lake."

The CPA friend gasped and put her right hand to her mouth. Linda Walton went pale and put both hands to her face. Gene McKinnon said, "Jesus Christ." Jane McKinnon stared at me with her mouth open and said nothing. Dave Walton took a long inhale through his nose and looked out across the water at the mountains to the west in New Hampshire.

"No cell coverage up there. I stopped to use a phone at a woman's house to call the state police," I said, crossing my legs to get more comfortable. "A cruiser from Bridgton got there pretty fast. Now the forensics people are there."

Trying not to be too graphic, I went on to describe what they were doing as I watched the scene: the police, the photos and turning the body over, how Lt. Merchand was on the radio when I left to come back here, that he would be in touch with me later and that the media would likely have the story soon.

"You said mutilated," Gene McKinnon observed. I knew he was an Army veteran and possibly had seen mutilated bodies himself. The others waited for my response .

"They're withholding specifics of what happened until later on," I answered. "I know there are lots of things they do before releasing information." I was trying to phrase my comments in a way that would "*not* share any details" of what eventually could be sensationalized by the media.

"I think it'll be very difficult for police to identify the body. Certainly it's going to take some time to contact any family," I added.

Dave was watching me more intently than the others, all of whom remained silent. Linda stood from the chair next to me.

"Would anyone like more coffee? I'm going to put water on for another pot of tea," she said, walking to the kitchen. Almost as if by a silent signal, the other two women followed.

Dave went to the chair his wife had just vacated and sat down. He leaned forward, clasping his hands together. I waited for him to grill me. Gene seemed to anticipate more information forthcoming, as well.

"You hear about some bizarre stuff these days," Dave said, breaking the silence.

I did the deep-cleansing breath routine – in through the nose, hold it longer than you would hold a normal breath, then exhale through the mouth. The equivalent, I guess, of a deep sigh. None of us speculated further about the body or the police.

From the kitchen I could hear murmurs unrelated to this dreadful topic. They were talking about going for a walk. Linda looked out at the thermometer on the porch and said that it was almost up to 30.

Six

Before going outside, the women put Thanksgiving leftovers on the counter separating the kitchen from the dining area. Linda said we should try to finish everything up because she wasn't taking anything back tomorrow. Too much fuss, and it would go to waste in the refrigerator at home.

Later on, Dave, Gene, and I fixed turkey sandwiches, and scooped out oyster stuffing, sweet potatoes, and an interesting cranberry/walnut/orange salsa that Jane had brought along two days ago, for the dinner on Thursday. We took plates downstairs to the family room and watched a college basketball tournament on TV. It was now a little after 1:00. Dave returned to the kitchen to get three soft drinks.

"I'm surprised you got the state police so quickly," he said, reviving the discussion from earlier. "It's always been my impression the Oxford County Sheriff handled things for the smaller towns." He handed Gene and me each a can of ginger ale.

"Could be," I replied. "But when I stopped at the house to make the call, the woman had the state police number posted next to her phone. So that's where I called."

I remembered that Helen MacRae did say both state police and the sheriff's office covered the Waterford area.

We ate, watched the basketball game and didn't engage in further conversation beyond occasional guys watching sports yips and hoots, reacting to some play from the game on the large wall-mounted flat-screen eight feet away.

After an hour, the women came back to the house. Within two minutes of returning, Linda appeared in the family room and asked again if I would stay for dinner.

"You know it's going to be dark. You don't want to be driving home tonight," she said.

I thought about it and decided that, no, I didn't want to drive across the frost heaves through New Hampshire in the dark. Better to leave early in the morning.

"OK. But I need be on the road first thing tomorrow," I said.

"Great. David, you're in charge of grilling the salmon," she said. "We'll make a big salad and I'm going to bake bread."

"What time do you want to eat?" Dave asked, as Linda started back up the stairs.

"Not early. Maybe 7:00, 7:30," she called back.

Rewind to an exchange we'd had over Thanksgiving dinner. Linda had started her "You'll want to meet Karen" banter. When she mentioned that her friend was a CPA,

Dave groaned, rolled his eyes, and made a crack about "Beware those wearing green eyeshades." Of course, he already knew her and was hamming it up for our benefit. It received only polite chuckles, and a crack from Linda.

"Right," she'd retorted. "Much better that we should tell some exciting *lawyer* jokes."

On TV from the Bahamas, the basketball tournament ended. Results: Villanova upset Kansas, 63-59.

"OK, let's bring in some firewood," Gene offered, rising from the sofa.

"Actually, if you want to help Mac, there's a dead tree I'd like to cut down," Dave said.

The three of us got boots, coats, and gloves, and headed outside. Dave got his chain saw and a plastic sled to hall the firewood back to the house. We were just getting started when Linda came out to tell me I had a phone call.

I came inside and Linda handed me the phone. I mouthed "Who is it?" and she shrugged to indicate she didn't know.

"Michael Hanlon," I said.

"We're about to go public on this." It was Lt. Merchand with an update. "But not until tomorrow morning. Colonel Hewitt is going to have a briefing in Augusta."

"So you got an ID on the body?"

"Not official yet," he answered, exasperation in his

voice. "We think it's a young college student from Connecticut. She and a friend started a Thanksgiving ski trip four days ago. They were going to Sugarloaf. Never arrived."

"You located the friend?" I recalled Sgt. Domina's comment about "this might be one of them."

"Negative. Both women spoke with their families before leaving Boston on Tuesday. They were taking the train to Portland. Never called or checked in at the resort and nobody's heard a word since." I didn't say anything, assuming that Merchand would go on.

"We got the first call Wednesday night. The father of one of the girls is a well-known doc in Connecticut. We think the dead girl is his daughter. Won't know for certain until tests are back later tonight." Silence at both ends of the line.

"You there?" he asked.

"Yes. Sorry." I was trying to shake the image of the body by the lake.

"Crime lab says she was killed in the past 36 hours. The butchering took place after she was murdered." He wasn't helping me to scrub the vision from my brain.

"Colonel Hewitt will say the body was discovered by a passing motorist when he meets with reporters tomorrow," he continued. "Eventually, he'll have to use your name. I didn't want you to get sandbagged by that."

As he spoke, I was replaying encounters observed at press briefings in the past. My experience was most reporters were attentive and alert to those giving the briefing, holding their questions for the right moment. But occasionally there was some asshole who thought *he alone* – I'd never seen a woman reporter act this way – should be given direct access to everything the police knew. And that he should have that information *immediately*, without regard to a victim's family or the general public.

"I know the Colonel will want to speak with you before reporters track you down," Merchand said.

"That's fine. I've decided to stay over tonight. You can give him this number," I said.

"Probably won't call today. He hasn't set a time yet for the press, most likely tomorrow afternoon," he replied. "It will be at headquarters in Augusta."

We agreed that I would wait for the phone call from State Police Col. John Hewitt. Merchand said that he would attend the press briefing on Sunday, and if I wanted to check in with him over the next few days, he'd keep me apprised of the status of the investigation.

When I went back outside to help with the firewood, Gene was doing the chain-saw work and Dave appeared to be supervising. They'd knocked down the dead cedar and were in the process of cutting it into shorter pieces for the fireplace. I put on my gloves and, because of the noise from the saw, tapped Dave on the shoulder to let him know that I was back.

As we worked on the wood, I told Dave about the phone call with Merchand, and that I was expecting another call from his boss, a Colonel Hewitt.

"Hoo-hah! You might get an audience with a real local hero, Jake Hewitt." Dave said, pulling the sled closer to the cut wood.

"Oh yeah? Who's Jake Hewitt?" I asked.

"The guy you're going to talk to. Native Mainer, high school and college sports legend. Appointed head of the state police at the ripe age of 39."

"Sounds impressive. You know him?"

"Not personally. But I've been hearing stories for a long time," Dave replied. "Everybody gives him high marks. Must be approaching retirement age. I first heard about him when I started coming up here in the late '80s."

Seven

"This your first opportunity to, uh... establish a niche up here in the woods?" Raley asked the big guy. His twang brought it out as *opper-tune-it-tee* as he hit each syllable. And *neach*, like peach.

They were standing between the Dodge Ram and the Jeep Cherokee. Raley watched the guy carefully. He wasn't sure that everything got through to this dude. He reminded Raley of some of the inbred shitkickers he'd known. Only this guy was bigger.

Dressed in a ratty gray sweatshirt and jeans falling down at the ass, the guy had a weird smile. Raley's matching denim jacket and jeans were more like a uniform for a country-music roady. His 5' 9", 140-pound skinny frame of a body looked like a stick figure standing next to a sumo wrestler.

The guy pulled a plastic grocery bag from under the front seat of the Jeep. Raley had the Glock in the back of his waistband and was ready, should this fucker try anything. The guy opened the plastic bag to show the cash, bundled with rubber bands. Raley relaxed.

"Why'nt you put that on the seat here and chill out for

a couple," Raley said, opening the driver's door of his pickup.

"I'll get the invoice and the parts your, uh... brother ordered yesterday." The big guy put the bag of money on the seat, turned and went back to the Jeep, leaned his large ass against the front of the rig and folded his arms across his huge stomach.

Raley stood at the door of the Dodge and, as Marco had instructed, did a quick count of the cash. The bundles were mostly separated into $10s, $20s, or $50-dollar bills. There were some bundles that had $100-dollar bills. All the currency looked as though it had been in circulation; no new, crisp bills. Marco said 25 grand would be the take. After nearly five minutes and using a small handheld calculator, Raley thought the amount looked right.

He walked around to the other side of the Dodge, opened the passenger door and, before picking up one of the boxes, pulled out the Glock, released the safety, and slid the gun into the box with the parts. Just in case we're not clear on how this works, he told himself.

He carried the box to the back of the Jeep. The big guy followed him and opened the tailgate. As the hatch went up, Raley looked inside.

"What the fuckin' catfish?" Still holding the box, he nodded his head at a jumble of balled-up plastic in the back of the Jeep. The plastic looked like it had gone through a car wash that was spraying red paint.

"Man! You got a real mess there," Raley said. The big guy still had the weird fucking smile.

"Helped my brother gut a deer." The guy could talk, hot damn.

Raley stood holding the box of parts. The big guy reached in and shoved the plastic out of the way. Raley put the box in, handed the guy the fake invoice, and quickly swiveled the Glock behind his back, but didn't return it to his waistband.

The guy stared at the invoice, looked at Raley, then back at the yellow piece of paper in his hand.

"In case you get stopped. Somebody might wanna know what you got here," Raley said. He stepped back from the Jeep.

"But what I'd do," he continued, "is take them brown packages off the bottom 'n' hide 'em behind that spare tire." The big guy looked at the tire mounted inside the rear compartment of the Jeep. He nodded.

"Course," he added, "somebody stops you and they have a German Shepard sniffer dog, you are shit outta luck, friend." Raley laughed. He wasn't sure the guy's weird smile had changed once in the few minutes they'd spent together. His fucking problem, not mine. Raley turned back to his pickup.

Checking the side mirror as he closed the door on the Dodge, Raley continued to look for any strange movement from the guy, like he might try something stupid. He saw that the guy was, in fact, putting two brown packages –

each the size of a cereal box – behind the spare tire. Then he closed the tailgate of the Jeep.

Raley turned the ignition key on the Dodge and the speakers roared to life again. He turned the volume down, hit the button to open his window as he put the truck in reverse, turned, and pulled forward. He gave the big dude a simple two-finger salute as he drove away.

Watching the rearview mirror, Raley slowly descended the logging road and started thinking about getting back to Nashua and that sweet hairdresser he'd met. She lived in the apartment above his. She really had nice hair. And a great ass.

He sang along with Tim McGraw, "*Babe, there's no red lights or stop signs around for miles...*"

Eight

A perfectly grilled wild sockeye salmon filet, garden salad with feta cheese, pomegranate seeds, and walnuts, and freshly baked bread. With a really nice California Pinot. Excellent meal.

"On a scale of zero to ten, this was a 9.2," I said to Linda. The others at the table offered approving murmurs and words of agreement.

"How do you keep the salmon so moist when you grill it?" I asked, turning to Dave.

"Smear it with a dab of mayonnaise, the *real* kind, a little lemon juice, and some chopped dill. Skin-side down first, then flip it after 3 or 4 minutes. And the grill has to be really hot."

"Where'd you get the idea of the avocado spread on the salmon?" I asked.

Linda pointed at her CPA friend, Karen, who gave me a smile.

"Actually I got it from a great restaurant in New Hampshire," Karen said.

"I created my own version," she continued. "Tiny bit of mayo, some horseradish, a little blue cheese herb mustard, lemon juice, a dash of pepper, and a ripe avocado."

"It was great," Jane McKinnon exclaimed.

"Peyton Place," Karen said. Linda laughed.

"That's the name of the restaurant. The name of the family who own it is Peyton," she added. "A really unusual menu and very good."

"I know where that is," I said. "Over on the Connecticut River, in Orford. It's probably 30 minutes from my house."

"Really?" Karen asked. "I didn't know the name of the town. I was travelling with a friend from DC two summers ago. She knew about it from an earlier visit."

"I've heard others talking about it, but I've never been there," I said.

More talk about food and restaurants, traditional fare versus unusual dishes, ethnic foods, all fresh ingredients, cooking good meals at home compared to eating out. It went on like that for more than a half hour, with each of us weighing in on some food favorite.

Linda made coffee and served leftover pumpkin pie with ice cream. We were still talking at the table when the phone in the kitchen rang. I looked at my watch. It was 9:25.

Dave answered the phone. While he was listening to the person on the other end, he looked at me and pointed.

"Yes. He's right here," Dave said. I got up from the table and started for the kitchen.

"Hold on just a minute, please." Dave put the receiver next to his chest to muffle the sound. "You might want to use the phone in our bedroom," he said, pointing away from the kitchen.

"Sure," I said. I went through the living room to the other end of the house. In the master bedroom there was a desk with a laptop computer and a phone identical to the one in the kitchen. I picked up the handset.

"Hello." I wasn't surprised when the caller identified himself as Colonel John Hewitt, Maine State Police. I heard Dave click off the extension.

Hewitt had a gravelly voice, but spoke clearly and deliberately. He repeated some of what Merchand had told me earlier about a planned media briefing scheduled for tomorrow. Yes, it would be at state police headquarters in Augusta at 1:00.

"The parents of the other girl are planning to be here," he said. "They want to make a plea for any information about their missing daughter. The FBI is sending an agent up from Boston. Our team will meet with him tomorrow morning."

"Lieutenant Merchand thought you might have some concern about reporters wanting to talk to me." I slid the chair out from the desk and sat down.

"Yes. Obviously, there are certain details of what was found – some of what you saw at the scene – that we are not prepared to release. We're asking that you don't discuss this with anyone at this point."

I thought about some law enforcement types I'd dealt with previously. Like the reporters, most were very professional and clear about what they would and would not share. But there was always the occasional big ego, self-important yahoo who was determined to suppress every piece of information until it could be released in a manner that made *him* look like "the Man."

"If you're available, could you meet with us before the press gathering tomorrow?" Hewitt said.

"I can do that. I was planning to head back to Vermont in the morning. I'll just leave a little later and come to Augusta first."

"Where are you driving from?"

"Kezar Lake. I'm staying with friends in Center Lovell."

"I'm afraid we're in the opposite direction. Just off 95, about two hours northeast of where you are," Hewitt concluded. "I can give you directions."

"Can't be that difficult to find. Is it Route 2 east to Augusta?"

"Better to take 302 from Bridgton. Pick up 95 north. Our headquarters is on Commerce. Follow the signs from exit 112-B. It's the same exit for the civic center."

We agreed that if I got to Augusta by noon that would allow us enough time to meet before the media scrum. Hewitt said to ask for him as soon as I arrived.

"Mr. Hanlon. We really appreciate your discretion here," he added.

I put the phone down and returned to the others in the dining room. Dave raised his eyebrows in a "what's up?" gesture.

"Looks like I'm here for breakfast. They've asked me to drive to Augusta tomorrow to meet with the top brass at state police headquarters. The body in Waterford this morning apparently is part of a bigger story," I said.

Nine

Insomnia wasn't something I'd experienced before. A prolonged illness and the not-so-distant death of my father; a gut-wrenching emotional roller coaster, with all the memories, during a lengthy divorce; lying and deceit from a trusted employer – *none* of that interfered with my ability to sleep soundly.

In fact, there were occasions when I could nap on command. Relax in a chair, recline the driver's seat in my car while parked at a rest area, and I could fall asleep in seconds.

Now my travel alarm showed 5:03. I hadn't slept more than a few minutes since getting into bed just before midnight. Too much wine, real coffee with dessert at 10:00 at night, a long, wide-ranging conversation with an attractive woman I just met? All of the above. I just couldn't sleep.

As quietly as possible I went to the upstairs guest bathroom and stood in the shower until I felt the hot water turning cold. After brushing my teeth and shaving, I spent a couple of extra minutes trimming my beard, toweled dry, and went back to my room.

It took only a few minutes to dress. I put dirty clothes in my travel duffel, stripped linen from the bed, shoved my wet towel in the pillowcase with the sheets, and carried them downstairs to the laundry closet. When I tiptoed to the kitchen to put on my shoes, Dave was sitting at the counter in pajamas and bathrobe, drinking coffee and reading the previous day's Boston Globe.

"Patriots have one more serious injury, that's pretty much it for the season," he said in a subdued tone, trying not to wake the others.

"I haven't followed them much. I normally don't pay attention 'til the playoffs."

"Slim chance this year," he said, putting the paper down. He stood, went to the automatic coffee maker on the opposite counter, took a clean mug from the cupboard, and poured coffee for me and another cup for himself. I stirred in a little half & half and sat next to Dave.

"You smell nice, but look a little whipped," he said with a chuckle.

"Didn't sleep all that well."

"I don't imagine. Seeing that body, who would?"

"You know, it was a bit more than I described yesterday. Somebody hacked at this person. Really gruesome and brutal stuff."

We sat in silence for a few minutes and drank coffee. Dave folded the newspaper and again got up from the counter, placed his coffee mug in the sink, and then held the pot out to offer it to me. I took a refill.

"I'm going to get dressed. You wanna take a drive?" he asked.

"Sure."

A few minutes later we were in Dave's Toyota SUV hybrid, heading north on the same route I had taken 24 hours earlier. It wasn't as cold as the previous morning. His dashboard gauge showed the outside temp at 34°F. Like yesterday, no other traffic.

We followed Route 5 through North Waterford, turned southeast onto Route 35, and headed toward Waterford. There was a sign, "*Welcome to Waterford – A Peaceful Village.*" I wondered how many residents knew about what was found in their peaceful village yesterday.

Passing the historical society, we approached the lake. You could see the yellow crime-scene tape. That was it, no other signs anything might have occurred there. I pointed at the spot.

"Do you miss being a reporter?" Dave asked.

"Ahh, sometimes. But mostly not. I like what I'm doing. And I sure as shit don't miss the long hours and marginal pay in radio."

He continued south on 35. We passed a sign showing we were headed for Bridgton.

"How many clients do you have now?"

"Only three. But one is a really solid company that's been around for a long time. I know the president and we work well together. Plus, they pay on time."

"What exactly do you *do* for this company?"

"You might call it *Woodchuck Ambassador*. In a way, I'm acting as their lobbyist on a small scale. With municipal governments and state agencies. And I advise a young woman at the company who writes their press releases, coordinates charitable events and community relations activities."

Dave nodded. I could tell this was almost as stimulating as handling a real estate closing. I babbled on.

"Two others are smaller businesses that need help with marketing. They can't justify paying big bucks to an ad agency, and I've really gotten into the photography aspect of PR, which helps them. Hell of a lot easier with digital and doing edits on a computer."

We eventually made our way full circle, arriving back just over an hour after we left. And like during the drive yesterday, I enjoyed the scenery. A mix of simple, modest homes, along with some down-and-out dwellings that were barely standing, and the occasional big spread with an enormous house up on the hill. Long white expanses of snow-covered fields running up to the tree line.

The atmosphere the rest of the morning felt like maybe we'd all had a night of insomnia. Nobody was particularly animated, and everyone appeared focused on going through the motions of getting packed and going home. Our goodbyes were cordial. I wondered if and when I might see Karen Genest again. I knew that I'd likely see Dave and Linda and the McKinnons in the spring.

At 9:45, I put my bag on the back seat of the CR-V and headed to Augusta.

Ten

"You count it?" Marco asked.

"Twenty bunches of 100s, rest in 50s, 20s, 10s and 5s," Raley said. "Twenty-five thousand exactly. I counted it again this morning." He shifted his cell phone so he could light a cigarette. He was still waking up.

"And the five grand you gave me on Friday," he added.

"Good man. Can't be too careful with new associates." Marco thought about the tough guy he'd dealt with before. The man had recently done a stretch in the new federal prison in Berlin, New Hampshire.

But the macho, now ex-con didn't yap about drugs, or bargain with the cops. If he had, Marco would've heard. And the money was always right, no skimming. Then the guy just dropped off the radar after his release from jail. No contact. Must've headed for the West Coast, or Florida. Maybe back to Chicago.

Over the past summer, the network had been shaky. Marco was afraid business might go elsewhere. He'd personally driven north on two occasions to check out prospective replacements, and was a bit nervous about the new arrangement with two brothers who lived in Bethel, Maine. The younger one was sharp enough. But the older brother, who looked like he could wrestle on TV, was questionable.

"So they got it right twice now," Marco said. "This trip and the run last month. No problems with the brother?"

"Fuckin' dude hardly spoke," Raley responded. "Parked his ass while I counted the money. Only mumbled a few words when we moved the parts to the back of his vehicle." It came out as vee-hickel. Raley said nothing about the plastic and the messy remains from "cleaning a deer."

"Tomorrow morning, 10 sharp. The Donut Shop near Rockingham Park. Turn left off 93. I see you pull in, I'll come out to your truck."

"Roger that, Cap'n," Raley answered. Marco decided not to admonish the kid for his smartass attitude. There was a lot to teach him. There would be time later.

Inside a dark, smelly, depressing trailer near Bethel, Maine – it was too far gone to be thought of as a manufactured or mobile home, which it might have been 40 years earlier – two brothers sat at a rickety, fold-up card table. It was 11:30 on a Sunday morning.

With so much clutter, there was barely room to move. The surface of the table had been cleared and now held dozens of small packets of crack cocaine, 10 smaller packages of black-tar heroin (carefully segregated to one side), and a pile of loose cash. A yellow pad and a ballpoint pen were in the center of the table. On the floor sat the now empty MOPA auto parts box.

Jarvis Blevens was a small guy. At 5' 5", he was shorter than most of the kids he'd grown up with, from first grade through high school. At 125 pounds, he looked like a middle-school kid. But he was 26 years old, and he was smart – smart being a relative term. He certainly was clever.

Leon Blevens, on the other hand, was huge. Topping out at 321 pounds and standing 6' 3", his bulk was mostly flab. It was hard to believe the two came from the same parents, now deceased. If one looked closely enough and studied them carefully, one could detect a similarity in the eyes, and maybe in the drab brownness of their hair. That was it.

Leon, three years older than Jarvis, clearly had the misfortune of starting life without the normal mental and emotional wiring. Childhood nutritional habits didn't help matters. By the time he was a teenager, he was an abnormally large and scary figure others routinely avoided. Leon spent all his free time either watching garbage TV, or wandering around in the woods, exploring but not seeming to learn much. Or at least it didn't show.

Jarvis also spent time in the woods. He taught himself how to use a rifle given to him by the elderly owner of a garage where he worked after school and most weekends.

The way car engines had changed in recent years, it was now uncommon to find an independent mechanic-owned garage. Still fewer young men took an interest in working on cars. The old man really liked Jarvis, and Jarvis liked him. For rural folk, it was an unusually close relationship.

Two years ago, when his parents died within a week of each other, Jarvis assumed the role of looking out for his brother. He moved back to the family hovel on cement blocks, vacating a small three-room apartment above the garage 10 miles away. Once he was back home, he never bothered to clean out the trailer. It still reeked of tobacco and stale disinfectant.

Their old man just croaked one night while watching hockey on TV. Jarvis wasn't surprised when, a week later, his mother went to the hospital and died the next day. The doctor said she had advanced lung cancer, most likely caused by second-hand smoke.

"Three drops yesterday," Jarvis said, holding the yellow pad in front of him, looking over the list of names.

"We get in the Jeep to make more runs tonight," he added. Leon grinned, but said nothing in reply.

"First I gotta see somebody in Gorham," Jarvis said. "It won't take long."

Eleven

The Maine State Police headquarters in Augusta is housed in a huge, nondescript, single-story former industrial plant.

A renovated computer manufacturing facility covering more than 40,000 square feet, the state police occupy a small portion of the plant, sharing the facility with public safety and other state offices. I entered at the side of the building and went directly to the reception desk.

"Michael Hanlon. Here to see Colonel Hewitt," I said to the dispatcher behind the protective glass shield. I slid my business card into the tray for him to examine.

He gave the card a quick glance, turned from the window, and picked up the receiver of one of the phones at his work station. He pushed a button, and 5 seconds later said something into the phone that I couldn't hear. Putting the phone down, he turned back to me.

"I'll buzz you through that door," he said, pointing to his right. "Follow the corridor all the way to the end, conference room on the left. Colonel Hewitt will be waiting for you."

Less than 30 seconds later, having followed the dispatcher's instructions, a man who appeared to be exactly my height and weight – 5' 8", 160 pounds – was waiting at the door. Despite any physical similarities and the perception he might be 10 years older than me, I had the impression this guy could do 20 one-hand push-ups before breakfast.

Clean-shaven, with short graying hair, he wore a crisp, slate-blue uniform with his name plate above the left breast pocket: Col. J.K. Hewitt.

"Mr. Hanlon," he said, extending his right arm. He made direct eye contact, we shook hands, and he took a short step back in the other direction. "This way," he added.

I followed him down the corridor and into a conference room. The room had a large American flag hanging at the front, extra tables and chairs stacked in a far corner. It looked as though it might serve for training classes and seminars. Probably could hold 50 people.

Lt. R. Merchand was standing when we came in. Another Maine State Policeman next to him stood up, and a taller man, probably 6' 2", dressed in a charcoal-gray business suit, also got up from the table.

"You've met the Lieutenant," Hewitt said. Merchand nodded to me.

"This is Detective Jim Reese of our criminal investigations/forensics unit." The other uniformed officer nodded, then shook my hand. "And this is Special Agent Gary Guidi, FBI." I shook hands with the guy in the suit.

"Please, have a seat," Hewitt said, gesturing to his right. The others returned to their seats.

There were two long tables pulled together, chairs for 14 people – six on each side, and two on the ends. Additional chairs lined the walls on both sides of the room. Hewitt took a center seat at the head of the tables. I sat to his right.

On the table in front of us was a multi-line phone console. Merchand was on Hewitt's left, with Reese and Guidi on opposite sides of the table. Each person had a manila folder in front of him. Hewitt had an additional blue folder, unopened, to his left.

"First, let me bring you up to speed on what we know," Hewitt began, "and then we'll talk about what happens going forward." It was my turn to give a nod acknowledging his comments.

"Thank you," I replied.

"The body you discovered is that of Marcia Farrand," Hewitt said. He paused, looked down at the open folder in front of him, picked up a sheet of paper and continued.

"Twenty-one years old last month. Senior at Northeastern University in Boston. The daughter of Dr. Nicholas and Katherine Farrand of Willimantic, Connecticut." He put the sheet of paper back into the folder.

"Detective Reese," Hewitt said, looking to his left. Reese opened his folder, removed a clip from some papers, and pulled one sheet out. He studied it a few seconds, then took a second sheet from the folder.

"Our tests indicate the woman expired before any of the butchering occurred. Time of death, between 4 and 7 AM, November 29. That was Friday. Not conclusive on cause of death." Reese paused, then went on.

"Lab says that'll remain uncertain until we locate the head." He slipped the two sheets of paper back into the folder. Reese looked at me, then back to Hewitt.

"As I said on the phone last night, we'll release some basic information to the press," Hewitt said, looking at a large, white-faced clock mounted at the far end of the room, "in just about 45 minutes. For obvious reasons, some details will only be shared with a small group of those who need to know."

He was giving me the look that clearly signaled "Got it?"

"Of course," I said.

"Lt. Merchand tells us that you used to be a reporter," agent Guidi commented. I turned to my right to face him.

"That's correct. I worked in radio for 24 years."

"Vermont?" Guidi asked.

"Most of it. I actually got started at a small station in Pennsylvania, then moved to Vermont."

"So you have a pretty good idea of how..." Hewitt interjected, paused, then continued, "of how persistent some reporters can be."

"I do."

"We can't control rumors, or leaks, or speculation. But

in consideration of the victim's family, and certainly for our work in finding the killer," he went on, "we ask that you give us your word that *you* won't be a source for 'anonymous' information."

It wasn't just Hewitt looking at me now; the others waited for my response, as well.

"You have my word. I know you have a job to do." I looked directly at Hewitt.

"It's never been my practice to put information out there just for the sake of being first," I added. "And I've personally seen families exposed to unnecessary media attention during a time of grief. It's irresponsible."

"I agree," Hewitt said. "Thank you." He reached over and again shook my hand.

There was a knock at the door. A young male state trooper entered the room. Hewitt turned to face him.

"Colonel, Mr. and Mrs. Turner have arrived," the trooper said.

"Take them to my office, please." Hewitt looked at the FBI guy, then at his watch.

"Yes sir," the trooper responded. He also looked as though he might be "fresh out of the academy." He retreated to the corridor.

"Stanley Turner and his wife," Hewitt opened the blue folder and looked at a sheet of paper, then added, "Carol. The parents of the other missing girl," Hewitt said. "Agent Guidi spoke with them on the phone last night."

"I'll go meet them now," Guidi said, rising from his chair and starting for the door.

"The feds, at this point anyway, will focus on the search aspect of the investigation. It's being viewed by all of us as a kidnapping," Hewitt said to me.

"The Turner girl is also from Connecticut. Both her parents teach at Yale," he added.

"Is she a student there?" I asked.

"No. She attends," he looked down at the papers in front of him, "Oberlin College. In Ohio."

Twelve

Jarvis Blevens pulled his green Subaru station wagon out of the driveway, turned, and headed west following Route 2. The drive would take 20 minutes.

Gerard Brousseau, a car salesman from Montreal, had told Jarvis that he'd be *interested* in acting as a silent partner for future business endeavors. The two met the previous summer at a strip club in Montreal.

When Brousseau learned that Jarvis was from western Maine, he told him that he often stayed with a friend in Gorham, New Hampshire. Jarvis said that was one town over near the Maine/New Hampshire line, close to where he lived. Today would be their second meeting since August.

The house was located on a winding road off the highway just over the border in New Hampshire, before you came to the central village in the town of Gorham. Brousseau called the house a ski chalet.

"Wish I had a Hummer," Jarvis thought to himself as he came to a stop in front of one, parked near the door of the house. Big, black, shiny with lots of chrome and high off the ground, raised white letter tires and alloy wheels.

The Hummer H3 license plate was from the province of Quebec.

Brousseau came out the front door as soon as Jarvis turned off his engine. He wore a hooded parka with fur trim, fancy jeans, and black loafers with tassels. He walked directly to the driver's door.

"I need some help," he said, before Jarvis could get out of the car.

"My friend isn't well. We're going back to Montreal." His French-Canadian accent seemed more pronounced than Jarvis had noticed previously.

"Today?" Jarvis asked.

"Yes. We have to leave now." He turned back toward the house. "Stephen will handle our arrangement."

Jarvis hesitated, then followed Brousseau to the front door.

Inside the chalet, on the lower level, there were boots, skis, poles, snowboards, and a wall covered with coats, parkas, scarves, and hats. At the end of the hall were stairs to the upper level. Brousseau had turned the corner and was going up the steps.

"Vivian," Brousseau yelled. "We're leaving. Now."

When Jarvis came up the steps behind him, he saw a woman lying on a sofa. The sofa next to a stone fireplace. Brousseau was shaking the woman's shoulder.

A small man, Brousseau was maybe 5' 7" and 130 pounds. Jarvis could see that the woman was considerably larger.

"Wake up, Vivian." The woman's head turned slightly. Brousseau motioned for Jarvis.

"Help me get her to the car." He maneuvered the woman's inert body so that she was now partially raised, not quite in a fully upright position on the sofa.

Jarvis stepped around a coffee table and stood to the other side of the woman. She opened her eyes, looked at Jarvis, smiled, then yawned and closed her eyes.

They wrestled the woman to her feet. Brousseau raised her left arm, pulled it around his shoulder, and grabbed her left hand. He placed his right arm around her waist and steadied her. She was a few inches taller, and Jarvis guessed she must weigh 50 pounds more than Broussseau. He tried to imagine them in bed together.

"Walk in front of us going down," Brousseau instructed Jarvis. "Don't let me drop her." They moved forward slowly.

"What about... the girl," the woman slurred as they descended the stairs. A loud belch and she put her right hand to her mouth.

"Don't get sick, Vivian," Brousseau snapped. "Stephen's coming back. He'll take care of the girl." Struggling, they got her into the passenger seat. Brousseau managed to recline the seat. He retrieved a blanket from the back, pulled it over the woman, lifted her feet in, and closed the door.

"Wait here for Stephen," Brousseau said. "He'll be

back soon." Jarvis studied the man's expression, but said nothing.

"I just have to leave. Right now." Brousseau climbed in front and started the Hummer. He backed up slowly. As he turned in front of Jarvis standing there watching, he lowered the driver's window.

"You can trust Stephen. This will work."

Thirteen

One newspaper reporter was in the lobby. He wanted to talk. When the press briefing ended, others packed up and left. I was doing the same.

"Sorry. I'm not going to be much help," I said.

"I really don't have anything to say. Maybe when it's all over," I added. We looked at each other and I gave him a palms-up *whaddya gonna do* gesture.

"Thanks," he replied, closing his notebook and walking away.

He stopped and turned back, fumbled in his shirt pocket, and gave me a business card. I looked at it. Syd Leavitt – *Portland Press Herald*. It had a physical address, two phone numbers, and an email address.

"When the time is right, would you call me?" he asked.

"Maybe."

It was almost 3:00 when I got into my car to head back to Vermont. Driving, I replayed the press conference in my head. Hewitt running the whole show, allowing Detective Reese to give the facts on the victim. Marcia Farrand, 21 years old, student at Northeastern University, hometown of Willimantic, Connecticut. Cause of death yet to be determined. FBI agent Guidi was next with a brief one-minute statement about the other missing student, then it was back to Hewitt to field the questions.

He was good, making sure reporters knew that information would be released *if and when* appropriate, but not going so far as to really piss them off. By my count, there were 11 people in the press group – two people each from three TV stations, four newspaper reporters and one woman from a radio station. Hewitt was succinct, and none of them pushed back on any of his answers. I wasn't surprised that he had the drill down cold.

The highlight, if you could think of it that way, was a plea from the parents of the other missing woman. Actually the plea came from the mother. The father appeared completely grief-stricken, and either unable or unwilling to speak to the media.

"Stanley and I extend our deepest sympathy to Marcia's family," said Carol Turner. She hesitated, took a breath and continued.

"Marcia was a beautiful, kind, loving, and talented person. This is such a horrible tragedy." The room was silent. The woman paused again, then went on.

"We want to know that our daughter is safe. And we want her back with us."

An attractive African-American woman, Mrs. Turner told reporters that she and her husband were offering a $25,000 reward for information leading to the return of their daughter. When one of the TV reporters started to ask a question, Agent Guidi held up his hand to wave the guy off. Guidi came to the podium, and Mrs. Turner stepped back. Guidi nodded to Detective Reese, who stood, walked toward the group of reporters, and began circulating copies of a photograph that included basic information on the missing woman.

DOB 8-25-94 – Ht: 5' 7" – Wt: 135 – Hair: black – Eyes: brown. The photo appeared to have been cropped from the shoulders up. It showed a smiling, lovely young woman. Where it listed her name, it read: Wilhelmina Bonita "Bunny" Turner. The FBI contact information was in large red type, all caps, across the bottom: 1-800-CALL-FBI.

"This has been sent to every police department in the state of Maine," Guidi said. "It's going out to every law enforcement agency on the East Coast."

As soon as Reese finished handing out copies of the poster, Hewitt stepped back to the podium. Guidi stepped aside and took his seat next to the Turners. Hewitt told the group that updates would be issued from his office on a daily basis. He repeated his earlier statement asking for cooperation from the public.

"Anyone who may have seen any vehicle in the area of Keoka Lake in Waterford, between 4 p.m. last Friday, November 29 and 7 a.m Saturday, November 30," he said, pausing for effect, "*any* vehicle, even if you think you know the owner, please contact the Maine State Police."

Before I left police headquarters, Lt. Merchand made

a point of thanking me again. I hadn't actually met the Turners. They were in another room with Guidi prior to the briefing, and returned with him to that room as soon as things broke up.   Dusk began to settle as I got off the Maine Turnpike and followed Route 25 toward New Hampshire. The shorter way home was through the Lakes Region and on to Plymouth, then over bumpy roads to the Connecticut River at the Vermont border. I'd get on Interstate 91 South to White River Junction, and drive another 5 miles to my house. I calculated that home was still 2 hours away.

Listening to commercial radio had become an effort I tried to avoid, except during baseball season when a Sox game was on. Scanning the dial I couldn't find anything appealing on either Maine or New Hampshire Public Radio. I flipped down the passenger visor and looked over the CDs in the case, all of which I'd listened to many times. None grabbed me at the moment. So I drove on without audio stimulation.

Watching for moose and deer kept me alert. With hunting season ending, deer were likely to be moving around. My thoughts went back and forth over the past few days. I replayed conversations in my head, and thought again about the scene at Keoka Lake in Waterford on Saturday morning. Maybe I *did* miss being a reporter.

Fourteen

Jarvis got back into his car, sat and waited. Nearly 30 minutes later, a silver-colored Audi R8 came up the drive and stopped next to the tired Subaru wagon. It was Brousseau's friend, Stephen, owner of the ski chalet. Jarvis had met him two months earlier on the previous visit with Brousseau. He didn't know the man's last name.

Stephen had a white scarf around his neck and was wearing the type of sunglasses that changed shades according to brightness, or being inside or outside. It was overcast. Jarvis was pretty sure the sun hadn't been visible all day.

He waited for Stephen to get out of his car first, knowing the man saw him sitting in the Subaru when he pulled in. But Stephen was turned away from him now and appeared to be fooling with something Jarvis couldn't see.

Finally, he opened the door of the Audi and climbed out. In contrast to Brousseau, Stephen was tall, but was also thin. He wore a suede, fleece-lined vest over a pink dress shirt, designer jeans and fancy western boots. And the scarf. His dark, longish hair reminded Jarvis of a kid from a nearby prep school who sometimes stopped at the garage where he worked. The kid's hair always looked oily.

Jarvis got out of his car and stood. Stephen had turned back to get something from the front seat. It was a dark green canvas briefcase with leather handles. He zipped the top of the case, pushed his sunglasses up into his hair, closed the door on the Audi, and clicked the locks.

"They left?" Stephen asked, looking around.

"Half an hour ago."

"O...kay," Stephen said, stretching out the O. "Let's go inside."

Jarvis followed him back to the chalet, back past the boots, skis, poles, snowboards, and the wall covered with coats, parkas, scarves and hats. Back up the stairs where the large drunk woman hadn't fallen, back to the living room.

Stephen put the briefcase on the coffee table. The table was large and made from a hatch cover from some old boat. He walked to a closed door off the living room, stood at the door, and listened. He checked the door handle, turned, and came back and sat on one of the sofas.

He adjusted the sunglasses a little higher on his head, but didn't remove them. A gold chain with some kind of medallion hung around his neck. He motioned for Jarvis to have a seat. Jarvis sat in a red leather chair.

"Gerard told me he wants to help get you started," Stephen said, putting one foot on the table. Jarvis looked at the fancy leatherwork of the boots. Silver, some turquoise beadwork and both light and darker leather.

"Yes," Jarvis said.

"Excellent. I love the entrepreneurial spirit." Jarvis thought he knew the word, but could not remember hearing it used this way before.

"Gerard and I are old friends. He must've told you." Jarvis nodded in agreement.

"I've been running up to Montreal since I was a kid. Great city." Jarvis thought of a girl he knew who used the word *great* in almost every sentence she uttered.

Stephen reached over and pulled the briefcase across the table, unzipped it, and removed some papers.

"Did you talk with Gerard about what you need to get started? And how much of, uh..." Stephen made quotation marks in the air with his fingers, and dropping his hands, "*silent partner* we can be?"

Even though Brousseau never discussed this, Jarvis wasn't surprised to hear Stephen use the term *we*. From the first meeting at the strip club last summer, Jarvis had wondered how much of Brousseau was for real and how much was bullshit.

Jarvis knew that Brousseau had plenty of flash, but did he have the connections? And a dependable source? Or, was he better off staying with Marco and hoping for a better cut later on? Jarvis shook his head.

"We didn't cover that. It's why I came over."

There was a muffled noise from the room where Stephen had stood by the door earlier. A dull thud; it sounded like someone dropped something. Stephen's eyes turned in that direction; Jarvis's, too. Neither man said anything.

"Let's go out to my car," Stephen said, rising from the sofa. He walked across the room and started down the stairs. Jarvis followed.

Standing next to the Audi, Jarvis saw the car had the Massachusetts vanity plate CARPE D. Stephen popped the trunk. But as Jarvis knew, it was the engine compartment in the rear of the car, no trunk.

Stephen reached behind a stainless steel cover over part of the engine, retrieved a small, flat container, and placed it on the fender. The container was black plastic, about the size of a thin paperback book. It had a magnet on its underside. When Stephen snapped the top open, Jarvis saw six packets of white powder, very similar to the packets back home with Leon. These appeared to be slightly larger.

"I'm going to comp you some really good stuff," Stephen said, removing two of the packets and handing them to Jarvis. Stephen was giving him a smile.

"Take 'em. No charge. You can get two thousand bucks for those." Jarvis accepted the packets and slipped them inside the pocket of his coat. He nodded to Stephen.

"We think there's some real promise around here," Stephen said. "Gerard says you're working with a guy from southern New Hampshire. What's your cut?"

"Ten per cent."

"We'll give you *15* to start. Six months, no problems surface, it goes to 20." Jarvis didn't reply.

"Think about it. Here," Stephen took a card from a thin leather wallet in his back pocket. "Get back to me in a couple days. I'm gonna be up here for a while," he said, walking back to the house. He stopped, turned to Jarvis.

"Or call Gerard. We can sync you into the operation in a week," he added before going inside.

Jarvis got into his Subaru and looked at the business card. It was a plain white card that read *CARPE DIEM* in large red letters, the name Stephen Rivera and a phone number, 413.278.3094.

He turned the ignition key, put the car in reverse, backed up while looking at the Audi R8, turned, and headed home to the trailer and his brother Leon.

Back in the chalet, Stephen went to the closed bedroom door. He removed a key from the watch pocket of his jeans, unlocked the door, and opened it.

The girl was sitting on the floor with her back against the bed. She appeared to be groggy. It was obvious she'd been crying. She looked up at him but said nothing.

Fifteen

Approaching Norwich, Vermont, I phoned C & A Pizza in Hanover and ordered a large pizza with mushrooms, onions, and black olives. A few minutes later, at Exit 13, I crossed back into New Hampshire, up the hill and straight to the pizza shop. In and out in 2 minutes, I drove the remaining few miles to Quechee, Vermont, where I live in a small, two-bedroom Cape.

Pulling into the garage, my dashboard clock read 6:49 PM. I hit the button on the sun visor, and the door went down behind me. I took the pizza inside and went back to the car for my duffel. It didn't feel nearly as cold here as it had in Maine. Who knew? I took the duffel into the house and dropped it on the floor in the kitchen.

Taking a plate from the cupboard above the sink, I opened the box and took out a slice. I got a paper towel, went to the fridge and pulled out a bottle of Wolaver's Oatmeal Stout, opened it, and sat at the kitchen table. As I took the first bite and before I could have a drink of the beer, the phone on the counter chirped. I instinctively looked at my watch: six minutes before seven.

The caller ID showed Private Caller. Telemarketer, I

thought. On a Sunday night?

It chirped a few more times before I decided to answer.

"Hello."

"Is this Michael Hanlon?" a male voice asked.

"Yes."

"Michael, this is Carlos Singleton. Do you remember me?"

Of course I remembered him. A high-profile, articulate, and seemingly level-headed Harvard law professor. He frequently wrote for syndication on various aspects of law, often the Supreme Court. Our local newspaper published his articles on occasion.

I'd interviewed Singleton when he spoke at Dartmouth College during the last presidential election campaign. That had been shortly after I decided to leave my radio job, but continued covering the election, feeding reports to other stations around New England. My interview with Singleton went for nearly an hour, and excerpts were broadcast on a Boston news/talk station.

"Yes. How are you?" I said, puzzled that he seemed to remember *me*.

"Not particularly well, I'm afraid. The missing girl in Maine is my niece."

The horrible vision of the body and the state police examiners flashed in my mind before it registered that what he'd said was "the *missing* girl."

"Carol Turner is my sister," he added. "When she told

me about the press conference this afternoon, I went online and watched it on a Portland TV station." Long gone the days when you had to wait for *film at eleven*.

"I was sure that I recognized you in the background with the police commander's opening comments," he said. "I remembered our interview at Dartmouth, but didn't remember your name. I asked Carol to get your number for me."

I took the phone to the table, sat down, and took a sip of beer. The pizza would wait.

"I'm truly sorry about your niece." I wondered how much detail he knew about her dead friend, Marcia Farrand.

"Her parents are stunned with fear. Stan can barely speak without breaking down." Stanley Turner's face and the obvious struggle for composure during the press conference came to mind.

"I'm driving up to Maine tomorrow. Depending on how things evolve, would you be available to help us?" The question caught me off guard.

Do what, I thought. Does he realize that I'm in Vermont, not Maine?

"The FBI, as I understand it, is coordinating the search for your niece."

"Yes, they are. And they have incredible resources. But you know and I know, there are some peculiar folk in northern New England. I've spent time in Maine and not everyone is going to be, enthusiastic, shall we say, about talking to a bunch of suits. Especially up there in the woods."

"I'm not sure that *all* federal agents these days are your stereotypical *suits*."

"I know that. But my mind has been racing since I got off the phone with Carol. I want to do anything and everything I can to help find Bunny."

"When I saw the video of the press conference," he continued, "and heard that you'd discovered the body, I recalled our interview 2 years ago. You impressed me at the time as a guy who *listens* to answers. Not everyone asking questions takes time to actually listen."

I didn't respond.

"I really believe that *any* assistance we get can speed this along," he added.

Maybe, I thought.

But I didn't say "maybe." What I heard myself say was, "Yes. If you think that I can be of some help, I'll try."

"Thank you," Singleton replied. "Is this the best number to reach you?"

"This is my home phone. Let me give you my cell. We have spotty coverage sometimes, but try the cell first." I gave him the number. He gave me his cell number.

"I'm meeting Carol and Stan in Augusta at 10:00 tomorrow morning. I'll call you after we've had a chance to see where things are."

After we finished talking, I took another bite of pizza. Cold. I turned the oven to 350°F and put the entire pizza on a tray and slid it into the oven, then took a long pull of the oatmeal stout.

While the pizza reheated, I took my duffel to the bedroom, took out the dirty clothes, and threw them in a wicker basket in the closet. I was removing a clean shirt from the duffel and placing it on a hanger when the phone chirped again.

Caller ID showed the 207 area code for Maine.

"Hello."

"Mr. Hanlon. This is Jake Hewitt." I was surprised at the informality of his greeting.

"Colonel Hewitt."

"I just want to give you a heads-up. You may get a call from the Turners. I gave Mrs. Turner your phone number. Hope that's OK. Seems you know her brother?"

"Yes. Just got off the phone with him 2 minutes ago."

"As you heard this afternoon, this is their only child. Apparently the girl is very close to Mrs. Turner's brother."

"That was my impression from his phone call," I said.

"I just want to emphasize again the importance of *not* sharing any details on the murder victim. Please leave that for us to handle when the time comes."

"You have my word."

"I'm sure we'll be in touch." He thanked me again for sticking around earlier in the day.

"You're welcome." We ended the call.

I put the phone on silent mode, checked the pizza, and drank my beer.

Sixteen

"**We'll leave in 5 minutes,**" Jarvis said. He placed the small packets back into the MOPA Auto Parts box with an old copy of *Car and Driver* magazine on top.

Leon looked up from the TV and said nothing. Sitting in an old recliner, the same chair his father had died in, he gave no indication that he was about to leap up and join his brother for the road trip.

Once Jarvis ventured into this new sideline business, he made an early decision that he *never* wanted customers coming to him. Partly embarrassment of where he lived, partly concern that some crazy might come back later to rob him. There were all kinds of stories of people doing really desperate things when it came to getting drugs.

So, Jarvis chose three different remote locations where he allowed people to meet him. Never would he be seen going someplace where customers lived or hung out. He was emphatic with instructions about *what time* a buyer could arrive, and staggered pickup appointments in 30-minute intervals. He would text or call them with the time and place to meet.

Jarvis figured most dopers knew about the others. That's how he got involved in the first place, talking with a guy who brought his car to the garage where Jarvis worked. The guy took Jarvis to a Montreal strip club, then later encouraged him to "establish a presence" in the North Country. Jarvis thought of the guy as sort of a weakling.

"All right. I'm set. Let's go," he said to Leon. "We'll take the Jeep. You drive."

It took Leon a few seconds to pick up the remote. He was mesmerized by an episode of *Ice Road Truckers*. Jarvis stood at the door holding the auto parts box. Leon hit the off button and got up from the recliner.

"I gotta whiz," he said.

"I'll be outside."

The Jeep was parked under a plastic-covered carport next to the trailer. Jarvis placed the box on the passenger-side front seat, then walked back to a beat-up metal storage unit at the end of the carport. His father had assembled it when they were kids. He kept a tool box and an old chest freezer plugged to an industrial extension cord running through a hole in the side of the trailer.

Jarvis opened the freezer. Inside were some black plastic trash bags. He felt the bags. They were frozen solid. Closing the lid on the freezer, he went back to the Jeep and got in. Leon came out, got behind the wheel, and grinned at his brother.

"Up to the truck stop first. I have to make some

contacts." In a black nylon holster strapped to his belt was a Samsung Galaxy II phone. Jarvis took it out and keyed the power button as Leon pulled onto the highway.

Stephen Rivera was anxious. Over a period of four days, he hadn't connected with the girl in any meaningful way. She had been knocked out most of this time with daily injections of chloral hydrate, a supply Branchik provided from previous activities. When she wasn't out completely, she remained groggy.

He offered food, but she refused it. Yesterday, she did eat a little cheese, some bread, and drank bottled water. When she was semiconscious, he walked her down the hall and allowed her to use the bathroom by herself. When she really started to come around, he gave her another shot.

Earlier in the day, when he left Gerard and the bimbo at the chalet, Stephen decided he wouldn't inject the girl again. He wanted her awake and responsive. It was a mistake to have asked Gerard's girlfriend, Vivian, to help clean the girl up the night before. Stephen told Vivian the girl had a serious drug problem and that he was trying to get her straight.

Would Vivian mind giving the girl a sponge bath and get her into fresh clothes? *Not* a good idea. Hindsight wasn't going to help now. Stephen was beginning to feel a little panic.

The fantasies and ideas that had excited him after she was brought here late Tuesday night had evaporated. She looked so young. Why had he thought it was OK in the first place? Because he was intimidated by that prick on two feet Branchik, no other reason.

Branchik was the one who said this was "ripe territory," even though it is more than 200 miles from Stephen's home base in Chicopee, Massachusetts. *Branchik* knew this area, he said, having been all over it in recent years. *Branchik* boasted he would provide "entertainment" anytime we wanted it. But now, Stephen thought, *Branchik* is completely crazy. Stephen had known others who were a little crazy. But Branchik is a truly dangerous psycho. Much worse since his release from prison.

Standing at the door, Stephen watched the girl. She hadn't said a word, hadn't risen from the floor next to the bed. He entered the room and closed the door behind him.

The clock radio showed 5:50AM when I opened my eyes. I'll take it, I thought. After a restless night and long drive home yesterday, eight-plus hours sleep is just fine. Slow shuffle to the kitchen where I pushed the button on the automatic coffee maker, which I always prep the night before. The obligatory return trip to the bathroom and I was in and out of the shower in less than 10 minutes.

Across the hills to the east it was getting lighter. I dressed, went back to the kitchen, poured coffee, and carried the mug to the living room window. I studied the sky for a few minutes. It was overcast, and having any sun today looked doubtful.

Notes from phone conversations last night remained on the kitchen table where I'd left them. Looking over what I'd written, my gaze went to *Turners, Augusta, 10 o'clock.* Below that was a phone number – 617.329.9393 - Carlos Singleton's cell phone. He said that he'd call after meeting with his sister and brother-in-law. We'll see.

Placing an English muffin in the toaster oven, I got a small container of yogurt and a large plastic jug of orange juice from the fridge, put both on the counter, and poured another cup of coffee. When the muffin was ready, I ate it dry, along with the yogurt. Unless someone else was in the house, I still drank juice directly from the container. My former wife had observed on numerous occasions, "That's juvenile and gross." She was right on both counts. I took another drink of the juice.

My guest room functions as a home office. Twin beds, antique bureau, a wicker chair and off to the other side is my desk and a straight-backed chair. I put the coffee mug down, turned on the power surge protector beneath the desk, and switched on the laptop.

Clicking first on my calendar, I looked over the week. The most important event was Tuesday, 10 AM – meet FM@GMB. Frank Montagliani is the President/CEO of a long-established Vermont construction firm, Green Mountain Builders, more commonly known as GMB.

The remainder of the morning I spent deleting and

responding to email, and reviewing GMB work, as well as other client files from the past few months. It was almost noon. I stood, stretched, and went to the kitchen. The large round thermometer outside the window above the sink showed that it was up to 40°F. No sun visible through the cloud cover, but it was getting warmer.

From my bedroom closet I took the wicker basket to the basement, put the dirty clothes in the washer, and went back to the kitchen. The pizza box from last night was inside the fridge and held three slices. Cold pizza is pretty good, too.

When I finished eating, I put on my coat and drove 2 miles to the village to pick up the mail. My post office box was stuffed from the past five days. Before leaving the building, most of what had been in the box was now in a blue recycling container in the lobby. Nothing going home with me looked all that exciting. Maybe the *Ebbets Field Flannels* catalog.

Seventeen

"Why don't you tell me your name?" Stephen said to the girl. Nothing.

"Bunny," she then replied hesitantly. And looked directly at him for the first time.

"*Where* am I? Who are you?"

"My name is Stephen. This is my house."

"Where's Marcia?" Stephen guessed this was the other girl in the car.

It had been nearly midnight the preceding Tuesday when Stephen saw headlights swing up the driveway. He'd gone downstairs to the door. He recognized the New Hampshire plates and Branchik's Chevy Impala.

"Got a gift for you, Stevo," Branchik had said, carrying the girl from the car into the house.

He was really popped up. On what, Stephen didn't know. He had seen many, many others who had *the look*.

Branchik carried the girl upstairs, glanced at the sofa, then took her to the guest room and put her on the bed. Returning to the car, Stephen following, Branchik opened the trunk and yanked out a suitcase and brought it to the house. From the interior light, Stephen saw another person slumped in the front seat when Branchik closed the trunk.

A teal-colored combination backpack/suitcase on wheels, Branchik dumped the contents on the floor next to the bed, came back to the living room with the empty suitcase. With his right hand, he took a solid grip on the back of Stephen's neck. Branchik had a big smile. Stephen noticed the new tattoos on his muscular right arm.

"Have fun, amigo." Laughing, he was gone as quickly as he arrived. Stephen stood at the open door watching Branchik get back in the Chevy and go back down the driveway.

As he looked at her now, his mind snapped back to the girl's question.

"I don't know Marcia."

She stared at him, then turned away again.

Stephen had placed her clothes on the overstuffed club chair near the door. When Vivian helped clean the girl over the weekend, she got her dressed in a clean pair of jeans and a light blue V-neck sweatshirt. Printed in yellow on the upper left front of the shirt were the words *Oberlin Yeomen, 2015*. The girl hadn't changed out of these clothes in three days.

"You want something to eat?" The girl turned back to him when he asked this.

Her skin was medium tone, most likely African-American. Maybe Caribbean. He was struck by her amazing complexion. No makeup, just remarkable skin. Branchik dumped only her clothes before leaving. No purse, no identification of any kind. She stiffened and sat up. She held herself in a rigid manner, still on the floor leaning against the bed. She raised her knees and wrapped her arms around them.

"Tell me *who* you are. Why am I here?" she said, almost shouting. "And *where* is Marcia?"

"I don't know Marcia. And I don't know where she is."

"You're lying," she screamed, tears in her eyes.

He stood from the bed and looked down at her. He thought she would start crying again, but she turned away and went quiet.

"Let me know when you're hungry." He walked out of the room.

Back in my car at the post office, my phone was on the passenger seat and the screen showed I had new voice mail. It was a message from Carlos Singleton asking me to call. I drove back to the house and placed the call from there. He answered immediately.

"Carol and Stan agree. All the help we can enlist is what we want," he said.

"Anything new from the police or FBI?"

"Not yet. We're meeting again tomorrow with the agent in charge. And the state police."

I remained skeptical. A) Could I find any realistic way that I might help? and B) If past experience held, law-enforcement professionals would *not* readily welcome the involvement of a "civilian do-gooder."

"I suspect you think this strange," Singleton said. "But my gut tells me that Bunny is alive. And I don't know how much time we have." He took a deep breath.

"Lots of wide-open land and some very small towns up there. She could be anywhere," he added.

No way he could know this, but one thing I'd done after our last phone call was to take out a road atlas and look over the map covering the state of Maine. Indeed, the western and northern parts of the state were relatively unpopulated, dotted with lakes, ponds, and plenty of small towns.

"I have an important meeting tomorrow morning, but everything else on my calendar is flexible," I said. "Maybe when you have a better sense of what you'd like me..."

"I already know what we want from you," he interrupted. "Carol jumped right on it this morning. When I told her about possibly involving you, she had the same thought. Somebody *besides* the feds talking with locals." Picking up on my hesitation, he went on.

"Look. This could be over tomorrow. Or soon. But if you'll just meet with me, we can agree on what the next step should be."

"I can do that," I replied. "Let me know what happens with your meeting tomorrow. We'll go from there."

Eighteen

Tuesday morning I drove to Springfield for the meeting with Frank at GMB. The offices and staging yard are just north of town, right off the interstate.

Founded in 1946 by two brothers from Springfield, both veterans returning from the war, the company had grown to become the largest contractor in the small state of Vermont. Good reputation, solid public image. With two other offices in the northern end of the state, GMB maintained corporate headquarters in Springfield.

Frank worked his way up to become head of the firm. We met four years ago when we both played in a winter indoor soccer league. He'd said that he was a regular listener of the station where I was working then. Later, when he learned that I'd started a media/management consulting business, he called and asked that we meet to discuss possible PR work for his company.

Arriving in the reception area, Bonnie Macklin came out to greet me. Bonnie is Frank's administrative assistant, so to speak. She isn't really a secretary, though some of what she does is clerical. She's smart, efficient, talented, and very personable. I guessed her to be in her late 20s, maybe early 30s. And she is *hot*. More than once Frank gave me the Groucho Marx bouncing eyebrows routine when he saw me in conversation with Bonnie. The meeting lasted 59 minutes. We covered everything Frank had on the agenda. He *always* had a short agenda written with bullet points on a plain sheet of paper, and rarely did meetings go longer than an hour.

It was unlikely there'd be much activity requiring another meeting until after the holidays. Frank was going to Florida to visit elderly parents for Christmas and said he'd call when he returned after the first of the year. Driving back to Quechee, I thought, well, *that's pretty convenient*.

Approaching the driveway, I spotted my neighbor, Millie Robinson, walking from the newspaper tube at the edge of her driveway. She was moving slowly, but steadily.

Millie is almost 90. She's one of those people you never hear complain about anything. I felt guilty that I hadn't been over to see her in two weeks. So, I left the garage door open and walked the short distance down my driveway to her house. She saw me coming and waited on the steps.

"Look what the cats dragged in," she said as I walked up her driveway. I waved and felt even *more* guilty.

She invited me in, and offered to fix coffee or tea, both of which I declined. Her handsome old golden retriever came out to sniff me. His name is Silvio and he's one of the sweetest dogs I've ever known.

We settled in her living room and had a nice, long visit. She has countless stories, a few that I'd heard before. She also has a great sense of humor and an infectious laugh. It was fun to catch up.

As I was about to leave, she gave me the startling news that she was considering a move to an assisted-living facility. At her age, I shouldn't have been surprised. But her independence and spirit made her seem 20 years younger, and I'd always assumed that she would stay in this house until the day she died.

"What will you do with Silvio?" He was asleep on the floor next to her feet. She bent down, patted him gently on the head and smiled.

"He's old, too. That's what's making this so difficult." It was all she could do to keep her composure.

When I got up to leave, she stood slowly and gave me a hug. I promised to come back for another visit over the holidays.

At 3:45 I heard the phone in the kitchen. It was Carlos Singleton, calling again from Maine.

"We just finished a long discussion with the state police and the FBI," was his opening remark. "Nothing has changed."

"I'm guessing they have the final lab reports on the Farrand woman?" I asked.

"I think so. The state police commander didn't have much to add to the meeting."

"Agent Guidi outlined what they know so far and what they plan to do going forward," he continued. "They're so goddamned officious." My sense was that I should say little here and just listen to what was on his mind.

"Carol and I, and Stan, we're not going to stand by patiently and see what unfolds in *due course*. We need to get some other activity started *now*.

You'd think Bunny is just another person on a long list they'll eventually check off," he said. The memory I had of the cool, no-nonsense guy I'd met 2 years ago didn't match the voice I was now hearing on the phone. But then, who wouldn't be rattled in a situation like this?

"I want to meet you as soon as we can," he stated. "Can you drive up here?"

"Augusta is about 4 hours from here."

"No. I want to go to Waterford. Where they found Marcia. The state police and the feds are here. But we don't think they'll find Bunny here."

"Did they discuss the manpower they plan to use?" I asked. "And who'll work the area where the body was found?"

"Yes. Apparently the state police work with the county sheriff's department. The FBI may send someone over. But Agent Guidi made it seem that his focus will be in Portland. The girls were last seen at the train station there Tuesday evening."

"Someone actually saw them leaving the station?" I said.

"It's not certain they left the station. An Amtrak conductor remembers them wheeling their suitcases off the train. We don't know beyond that. And they appear only briefly on a security video inside the station," he added.

"I repeat what I said Sunday night," Singleton continued. "This might end soon. Or, it might drag on. We're not prepared to just wait it out."

"Can we meet in Waterford tomorrow?" I replied.

"I'd be truly grateful," was his answer. Again he went on. "I promised Bunny's parents that I would handle this. It's not something they should be burdened with."

Looking out across the hills, dusk was moving in. Which reminded me that this time of year, daylight also comes later. I'd prefer not to be on the road much before sunrise.

"If I leave here by 7 in the morning, I should make Waterford certainly before noon."

"Is there someplace I can meet you?"

"Yeah." I remembered the country store and café between Waterford and North Waterford.

"There's a store and café," I told him. "It's right on Route 35, I think. Heading north. Big building, gas pumps out front." My brain was scrambling to call up the name of the place.

"Melvin's, Melby's. Something like that. There's

another gas station, but this store is the only one around with a dining area, so you'll know the place I mean."

"I'm sure I can find it," he replied.

"I drive a silver Honda CR-V. I'll park where you can see it. Vermont plates."

"Noon tomorrow."

"If anything happens, I'll just wait. Uncertain cell coverage in that part of the state."

"I'll be there," he said.

We hung up and I began preparing for another scenic drive to Maine, a *state of mind*. Or, was it *Lobster Vacationland* these days?

Nineteen

Jarvis now had more cash than he'd ever had in his young life. And he still had the two bonus packs.

The 'comped' stuff might not fetch the $2,000 Stephen boasted, but they could put Jarvis over $20,000 for this haul and the smaller take a month ago. He knew he could do better.

It was late; Leon was inside watching TV, and gave no attention to the money. He just liked being with Jarvis, and Jarvis liked having him along. None of the buyers knew anything about the big guy who stayed in the Jeep while Jarvis was making a sale.

Carefully placing the last bills into a re-sealable plastic sandwich bag, then into an empty plastic one-quart motor oil container, he put it next to three matching containers in a cardboard box. The box would go back under the trailer. He'd have to remove two cinder blocks at the far end, slip the box under the trailer, and then replace the blocks.

Back to work at the auto-repair garage in the morning, and he'd call Brousseau in Montreal. No more moonlighting until next weekend.

Stephen Rivera sat at the foot of the bed. The young woman was now leaning against the headboard and avoiding eye contact. She'd gone silent after the brief exchange Sunday night. She ate little of the food he offered and drank only bottles of water. He now allowed her use of the guest bathroom on her own. He knew that she'd showered the day before.

"You can come out of the bedroom," he said. No response.

"What's your real name?" Nothing. "Do you want me to call you Bunny?" No reply.

They sat in silence for another minute. Stephen got up and went to the door. She didn't move.

"The door's unlocked. Come out whenever you like."

MapQuest provided a better route for this trip. In just over 3 hours, I was on the eastern side of Rattlesnake Mountain following a road named Crooked River Causeway, a shortcut from Route 2 in Bethel to routes 5 and 35 in North Waterford. Coming over a slight hill, I spotted Melby's Market & Eatery just ahead on the left. The dashboard clock showed 11:26 AM.

Across the street in the parking lot were a dark-blue, rusty older SUV and two pickup trucks, one white and the other dark green. In front of the pumps was a guy in a plaid jacket and pork pie hat. He was putting gas into an older maroon-colored Chrysler convertible with a black top.

Parking next to the pickups, I positioned my car so it could easily be seen from the highway, and then walked across the road to the café.

Up front there was a cash register counter with a lottery terminal. Directly opposite the register was a rack with newspapers and magazines, beer and beverage coolers to the left and another cooler with prepared meats, cheese, eggs, butter, and milk to the right. The store gave off a pleasant aroma of food being cooked, and freshly baked pastries or bread.

There was an ATM near the entrance. Off in another section were shelves holding wine and liquor bottles. A sign above indicated the store was an authorized Maine Agency Liquor outlet. And there were shelves with grocery items.

Adjacent to the entrance was a larger area that held four tables, and a lunch counter with several stools. At the far end of the room there were two more tables that could accommodate maybe ten people.

Two men sat talking at one of the tables. Both were older guys, maybe in their sixties. Each wore the uniform I'd seen on a thousand guys around rural New England: work pants and leather boots, a barn jacket with flannel lining and different baseball-style caps with some company's name embroidered above the brim.

At the counter, one guy ate alone. He appeared to be on his last lap around the track. I guessed him to be late 40s, although scraggly hair, several-days' beard growth, and thoroughly worn clothes – bleached-out green military jacket, grease-stained brown logger's pants - you could easily believe he was 20 years older. He was eating and didn't look up.

The two older guys nodded to me as I went to the end of the room and a table next to the windows. This was on the side of the building facing the road, so I took a seat there. A woman came from the kitchen behind the counter with a menu and a glass of water.

"Could I have coffee, please? Cream on the side."

The menu was a sheet of yellow paper in a tri-fold format. Inside was a section *Breakfast - We'll do it Anytime, Morning Noon or Night*. Biscuits and gravy looked good. The waitress returned with a mug of coffee and a handful of small creamers, which she placed in a bowl on the table. She was ready for my order.

"I'm expecting someone to join me. I'll wait 'til he gets here to order."

"Certainly," she said and went back to the kitchen. I noticed the guy at the counter giving me a glance while I studied the menu. He was quietly finishing his meal.

I stood and went back to the news rack, got a copy of a paper called the *Sun Journal,* paid a man at the register, and returned to my table. The two older men were getting up to leave. The taller man placed a $20-dollar bill on the table next to the dirty plates.

"We're all set, Charlene," he hollered. I presumed this was to the woman in the kitchen.

"Thanks, Dana. See you tomorrow," she said, popping her head from the kitchen.

The men went outside and stood talking for a minute, then crossed the road, each getting into a pickup and driving off in opposite directions.

Flipping through the *Sun Journal*, I read some of the news from Lewiston/Auburn, Franklin, Oxford Hills, River Valley, and Bethel. I scanned obituaries, local sports results, and the opinion page. If letters to the editor and columnists were any indication, without question this paper had a conservative slant. But then again, how many liberal publications did one expect to find in northern New England?

A sporty looking metallic-blue Volvo C-70 with Massachusetts plates pulled into the lot across the road. Stepping from the driver's seat, Carlos Singleton looked much the same as when I'd met him 2 years ago. Just under 6 feet, probably not an ounce of fat, he wore a navy-blue ski parka over an ivory-colored fisherman's crew-neck sweater, loose-fitting jeans, and brown-leather hiking boots. He reached into the car and retrieved a gray-knit toque and put it on. He clicked the key fob to lock the car.

Singleton saw me at the window and waved as he approached the side of the building. The scraggly, disheveled guy at the counter gave a more obvious stare at Singleton when he came inside. It occurred to me this guy maybe didn't encounter many non-whites in his daily travels. I wondered if he'd ever been beyond the county line.

Standing at the table I extended my right hand as Carlos came over. He gave me a firm grip.

"Thank you for doing this," he said.

Holding my hand longer than one normally would in a handshake, he put his left hand on my shoulder and held eye contact. He released my hand, removed the ski parka, and placed it over the empty chair across from me.

As we sat down, the waitress was on the spot. She held a mug in one hand and the coffeepot in the other.

"Could I have decaf, please?" Singleton said. She placed the mug on the table in front of him, smiled and went to exchange coffee pots.

The guy at the counter got up, put a tip on the counter, went to the register, and paid his tab. The waitress returned with the decaf and poured the coffee. She handed Singleton a copy of the menu.

"I'll give you a couple minutes," she said and went back to the kitchen.

When she returned Carlos went for a Southwest BLT wrap, with a side order of shoestring fries. I ordered the biscuits and gravy with one egg, sunny-side up.

Twenty

The girl stood on the bed trying to look out the window. A narrow rectangular style, it wasn't very large and not meant to open. An identical window was on the other side of the room, also up high. They were installed to allow natural light in, not to open for ventilation or egress.

The trees that were visible were pine trees; some had splotches of snow on the branches. She had no sense of the time of day, but it was light out. All she knew was light and dark. Since regaining consciousness completely, she remained fuzzy-headed, with sleep coming on and off. Her internal clock told her at this very moment it was still morning.

She'd stopped crying two days ago. Refusing most of the food the man brought, she ate only pieces of cheese and some bread. She drank lots of water, but that brought on the urge to pee, so she slowly drank only one 20-ounce bottle a day. She knew her body was not right. She felt weak and missed regular physical activity.

Repeatedly, she tried to remember everything that had happened since they'd left Boston. It all fit and was easy to recall, *until* they got off the train in Portland. She remembered other people leaving the train, but they went to cars in the parking area, or to taxis in front of the station.

She and Marcia were waiting for a shuttle van that would take them to the ski area. It wasn't out front. It was dark, and they worried the shuttle might have left before their arrival. They went back outside again to check.

There was a man standing off to the left, smoking. She thought he'd been inside the station when they arrived. Now he approached and she thought he was going to offer a ride. Her mind was a blank after that. She recalled being awake momentarily, and a woman helping her get dressed. She thought it was a dream. But the jeans she wore now were *not* the jeans she'd worn on the train.

She had no recollection of arriving in this room. Her clothes were piled on a big chair; on the floor, the suitcase was gone. Her travel handbag and phone were gone.

She thought about Marcia and wondered where she was. She thought about her parents. And her friends waiting at Sugarloaf. The thoughts brought on both anger and sadness. Determined not to cry, she refused to go to other parts of the house, or to talk with this stranger, or to let him fool her into having any contact.

The man, he said his name was Stephen, was not the man from the train station. It was dark, but that man was larger. She tried to remember his voice. She did recall that he was very casual and didn't seem threatening. He'd spoken to both of them, and Marcia had responded first. It was just a blank after that.

Stephen Rivera was not accustomed to uncertainty. Since his earliest days on the streets of Chicopee, other kids acquiesced to his personality. He had initiative and was quick to take control of situations.

In high school, they always had girls. Even *shared* girls. But this was different. The girl in the bedroom was young, probably 20 years younger than Stephen. He was afraid to get close to this girl. The fear went beyond how young she was and he knew why. Branchik.

At first, it was good to have someone like Branchik. Stephen was beginning to establish himself, carefully targeting areas that were underserved. It was crucial to have some muscle. At the time, nobody else knew Branchik. When they'd met nine years earlier, Branchik had come to Springfield from just across the Connecticut line. He told Stephen that he was from Chicago, and had come east to get away from family, as well as certain "friends."

Stephen thought he could rely on Branchik to handle difficult situations, which he did on several occasions. But then Branchik began spending more time in northern New Hampshire and Maine. Five years ago he was busted for his role in a group that targeted companies in the

Northeast, stealing catalytic converters from cars and fleet trucks, then shipping the stolen parts to Canada and Mexico. Branchik got off with a three-year sentence.

Just as soon as he was paroled, he came to see Stephen. That was a year ago. And here we are now.

Richard Marco had contacts all over the place, even in the most rural reaches of the Northeast. Word was out that others were starting to jockey for untapped territory north of the Massachusetts border.

Sitting in his office in Lowell, Massachusetts, Marco ruminated over the routes, the risks, and the rewards, an exercise he'd done before. He even compiled a spreadsheet with several different *what-if* scenarios. At 63, he felt as sharp as he'd ever been. And still looked carefully at details before taking a next step.

Vermont was small, but had a more affluent population than most people realized. New Hampshire had twice the population of Vermont; and Maine was larger, but had pretty much the same population as New Hampshire.

Compared to Massachusetts, with an average of 800 people per square mile, the three northern states averaged about 40 people per square mile. With a combined population of just over 3 million, somebody was in for a lot of driving. Marco was OK with that. As long as it was *his* somebody doing the driving. And the deals.

"We're not giving it to the fucking Jibaros," Marco had said more than once. "Not now, not ever."

"We really need to go talk with Lt. Merchand," I said. Singleton looked puzzled.

During lunch, he had more thoroughly recounted the state police and FBI discussions of the last two days.

"He's in charge of this area. I met him when I found the body," I said.

"But he must get his directions from the commander in Augusta," he said.

"No doubt. But Col. Hewitt, as far as I know, hasn't spent a lot of time around here. Merchand's gotta have a fix on the locals. Especially the bad ones." Singleton didn't reply.

"I said I'd help any way I can. My experience as a reporter is that *no* law enforcement agency really welcomes outside unsolicited assistance. I'd feel more confident of my ability to actually help *if* I don't have to worry about tangling with the cops."

Singleton took another sip of coffee, placed the mug on the table, and wiped his mouth with a paper napkin.

"You think I should go with you to see this guy?"

"Yes. No matter what I say to him, or what we say, he's going to be on the phone with superiors. It's *your* family that asked me to help. He needs to believe that."

Reaching into his back-right pocket, Singleton pulled

out a thin black wallet. He removed a credit card. I assumed he was about to pick up the check for lunch. He slid the plastic card across the table.

"This is for you," he said. "I went to the Bank of America branch in Augusta. It has $2,500 on it."

I looked at the card. The bank name and logo were imprinted on top, and the bottom right indicated that it was a VISA Debit Card.

"When I get back to my office I'll send you a check," he added.

"This is fine. I don't expect much in expenses the next few days."

"Let me know what you need. Invoice me from your company, if you prefer."

My quick thought was that the IRS and the Vermont Department of Taxes probably didn't care a whole lot *where* my income came from, as long as it was legal. And as long as I reported it.

Singleton stood, removed his parka from the back of the chair, and put it on. My coat was in the car. We walked to the front of the café where he again took out the wallet, this time giving the man at the register an AMEX card.

Walking to the parking lot, I looked at my watch. It was 1:35.

"You want to follow me? It's about 15 miles to Bridgton," I said.

"Sure."

I touched the button on my key; the doors clicked and

lights flashed.

"Wait a second," he said as I started to get into my car. I got back out.

"Listen. Two things you need to know." I waited.

"First, let me repeat what I said on the phone. I'm an optimist. I believe Bunny is still alive." He inhaled deeply and let the breath out.

"And my sister, and Stanley, we're truly grateful that you are up here and willing to help us find her." I nodded in acknowledgement.

"Second, you need to be prepared for *other* dynamics that could come into play." He picked up on my quizzical expression.

"For more than 30 years, I've learned to ignore the narrow thinking and prurient speculation of people who are either too bored or too ignorant to allow others to live their lives," he went on.

"My sexual orientation is pretty well known. If it comes up, I suggest you thank others for their interest and tactfully suggest that they take a flying fucking leap."

I laughed. Somewhere along the way I'm sure I must have read, or heard, or discovered that Carlos Singleton was gay. But it really hadn't entered my mind during conversations over the past few days.

"One of my specialties," I said. "I got a blue ribbon in tactfulness."

Twenty One

The music sounded like she was in an IMAX theater.

Or, the Cleveland Orchestra concert last summer at Severance Hall. Full, rich and enveloping the entire house. She tentatively opened the door a few inches.

She knew this track. The Latin percussion, the guitars, the voice. One of her friends had sent her a YouTube link. She opened the door wider. The speakers were somewhere above her. It was a concert audience in a large auditorium, singing along with the artist.

She stepped from the room. The man was nowhere in sight. He must be here, the music didn't start by itself. It came to her. Shakira - *Antologia*.

Carefully making her way into the room, she saw a stone fireplace. There were two ivory-colored sofas opposite each other, a red leather chair, and two matching chairs of dark-green cloth. A large wooden coffee table was between the sofas. The rug on the floor was a thick, deep blue. There were large windows on the other side of the room.

She stood next to the fireplace. Above her were exposed wooden beams that looked old. Recessed light fixtures were scattered throughout the ceiling. The off-white color of the lights matched several small, round speakers in the ceiling. The woman singing had a beautiful voice.

A door opened upstairs. Bunny quickly went back into the room and quietly closed the door.

The call from Branchik heightened Stephen's anxiety. He was coming back and could be here any minute.

"I need to get my hands on some cash. And we need to talk, Stevo," he'd said on the phone.

No one else called him that. His name was Stephen. When he was younger, a few had just called him Rivera. But he stopped that when he was 18.

He went to the living room and lowered the volume of the music. Before going upstairs to shower, he'd put the CD in. While he was getting dressed, his phone beeped. Now he'd wait to see what this was about. Was Branchik bringing the other woman? Was he planning to leave her here, too?

Stephen went to the windows that looked out to his driveway and the White Mountains. Only the Audi, no sign of Branchik. Yet.

Timing is everything. Sometimes you hit it right, I thought, turning into the side lot of the state police barracks in Bridgton.

Lt. R. Merchand was walking from a parked cruiser

toward the building. He recognized me and stopped just as Singleton's Volvo pulled in next to me. We both got out of our cars and walked to where Merchand stood.

"Lieutenant."

"Mr. Hanlon," he replied.

"This is Carlos Singleton. Bunny Turner is his niece." Merchand extended his right arm and they shook hands.

"I recognize you from your photo," he said. "Colonel Hewitt said you were at headquarters. I did a Google search." Singleton gave a quick glance from Merchand to me, then back to Merchand.

"Nice to meet you," he said.

"Do you have a few minutes?" I asked Merchand.

"Come in." He gestured with his left arm to a side door of the building. We followed him through the reception area where a dispatcher behind a window was on the phone. Merchand nodded to him.

He took us to an office in the rear of the station. It's a small building; his office was 10' x 12' at the most, with a laptop on a metal desk and a four-drawer file cabinet in the corner. He removed his trooper hat and placed it on top of the file cabinet.

"Have a seat," he said. Two folding chairs were leaning against the wall. We pulled them out and sat down. Merchand went to a chair behind the desk.

My impression of Merchand from the morning I found the body, again at the press conference last Sunday, and my brief meeting with police and the FBI agent before the media arrived, was of a real 'spare the chitchat and bullshit, just get it done' kind of guy.

"Professor Singleton has asked that I help the Turners with finding their daughter."

Merchand looked directly at me, but didn't comment. It may not have been visible to him, but I squirmed slightly on the metal chair. He shifted his gaze to Singleton.

"You know the FBI is leading the search," he said.

"I do," Singleton responded. "I met Agent Guidi. Twice, in fact. He made it clear that his office, along with field agents here in Maine, are all over that. And I know that in situations like this, the FBI works closely with other law enforcement agencies." No reaction from Merchand.

"My intention is to try to talk with some locals. Starting in Waterford," I interjected. "See if I can dig out any information that I would pass along to you. And the feds."

Now Merchand slowly half-turned back to me, but he said nothing. And we said nothing more.

Pushing his chair back, Merchand opened a drawer on the right side of his desk, lifted out a file folder, and opened it. He studied it for a few seconds, closed it, and left it on the desk in front of him. It could have been a folder from the media gathering on Sunday.

"You're gonna want to be careful," he said, speaking to me. He paused, then went on.

"People see Vermont plates on your car, they might

think you work for Bernie Sanders." He didn't smile and I didn't hear it, but I sensed there was a snicker in his voice. He knew that I knew that many people in the state of Maine might be a tad wary of Vermont's Independent, media-savvy junior US Senator, Bernie Sanders.

"I don't think that'll be a problem," I said.

"We know that you and the FBI will do everything you can to find Bunny," Singleton said. "This is not about a lack of trust in law enforcement. We simply believe there are some people, for *whatever* reason, that are less inclined to be forthcoming with cops."

Merchand looked back to Singleton. He waited a beat, then spoke.

"This is a horrific crime. No matter when the details emerge, and some of it *will* get out, and no matter *how* we go about searching for your niece, citizens will be ready to help."

"I hope that you're right," Singleton responded.

We sat for a few seconds without further discussion. Merchand opened the center drawer of his desk and took out a card. He wrote on the back and handed it to me. It was the same business card he'd given me the morning the body was discovered.

"My home number and my cell phone."

"Thank you."

We stood. Merchand shook hands with us again before we left.

Twenty Two

"She's no longer with the program," Branchik said.

Pushing by Stephen, he went upstairs first to the living room, then to the kitchen and to the refrigerator. He opened one side, held the door wide, and seemed to be surveying the contents, then opened the freezer side.

Thinking, *hoping* that he'd changed his mind about coming back, after several hours Stephen concluded that Branchik would stay away. Wrong. Here he was.

Stephen had gone down to meet him at the door. When Branchik got out of the car, alone, Stephen's first question was, "Who is this girl?'"

"Where's the other girl?" he'd asked, trailing behind Branchik up the steps. He'd gotten the smartass "no longer with the program" reply.

Branchik pulled a bottle of Grey Goose vodka from the freezer, took a glass from a cupboard, and poured several ounces into the glass. Stephen came into the kitchen. Branchik held the glass up in a toast to Stephen, then took a long swallow.

"So we can take this girl back with her friend," Stephen said. Branchik didn't answer. He took a second drink of the vodka.

"You got any good stuff with you?" Branchik asked. "I'm gonna see a guy in Portland. He's good for a few thou. Maybe more." Branchik now sniffed the vodka, then took a smaller sip.

"Yeah. I have something. Tell me about the girls. Where'd you meet them?" Stephen said.

Branchik didn't answer. He held up the vodka bottle toward Stephen, who shook his head no. Placing the stopper back in the bottle, Branchik returned it to the freezer. He picked up his glass, went to the living room, and sat on one of the sofas. He swiveled and placed both feet on the coffee table.

Stephen stood at the breakfast bar between the kitchen and living room. He pulled out one of the stools and sat.

"Where are they from?" Stephen asked. Branchik took another sip of his drink.

"Fuck if I know!" he answered.

"But you picked them up *somewhere*? Like the French babe this summer?"

"Portland. They needed a ride."

Stephen had been speaking to the back of Branchik's head, so he walked around and sat across from him on the other sofa.

"This girl doesn't look like she's *18*," Stephen said. "How old's the other one?"

Bunny Turner began to sob. Her body was shaking. Listening to the men talking, she knew something had happened to Marcia.

Afraid to open the door, she heard the exchange in the living room. She wanted to see the man who said "they needed a ride.'"

Trying to remember what he looked like, in her mind she went through the encounter outside the train station. While she was taking her phone from her bag to call the ski area, the man approached and spoke to Marcia. She remembered having her phone in her hand. She couldn't remember speaking with anyone.

Now she tried to get her breath and tried very hard not to cry.

Just a comfortable bed and a hot shower. What else do you need? So, I was OK with a room at the Greenway Inn, a small motel located halfway between Bridgton and Waterford.

Carlos Singleton went back to Augusta to see the Turners before returning to Boston. We agreed that I would call the following evening, unless something occurred sooner.

Glad to find a place to stay and get settled, I wanted to venture out and get a better take on this neck of the woods. It appeared to be a little different from the area around Kezar Lake. More ponds and lakes for sure, but if there were any upscale homes, they must be tucked away.

It was 4:30 and getting dark. Locking the door to my room - with an actual key, not a plastic card - I went to the car and drove back into Bridgton. The woman at check-in said the population was around 5,000 and that it was the largest town in the area.

The town website might provide basic information. I would check that later. But I wanted to see firsthand what was out there, especially in the way of bars or clubs. One of my early broadcast mentors regularly imparted his wisdom to me. In your Top-10 list of things to do when you're new in town, he said, go see who's hanging out in the bars.

Thirty minutes, around downtown twice, and I had an idea of what was here and what wasn't. The "here" column included a book store, an artists' cooperative, one barber shop and one salon, antiques store, four churches, two clothing stores, community-access TV, a Dunkin' Donuts, food store/deli, jewelry boutique, land-trust office, laundromat, three law offices, library, movie theater, house of pizza, two real estate offices, four in-town restaurants, ski and sport shop, thrift store, and only one tavern. I knew there were more on the outskirts of town.

The "not here" column? I had to think about that. If it was somewhere else and *not* here, did it really matter? Isn't it debatable, what some towns have and others don't? Or, did the old New England country store dictum apply: If we don't have it, *you* don't need it.

This late in the day, stores were either closed or in the process of closing. A few pedestrians were on Main Street. During my second cruise around town, I'd spotted a restaurant that I would try for dinner, but it was too early. So I parked and decided to have a walk around. First, I wrote a couple of observations in my notebook – names of businesses – then locked the car and headed across the street to check some windows.

After 45 minutes of scoping things out, I made my way back across Main Street to the Mai Thai Restaurant. It looked small, but I like Thai food. Turned out to be a good choice. Quick, attentive service and spicy enough for me. I elected to play it safe ordering a Thai curry dish, stir-fry vegetables, and a bottle of Shipyard Brown Ale. Like many Thai restaurants, the menu indicated a hotness scale of 0-5 stars. I usually stayed around the 3 rating.

The tavern in town looked a little too "family oriented" for my purposes, so I skipped it and drove back up Route 117 toward Waterford. Within 5 miles I slowed down when I spotted a building with two cars, an SUV, and five pickup trucks out front on a Wednesday night. Four neon beer signs in the window and no reference to Sunday Brunch. I pulled into the lot of *The Skidder*.

I stood next to my car and made notes on all the license plate numbers and make of the vehicles in the lot. All had Maine plates. The SUV, I was certain, was the same one I'd seen earlier in the day at the café – an old, faded, midnight-blue Isuzu Trooper. It had a little rust, but good tires. I don't think they've made that rig in more than 20 years.

Inside, a half-dozen tables, four booths along the wall, and eight seats at the bar, plus two video-game consoles and a jukebox. Lots of white Christmas-type lights at different spots around the room. At the far end was a small stage with a microphone stand, a couple of speakers on the floor, and chairs against the back wall. The stage area was dark.

Using the *how many people at the public hearing* approach, I made a quick head count: 14, not counting the woman behind the bar. Five patrons were at the bar. Taking a seat, I realized that three stools to my left was the guy with scraggly hair and the faded military jacket, same character I'd seen at the lunch counter earlier in the day.

Twenty Three

"**Whaddaya have on tap?**" I asked the bartender. She slid a laminated drinks list across the bar.

"Allagash White, Baxter IPA, Geary's, Brooklyn Lager, Harpoon, Sam Adams, Seadog," she said.

"More in bottles," she added, turning back to the shelves behind the bar. She picked up a bottle of José Cuervo, poured a double shot, and walked to the other end of the bar. Attractive, early 40s, upbeat manner. Most likely a good bartender who got good tips.

Reading the beer list I counted another 10 bottled selections in addition to the brews she'd rattled off. When she returned, I ordered a pilsner glass of Baxter IPA. She carefully poured off some of the head, finished filling the glass, and placed it on a coaster in front of me. There appeared to be a kitchen behind the bar. I didn't see anyone with food.

Music playing on the jukebox was nothing I recognized – a woman singing some country crossover number with pretty good steel-guitar backup. A small dance area was in front of the stage, but there was no one dancing.

Two couples sat at one of the tables. The two women were talking with each other; the two men were drinking from bottles and didn't seem to be much into the conversation. One of the men looked pretty far along with the alcohol.

At another table, three younger men – early 30s was my guess - drank beer and were involved in an animated discussion about Tom Brady and Peyton Manning. One guy got up from the table and mimicked a quarterback jumping around behind the line of scrimmage. He was hamming it up and his two friends were laughing.

Across the room in one of the booths was a couple – late 60s, maybe. The man looked about 225 pounds, twice the size of the woman. Each had a mixed drink in front of them. If they were conversing, it must be halftime.

Trying to be nonchalant, I scanned others at the bar. A man and a woman sat to my left. I assumed they were together. The scraggly hair guy sat beyond them. And two guys were on my right, with an empty stool between us.

None of the talk I heard led me to conclude that any of these particular patrons warranted much of my time. The exception might be the two guys on my right. One occasionally said something I couldn't hear, and the other guy would nod. Their clothes made me believe they worked in the woods. After a second glass of beer, I checked my watch; 8:20. The Miller High Life clock above the liquor shelves showed that it was 8:30. Deciding that my timing of stopping here was off, I put a tip on the bar and thanked the bartender. It was probably too early in the evening to observe anything more than I'd already seen.

"Come see us again," the bartender said as I got up.

"You serve dinner? I asked.

She produced another laminated menu and handed it to me. I looked it over for a few seconds, then handed it back.

"Fried shrimp might be good," I said. "Maybe later in the week." She gave me a nice smile.

Walking past the others I had a brief glance at the mirror behind the bar; it was obvious that Mr. Hair Needs Washing guy was giving me a look.

John LeCarre is the best contemporary fiction writer alive, my thought as I placed the book on the nightstand next to the bed.

I was reading *The Naïve and Sentimental Lover*, one of LeCarre's earlier works, for maybe the fourth time. I knew there were authors I hadn't read, or even *heard of*, that others thought were pretty good, too. Like food, like music. Subjective, I guess.

I got up, went to the bathroom, brushed my teeth, relieved myself, then got back into bed. The motel's digital clock said it was 11:03. My analog travel alarm showed that it was really 11:05. I set the alarm for 6:30, switched off the lamp, and was asleep in less than a minute.

Twenty Four

Thursday morning arrived as expected. The bed was OK and, if anything, the room was too warm. If I continued to bunk here, I'd have to get the hang of the temp control settings on the wall-mounted heater/AC unit.

Standing in the shower, I thought how most of us just assume the next day will arrive. Optimists think it'll be better than today. Or yesterday. But *today* hadn't arrived for Marcia Farrand.

How do parents cope with something so terrible? A woman so young, the rest of her life filled with promise. How many young people, and *children*, all over the world, gone in a flash? Today would not arrive for them.

Opening the draperies to the parking lot, I toweled off while thinking more about the untimely deaths of young people. Skipping the in-room coffee, I got dressed and went to the lounge and had the continental breakfast – bagel with cream cheese, fruit and yogurt, coffee to go. I confirmed with the young man at the desk that I would stay another night.

The weather channel in the motel lobby indicated this part of Maine could expect clouds, some afternoon flurries, and temperatures in the mid-20s. Driving shouldn't be an issue. Two minutes later, when my car heater was ready, I was ready.

Before I got into reading last night, I looked over the Maine Atlas and Gazetteer for a few minutes and decided the first part of the drive today would be back through the Waterford area and around the lake, checking any side roads that looked interesting. Depending on how that went and after lunch somewhere, I'd think about the rest of the day.

Based on what I might see and with whom I might speak during the morning, the afternoon plan could be adjusted. There was no shortage of roads to travel, but I was less certain about information I'd get.

Initiating conversation with people I don't know is something I'm accustomed to. Doesn't take much effort to start with a brief introduction. I did recall an old Vermonter once who just stared at me without saying a word as I babbled on about who I was, why I was there, and could he tell me anything about a local business owner who left town with a lot of other people's money? It was a short and not very productive conversation.

Taking Route 117 north, I turned onto 35 towards Waterford, and looped around on Mill Hill Road to Passaconaway Road. For quite a distance it wasn't possible to keep the lake in sight. I turned onto Johnson Road, which brought me to Route 37 and eventually to the Town Common. A few houses, lots of trees, several trails and old logging roads visible, but nobody flagging me down with information to share.

"Are you a fucking queen? You need a little 'show me how' here?" Branchik was staring at Stephen, who didn't respond.

"All that time you got organized down in Mass. and you can't *handle* a little action up here in the woods?" Still no reply. "That nympho Frenchy didn't straighten you out?"

Branchik was standing in the kitchen wearing only jockey briefs. Stephen was at the breakfast bar drinking coffee. He had allowed the girl out to go to the bathroom and offered food again. She took just another bottle of water. Hungover, in an upstairs guestroom, Branchik heard the talk downstairs. By the time he came down, the girl was back in the bedroom.

"I brought her here for *your* entertainment," he declared. Still no reply from Rivera.

Stephen had yet to get a handle on his fear of Branchik. That's clearly what it was, fear. He remembered a similar feeling as a kid when this older, really mean high school drop-out in the neighborhood terrorized everyone.

"What a fuckin' waste," Branchik said, scratching his balls as he turned to go back upstairs.

The previous night, Branchik had continued drinking. The conversation was mostly Branchik boasting about people he'd met since his release from prison. Some very rich and some very stupid, he'd said. And *all* of them want good stuff, the sooner, the better.

A regular supply of drugs this far north was hard to come by. It was like he was making a play to become a full partner. That couldn't happen. Stephen knew Branchik was effective in *some* circumstances, but he also knew that he was unstable. They'd stopped talking after midnight.

She had a clear view of the man doing the yelling.

With the door ajar, she first saw him from the back; then briefly, as he came from the kitchen, a quick view from the front. She saw tattoos on his back, both arms, and the calves of his legs. She thought he was about the same size, just as large as the man at the station. The face looked like him, but he'd been dressed then and wearing a hat. Now she could see that his head was clean-shaven.

Like violin lessons when she was little; repeat the same exercise over and over. She went through the exchange outside the train station. The man approaching, flipping a cigarette into the street. He'd said something, then bumped directly into Marcia. While Bunny was fooling with her phone, the man had reached toward her. She dropped the phone and tried to see Marcia. Blank.

She sat on the floor and leaned against the bed. Waiting. One, or both of them, she knew, would come into the room.

Twenty Five

Carlos Singleton watched students going into Langdell Hall. It was almost noon and he was scheduled to lecture at a 1:10 class.

Standing at the window of his fourth-floor office in Hauser Hall, for the first time in nearly a week Singleton felt frightened for his missing niece. With no children of his own, Bunny was like *his* daughter. From the day she began to crawl and pull herself up, through elementary school days and the beginning of her love for music, to the blossoming young woman now about to graduate from college.

Two young women and a man were standing on the steps, engaged in conversation and laughing. One of the women could be his niece. Same height as Bunny, taller than her friends, and from what he observed, same easy manner.

A movie trailer of memorable scenes. Visits to museums, picnics, Bunny riding on his shoulders, riding the subway in New York City, visiting Bunny and her teenage friends at camp. Having dinner with Bunny and her parents, the bursting pride in their accomplished, beautiful daughter. Now she was becoming an adult. Now she was missing.

He walked from the window, collapsed in the chair behind his desk, and began to sob. Until now, he'd been like a rock. Comforting his sister and brother-in-law, doggedly questioning authorities without losing his cool, focusing on *other* avenues to pursue in trying to find Bunny. Relentless, like his earliest days as a young practicing attorney and more recently as an academician.

After 30 seconds, Singleton took a handkerchief from his pocket, wiped his eyes, and took deep breaths. He walked to the upside-down water jug dispenser in his office, drank two cups of water, and calmed himself.

Bunny was alive. She had to be.

Welcome to Waterford, a Peaceful Village. Maybe a peaceful ghost town, I thought.

Deja what? My second time in this quaint, lovely village and I'm *not* seeing people. Is there some assignment of time slots when folks go about their daily routine, get in cars and drive somewhere, go for a walk?

On the first pass this morning, after taking various roads around the perimeter of Keoka Lake, I'd come through Waterford and nothing was stirring. But that was shortly after nine and I wasn't surprised by the absence of people. I'd doubled back on Route 37 north, then traveled along Route 118, the Norway Road, and now it's 11:15 and here I am across from the Village Common.

133

Less than 50 yards from where Marcia Farrand's body was found, the doors at the Historical Society are locked. Read the sign. Hours: Mon, Weds, Fri – 2 to 5 PM; Sat 10 to 2. I remembered the Town Offices being located south of the village on Route 35, so back in the car.

Deputy Town Clerk Barbara Pietrowski was cordial, professional, and willing to provide a copy of the town map, including a trails map. She didn't ask and I didn't volunteer *why* I was in town. Just visiting the region for a couple of days and curious about the different towns. Right.

Five minutes later I'm on a return visit to *Melby's.* This time I take a seat at the counter. Same waitress as yesterday, Charlene.

"Could I have the soup and sandwich special," I ask, looking at the selections written in different colors on a blackboard. It says French Canadian Pea Soup is today's feature.

"Grilled cheese with tomato and onions."

"What kind of bread would you like with the grilled cheese?"

"Uh, do you have rye?"

"Sure thing." She notes that on her pad and goes to the kitchen.

It's not quite lunchtime and there's no one else at the counter. Two women are having tea and scones at one of the tables. They appear to be in their 60s and bear a facial resemblance. Sisters?

Waiting for the grilled cheese and soup, I opened my notebook to consider all I'd jotted down over the past few days. Two pages of names and contact information from phone conversations going back to last weekend. A short list of places to stay in the Bridgton/Waterford area. Two businesses on Main Street and a list of eight license plate numbers and shorthand for each vehicle they represent. My eyes stop on 483 ABQ (ME) dk blue Trpr.

Charlene is back with my lunch and asks if I want coffee. I tell her that I'm OK with just a glass of water.

"Could I ask you about a fellow I saw here yesterday?" She turns back to me.

"Who's that?" she replied.

"When I was having lunch with my friend," I gestured to the table where we sat, "there was a guy here at the counter. Old green army jacket. Long hair."

"Lou. Comes in almost every day."

"You know his last name?"

"No. I've only heard him called Lou."

"He looks like a guy I knew from high school," I lied. "Does he live around here?"

"Don't know where he lives. He's only been coming in here for the past month or so."

"Thanks." The sandwich is pretty good and the soup is outstanding.

Standing at the rack near the front register after paying for lunch, I scanned several newspapers looking for stories related to the body and the missing girl. Nothing in today's editions. It occurred to me earlier, but I didn't go back, that maybe a visit with the woman who let me use her phone last week – Helen MacRae – might help me connect with some others.

I bought a large oatmeal-raisin cookie, an apple, and a bottle of water. My watch said 12:50. Back on the road.

Twenty Six

"Here's what we need to do, Stevo." Branchik had dressed and come back down to harass Rivera.

Stephen remained at the breakfast bar looking through printed information sheets on commercial real estate investment properties in New Hampshire. A handheld calculator was on the counter next to his briefcase and cell phone.

"*You* give me some of the best stuff you have. And *I* head back to Portland." He watched for Stephen's reaction.

Tapping the papers in front of him into an orderly pile, Stephen used a large clip to hold them together, then placed them inside the briefcase. He was slow and deliberate, hoping to convey that he was cool and that *he* was still in charge here. If this registered with Branchik, it didn't show.

"Let's go out to my car," Stephen said, standing up from where he'd been perched for the last hour.

Branchik stepped aside and waved his arm like a maître d' escorting diners to their table. Stephen retrieved his car key from the briefcase and walked in front of Branchik down the stairs. Once out the door he hit the button on the key. The lights on the Audi flashed, and there was the click of the doors unlocking.

Opening the driver's door, Stephen bent at the waist to reach under the seat. Branchik stood back and kept his hands at his side, his coat open. The always handy Sig P220 was in his left-inside pocket and very easy to reach.

Stephen stood-up holding a flat black, heavy-duty plastic container that had metal trim, identical to the two he kept attached with magnets inside the engine compartment. Only the contents of this container was different from the one opened for Jarvis Blevens a few days earlier.

He turned back to Branchik and slid the lid open on the container. Inside were a half-dozen thin, light-brown envelopes, each about the size of an index card.

"This is as good as it gets," Stephen said. "The best from Bogota. My entire supply for another month." Branchik took the container from Stephen's hand and lifted one of the envelopes. He opened the flap and sniffed.

"How much's here?"

"Four ounces each pack. Five grand a pack."

"You got any Blue?" Branchik was still holding the container with the individual packets of cocaine.

Stephen hesitated, then turned to the car. Reaching again under the driver's seat, he came up with a clear plastic prescription bottle. It was full of light blue pills.

"A hundred pills, 30 milligrams. You can get 25 bucks a pop for these." Branchik took the container and placed it in his right coat pocket. He gave Stephen the sleazy smile.

"I'm your man, Stevo. Best advance man you got. We'll settle-up when I get back."

"When is that likely to be?"

"Saturday. No later than Sunday. Depends on the main man in Portland."

Branchik opened the door on his Chevy, sat behind the wheel to start the engine, then climbed back out to continue the conversation.

"When I come back, we'll get the girl back with her friend. My advice to you, partner, make her *your* friend now." Stephen didn't respond as they stood looking at each other. Branchik got in behind the wheel and held the door open with his left leg still outside the car.

"Whatever you do," Branchik added, "do *not* let her leave here." He watched Stephen when he said this.

"She leaves on her own, we're in shit deeper than you even wanna think about."

Branchik closed the door and pulled away.

"Partner. Not in this lifetime," Stephen said to himself, watching the Chevy go down the driveway and toward Route 2.

Carol Turner tried to comfort her husband. The lobby was quiet at the Senator Inn & Spa in Augusta. She brought him a cup of tea, placed it on the table in front of him, sat, and took his left hand in both of hers.

"Stanley, we have to be strong," she said in a soft voice. He offered a weak smile, picked up the tea, and took a sip.

No one else was in the lobby, only a young woman at the reception desk. It was late on a Thursday afternoon and very quiet.

"We'll stay right here until they find Bunny." She watched him close his eyes again, something she'd seen multiple times over the last week. Something she knew was a refuge he went to during difficult times in their life together. Finding a place to absorb whatever he was coping with at the moment. And there had *never* been anything like this.

Earlier in the day, Agent Guidi asked to go over some information they'd covered before. He said it was to see how it fit with details learned in a meeting with Dr. Nicholas and Katherine Farrand, Marcia's parents.

Waiting until after the Farrands had a chance to process some of the grief from their daughter's horrific death, two FBI agents out of the Hartford, Connecticut office went to the couple's home in Willimantic. They'd spent the morning talking with them, rechecking all they knew about the girls' plans before the disappearance a week ago.

And it did fit. Both families relayed the same basic information.

Marcia and Bunny were to meet with three other friends – all three were female students at other colleges in the Northeast – for a long Thanksgiving ski holiday at Sugarloaf Mountain in the Carrabassett Valley of central Maine. The trip was organized by one of the friends, a student at Colby College in Waterville. She'd reserved a condo and made arrangements for rental equipment and ski lessons for three of the girls in the group.

All friends since their teen years together at summer camp, they had made a similar trip two years earlier when the five of them went to Barbados over Easter break. Now, they were about to move from college to graduate school, professional careers, possibly marriage and other challenges. They wanted this trip together before getting on with their lives.

Bunny traveled the longest distance for the ski trip, flying from Cleveland, Ohio to Boston, where she met Marcia, who was a student at Northeastern University. The three other women arrived at Sugarloaf from their respective schools. At first they were unconcerned, as Marcia had told one of her friends that she and Bunny would try to get there Tuesday night, but might not come up until Wednesday. By late Wednesday afternoon, troubled they hadn't received any phone or text messages, one of the friends contacted Marcia's parents in Connecticut.

Dr. Nicholas Farrand then called the Turners in New Haven. The two families' last word from their daughters had been phone calls late Tuesday afternoon as the girls were about to leave Boston. After confirming this information, Farrand made his first call to the Maine State Police in Augusta late Wednesday night. He was truly concerned.

Sitting quietly now with her husband, Carol Turner thought about her phone call with the other three girls. They had been completely in the dark and just as anxious as everyone else on Thanksgiving and the next day. That all changed after the discovery of the body and interviews conducted by Maine State Troopers who traveled to Sugarloaf late on Saturday, before the FBI became the lead in the search for Bunny Turner.

Nicholas and Katherine Farrand sat with their priest, Father Thomas Calcamuggio. It was the third meeting this week.

Father Tom had been of tremendous help, but Katherine Farrand was near catatonic. Her husband initially considered asking a colleague to prescribe medication for his wife, but after consultation decided on herbal capsules. She'd been taking them for only 3 days.

Now, watching her, the middle-aged pediatrician was uncertain that *any* medication would ever help to restore the slightest semblance of her former life. And he knew that he could hold up for only so long. His biggest fear, now, was the immeasurable impact this was having on their 13-year-old son Nicky, Marcia's little brother.

Twenty Seven

Guidi glared at Colonel Jake Hewitt. He adjusted his necktie but said nothing.

Leaning against the back wall in Hewitt's office, State Police Detective Jim Reese rolled his eyes and pretended to be playing a violin. With his back to Reese, Guidi was unaware of the detective's mime.

"Agent Guidi, with all due respect, this is *not* a court you may be used to playing on." Known for doing his homework, Hewitt's crack was a not-so-subtle dig at the FBI agent's days as a standout college basketball player at Holy Cross.

"I have every confidence in *my* men and women." He paused, then added, "You keep *us* informed, we'll keep *you* informed. It's really that simple."

Hewitt's comments were in reaction to what he interpreted as condescending remarks made by one of Guidi's fellow agents in the FBI Boston office. During a conference call, apparently forgetting he was on speakerphone, an agent in Boston said to Guidi that he was sure the Maine State Police would eventually make a contribution to the case.

"If they get the fuck off the turnpike for a while," the agent said, "and pay a little more attention to figuring out how to get in line with something more serious than overweight trucks."

With the call ended and the speakerphone switched off, Hewitt emphatically told Guidi that all information regarding the murder investigation would flow through *him*, just as he'd stated at the media gathering the previous Sunday.

"That's not going to change," he'd said. "Irrespective of any attempts at grandstanding by your associates in Boston."

Now, here they were in Hewitt's office, doing the macho stare-down.

Guidi rose from the chair and pulled his jacket on. Hewitt sat behind his desk and chose not to expand on earlier comments.

"Not a problem," Guidi said. He turned to leave, glancing at Reese on his way to the door, then turned back to face Hewitt.

"Agent Heinzer in Boston," said Guidi. Hewitt waited for him to continue.

"He's always been an asshole." With that, he left and closed the door behind him.

Hewitt shook his head slowly and looked at Detective Reese.

"Suppose they have more than one?" Hewitt said.

"**From W H Y Y in Philadelphia.**" The voice came at me as I stepped outside Melby's Market.

It was the disheveled character who'd been here yesterday, at *The Skidder* last night and the waitress just told me is Lou. Now, leaning against the side of the building, he gave me what could only be regarded as a smirk.

"You're the radio guy, eh?" he said. The "eh" was added for affect.

Seeing him up close, I realized maybe he *wasn't* in such tough shape after all. He appeared to have good teeth and maybe all of them. A bit of sparkle in his eyes. The scraggly hair and three-day beard threw me off. His clothes were indeed old and thoroughly worn, but his boots looked better than average. Not shiny and new, but well cared for.

"Uh, yeah. I guess," I replied, wondering how he knew anything about me. This was only my second trip to the area. I really didn't know anyone and didn't think anyone knew me. Or anything about me.

"I've spent a few hours behind the microphone," he said, pulling off his greasy CAT baseball cap, scratching his dirty hair, first on top and then on both sides of his head. He put the cap back on.

"Ragsdale," he added, extending his right hand. "Lieutenant Merchand told me about you".

"Michael Hanlon. But you seem to know who I am," I shook his hand.

"Michael Perry Casey Hanlon," he cracked.

Jesus. My mouth dropped when he said this. Not many knew my full name.

"Hotshot news guy from the Green Mountain State. You got a lot of play when the state's attorney got blown up a couple years back," he went on. "My sources say you're OK." He was still smirking.

Flashback: it was the winter of a New Hampshire primary election season, with the usual hordes of media roaming through northern New England. Most were covering Republican candidates in the primary, but then across the river in the peaceful little Republic of Vermont, an explosion. A *real* explosion, as in a brand-new Prius on the main street of Norwich at 1:30 in the morning.

Inside the Prius was a smart, over-educated, politically correct, politically astute and very ambitious State's Attorney. Perceived as a "golden boy" in the state Democratic Party, he was now a *very dead* State's Attorney.

Our station broke the news and stayed on the story for months. As the case evolved, I did a series of interviews with the attorney's colleagues and friends, trying not to sensationalize developments.

Eventually, it came down to a couple of thugs from upstate New York, hired by a crazy right wing type who had relocated to Vermont. Seems he didn't care for liberals in general, and especially didn't care for this rising star Democrat.

"You work in radio?" I asked Lou Ragsdale, now standing in front of me.

"*A long, long time ago.* Like Don McLean, back in the day. Did sports play-by-play. Weekly oldies show at my college station." The guy's eyes really did seem to sparkle and maybe the smirk was his normal expression.

"Got a minute?" he pointed to the old dark-blue Isuzu Trooper in the parking lot.

"Warmer in my rig." I followed him across the road and got in the passenger side. The engine was running and the heater was going full tilt. He turned the fan lower.

He reached under the driver's seat and I tensed. But he pulled up a thermos and a plastic sleeve of disposable paper coffee cups. He handed me the thermos and the cups. Then, reaching inside his jacket, he pulled out a small leather case, flipped it open, and laid it on the center console next to me. His photo ID. And a badge.

I put the bag holding my apple, cookie, and bottle of water on the floor. Placing the ID case on my lap, I poured coffee into a cup for him, then poured a cup for myself.

RAGSDALE, Louis James. The ID gave his height as 6 ft – weight 185 – brown hair, brown eyes. DOB 2/17/65. And it showed that he was assigned to the Joint Northeast Counter-Drug Task Force.

I looked up from the ID and the smirk hadn't changed.

"Good cover," I said.

"We try," he said, taking a sip of the coffee.

"Course with some of these fucking crackheads, you could get away with a Sponge Bob outfit."

"That was Carlos Singleton yesterday," he went on. "Merchand told me you had a visit with him, too."

"Yeah. When Singleton found out I was the guy who discovered the body last week, he hired me to work for his family." Ragsdale gave me a puzzled look when I said this.

"I met Singleton two years ago. I interviewed him. He thought I did a good job and remembered me. I showed up on TV last week at the press conference with the state police. The family's anxious to find the girl and he tracked me down back in Vermont."

"So now you're a private eye? An 'investigator'? No more Radio Rick stuff?"

"Well, no. I'm not really an investigator. And maybe like my former wife says, don't have a clue, let alone a license."

"And yes, no more radio," I added. "Left 2 years ago. Got tired of the bullshit. And the long hours." Ragsdale seemed content to let me go on.

"Now I do PR work for some companies in Vermont and New Hampshire."

"Gonna have to serve somebody," he quipped.

"So. You're obviously plugged into the Maine State Police. It's my sense they have a very tight lid on any and all information related to this murder," I said.

Ragsdale hit the button to lower the driver's window a couple of inches. He took another sip of coffee and put the cup in the holder between the seats.

"No surprise," he responded. "They're not doing hand springs now that Boston TV stations have discovered that Maine extends farther than Freeport. You'll hear things *if and when* Merchand and his brass want you to. Not 5 minutes sooner."

I watched Ragsdale as he watched a grey Jeep Cherokee pull up to the gas pumps in front of Melby's. A really huge guy got out and started pumping gas.

"Are you working on this case? The body in Waterford." I asked.

He turned back to look directly at me.

"We have an interest in mutual constituents," he said. He pulled a card from the photo ID case and wrote a phone number on the back.

"I'm gonna pull out here in a minute. That's my cell. Give me a call this evening. Around six." He handed me the card.

"Where in hell do you get coverage out here?" I asked.

"Back down the road, just before the intersection of 5 and 118. You get five bars like you're in the middle of a TV commercial." He closed his window and pointed at my door.

I got out and Ragsdale slowly backed up to turn around. He pulled away and at a distance followed the Jeep Cherokee.

Twenty Eight

Rivera is a spoiled fucking pansy. He had some lucky breaks when he got started, but he doesn't have the *balls* to do what it'll take to get control of bumpkin country. Goddamn Girl Scouts selling cookies would do a better job.

Driving on secondary roads through New Hampshire and Maine, these were the best thoughts Arnie Branchik could muster.

But Rivera had been his source for both drugs and cash for the past year. He'd been impressed by Rivera's flash, his friends and his willingness to reconsider an ex con. Thinking back now, Branchik decided that should've been a sign. Rivera's "willingness" may have something to do with his "waffleness." Who's gonna take charge? Who decides which people get to *stay* and which people are no longer useful?

Pulling into a convenience store in Limerick, Maine, he filled the gas tank of his Chevy and went inside to piss. Restrooms in most chain-operated convenience stores were a good place for a quick toot. He folded a paper towel and laid it on the sink, then carefully sifted a little coke onto the towel. He rolled up a dollar bill and inhaled two good hits.

'Better than ejaculation.' He remembered that description from his introduction to cocaine years ago. It was still true. Back in the car, his mind was ablaze with the events of the last 2 weeks.

A vivid image of another recently paroled roommate from the federal hotel in Berlin, who knew a *slick* with a fancy house out in the Maine woods. What a contrast to that pansy Rivera's ski place! An image of the girl and the nonstop, all-night party. Couldn't go back there anytime soon.

Portland. *That's* where I need to be right now.

Always careful to stay under the speed limit, very hard to do when you feel like *this*, Branchik stayed on course to Maine's largest city and to establish contact with his newest friend.

"Why are you keeping me here?" Bunny Turner had asked Stephen Rivera.

Darkness was coming on. Minimal light from the high windows only added to the gloom. Inside the house, silence. No yelling, as there had been earlier between the two men. No music from the ceiling speakers, as there had been yesterday.

Standing at the open doorway in the room where she was being held against her will, Bunny looked at the man who said his name was Stephen. He sat at a counter across the room. He turned to face her when she spoke, but offered no reply.

"Where did your friend take Marcia?"

Rivera got up from the stool and walked toward her. He noticed the tone of her questions had a ring of defiance, not the fear and resignation he'd heard in her voice during the past week. Until now, she had said very little.

"Come out and we'll talk." Rivera moved to the center of the living room and sat on one of the sofas facing her at an angle. She didn't budge from the open door.

Crossing his legs, he raised his right hand to his chin, index finger rising over his closed lips. Placing his left arm across his lap, he used it to support his right elbow. After perhaps a full minute of this standoff, Bunny still at the door with arms crossed at the chest, Rivera lowered his arm and positioned his right hand over his left wrist.

"I don't *know* where she is. But he's coming back. Maybe she'll be with him."

Now he raised his arms and crossed them, unintentionally mimicking her posture.

"I'd like to use the shower again," she said.

"Sure. I'll get you a clean towel." He rose from the sofa, walked past her to a closet along the narrow hallway, and produced a large bath towel and wash cloth. He turned and handed them to her.

She took the towel and cloth, and stepped back into the bedroom where she retrieved a fresh shirt and undergarments. She came back to the door and hesitated.

"Use the same bathroom," he said, gesturing toward the hallway on her right. She went in that direction. After a minute, Rivera heard the water in the shower.

Twenty Nine

Perhaps not the Twilight Zone after all. There was a real person.

Stepping off the side porch of Helen MacRae's home in the village of Waterford, I saw a woman walking an energetic German Shorthair Pointer on the road near the driveway. She stopped when she saw me coming back to my car.

"Hi," I said, with a wave. I walked over to where she stood as she pulled on the dog's leash.

"Hello. I was hoping to visit Mrs. MacRae. Guess she's not home." I sensed reluctance from the woman, so I went on.

"I was here last week and had coffee with Mrs. MacRae. Thought she might be able to help me with a project I'm researching."

Polite smile, another tug on the leash, but no reply. More than 25 years in New England and I'm still struck by how reserved some folks could be – and without much effort.

"She may have gone shopping," the woman finally offered.

Of course, I'd said "Mrs. MacRae" not "Helen." Maybe that put this woman on alert. Strangers asking about neighbors. Maybe she wasn't "Mrs."

"Thanks. I'll stop back later." I turned to the car. When I backed out of the driveway, the German Shorthair, nose to the ground and displaying lots of energy, was leading the marginally helpful citizen farther up the road.

More of the scenic tour and yet another human encounter. This time, surprisingly, with a loquacious man at a service station south of the village.

It was an old-style gas station in a small building. No convenience store component to it, and no service bay for repairs. Just one set of pumps out front and a kerosene pump on the side of the building. I was amazed this guy could still purchase gasoline for resale.

"How's the deer herd in Vermont this year?" was his opening greeting. He'd quickly come out to pump my gas and spotted the plates on my car.

"Haven't heard. I'm not a hunter." He looked at me like I might be a Martian. I realized the mistake and tried to recover.

"One of my neighbors is a big hunter. Takes 2 weeks off every November. But I haven't talked with him recently."

"I usta hunt over near Rutland," he said. "My wife was from there. Hunted with her dad and brothers."

While the gasoline was pumping, he was talking.

Stories of deer that field-dressed at close to 200 pounds, deer that were "real skittish" and, of course, deer that got away. I shifted from one foot to the other. When the pump stopped, he went on for another 30 seconds.

I followed him inside the small building. When I attempted to pay with a debit card from my local credit union – *not* the card Carlos Singleton had given me the day before – the topic shifted but the flow continued.

"Don't take credit cards," he said. "Damn banks and credit card companies do pretty well on 'em. Little guy like me, don't pay."

Handing him two 20s and a 10, he gave me three dollars and a dime in change.

I asked how long he'd been around this area and got several more minutes of material. Maybe this guy didn't get many customers. But then he said something that got my attention.

"Some crazy, mean people in the world, let me tell you, Mister Man. Found a body 'tother day up the road at Keoka Lake. All chopped up!" He watched for my reaction.

"Some college kid from away," he added.

I was surprised at the "all chopped up" reference but didn't let on that I knew anything about the body.

"God. That sounds awful," I replied. "What happened?"

"Don't know. My daughter knows a sheriff's deputy. Says it's all hush, hush."

Right. Local law enforcement here is shared by the state police *and* the county sheriff's office. Somebody's yacking.

"You folks have gang wars up here?" I asked, hoping he might offer more. He only shrugged, with his palms up and raised eyebrows.

"Maybe some logger got pissed off at somebody?" I suggested.

"Nope. They'd jes' shoot 'em. Or fix their rig so it ain't gonna run for a spell."

It was late and would be dark soon. I headed back to the motel, took a 10-minute shower rather than a 3-minute spray, got dressed, and read my book for a few minutes. At 5:50, I put my coat on and headed out to make phone calls and have dinner somewhere.

Thirty

"Yes?" A terse response on the other end of the phone.

It was the number Ragsdale had given me for his cell phone. He'd said to call around 6:00. My dashboard clock showed 6:03PM - 30ºF.

"This is Michael Hanlon."

"Didn't recognize your number on caller ID."

"Yeah. I'm in my car about to go eat. Thought I'd try you first."

"Where you planning to eat?"

"Haven't decided. I'm staying at The Greenway Inn. Think I might pick someplace in Bridgton. Went to the Thai restaurant last night."

"There's a good Italian place on 302. Near Fryeburg. Only a few miles west," Ragsdale said.

"I like Italian. Maybe I'll run over."

"You want, I could meet you there," he paused. "Half an hour or so?"

Company for dinner wasn't in my plan. But after our brief conversation earlier in the afternoon, it was clear to me this guy was, as I'd said at the time, "plugged-in." There was a chance I could learn something.

"Sure. I need to make a couple calls first. Could we make it, say, 7:30?"

"That'll work."

"What's the name of the place?"

"Tony's."

"You're making that up," I said. He laughed.

"No. That's the name. And this is *second-generation* Tony. Good food."

"And it's right on 302?"

"Yep. Coming from Bridgton, on the right, before you come into town."

"See you at 7:30," I said.

"*Scenes From An Italian Restaurant*, Billy Joel," he said and ended the call.

Parked there with strong cell coverage in the lot of the US Post Office, Bridgton, ME 04009, it was a good place to stay and make my other calls.

First, to my sister, Laura, in Alameda, California. It was December 6, her birthday. With the time difference, it was near the end of her workday and, not one to let a short call stay short, she kept me on the phone for almost half an hour. Lots of questions and variations on the *same* questions: what was I up to, was I staying healthy, was I going back into broadcasting, how's my love life, wasn't I tired of the long winters in Vermont? An elementary school teacher in an urban district, I heard about some of her ongoing challenges - budgets, students, parents, administrators. *No* thank you, I thought. We talked about her workaholic husband, Gil. We talked about cousins. We didn't talk about what I was doing at the moment. I finally was able to wiggle off at 6:34PM – 27°F.

Seeing the time and not having anticipated the length of this call, it made sense to drive toward Fryeburg and place my call to Carlos Singleton from there.

Tony's Italian Ristorante was easy to find. Just like he said, Route 302 on the right. I found a spot at the far end of the lot and parked facing out so I could see Ragsdale when he arrived. I turned off the engine and tapped in the numbers for Singleton's cell phone.

Branchik arrived at the East View condominiums in downtown Portland.

The directions were on the money. Take Congress Street to State Street, turn right, go six blocks to Cullman Lane. Four-story brick building on the corner, 5 minute walk to the waterfront. Nice spot. Money.

The desk clerk would be informed that a visitor was expected. Tell him you're here to see "Mr. Lazelle" in 401. That's exactly what Branchik did, and the elderly man behind the desk gestured to the elevator off the lobby.

"Fourth floor. It's the unit on the left." The clerk didn't smile, didn't blink and, Branchik figured, probably didn't give a damn.

Small rectangular mirror above the controls, floor numbers indicated with raised brass buttons inset vertically on polished brass. Rich walnut paneling, probably antique. The whisper of the lift was imperceptible. Branchik wasn't sure the elevator had even moved until the door opened again.

Before stepping off, he double checked what he had. Two packets outside left coat pocket; pills in the right pocket; flip phone, right pants pocket. Sig P220, inside left. Knife case strapped under his slacks on his right calf. He looked in the elevator mirror and stepped into the corridor.

On the lower left next to a door marked 401, a round shell-colored button no bigger than a dime was mounted on yet another polished brass plate. The door opened silently two seconds after he pushed the button.

"Glad you could drop by," said the man.

Six foot, some gray showing in his mostly dark-brown hair, better looking than Branchik recalled. Custom-tailored royal blue shirt with white collar, open at the neck; charcoal gray slacks and burgundy loafers.

"Please, come in."

"Thanks." Arnie Branchik was not one who normally expressed gratitude, regardless of circumstances. Not much call for it in his circles.

The room was vast, maybe 1,500 square feet. High ceiling with several skylights, parquet floor with expensive-looking rugs scattered around the room. At first glance, Branchik counted three sofas, as well as numerous chairs and lamps. Mixed art, small pieces of sculpture on pedestals and a shitload of paintings, some very dark, others with bright colors.

"Make yourself comfortable, please. Can I offer you a drink?"

Branchik had not underestimated the man. Classy place. Treats me like one of his sailing pals. I'm *also* glad I could drop by.

"Vodka?"

The man went to an antique sideboard near an archway leading off to another room. He stooped, opened a carved door and took out a bottle of Absolut. From the upper section of the cupboard he removed a tall, blue-tinted glass, and brought it to a table in front of one of the sofas. Branchik remained standing.

"Have a seat, please" he gestured to the sofa. Branchik sat. The man poured vodka, probably 2 ounces, Branchik thought. Maybe he'd been a professional bartender early in life.

The man sat in a chair to Branchik's left and crossed his legs. Navy over-the-calf socks, tassels on the loafers. In their first meeting two weeks earlier, Branchik guessed the man was probably 60 or so. But it was dark then, parking lot outside a restaurant. Somebody else Branchik knew arranged the meet. Told him *this* is a good contact. "Nurture him," is friend said.

"I believe that we have a mutual acquaintance." The man had one of those smooth-as-silk voices, like a Chicago undertaker. Branchik sipped the vodka. Maybe better than Grey Goose.

"You mean Rogers? Guy that had you meet me last month?"

"No, besides him." Branchik studied the guy a little more carefully. He couldn't imagine who else *he knew* that would also know *this* guy.

When he did the deal in the parking lot before Thanksgiving, the guy gave Branchik a slip of paper with a phone number written on it. He'd asked Branchik to call "next time you're in town." The meaning was clear – next time you have some product. Branchik called and here he was.

"Who's that?" Branchik asked.

"Richard Marco. He's an associate of mine. I think you know him."

Fuck me! This guy knows Marco? Holy shit. He wracked his brain trying to recall exactly how he'd parted with the stealth racketeer in Massachusetts.

"I'll be damned. Yeah, I know Marco." He wondered if the earlier charade in the restaurant lot had been a setup. What the fuck's going on here?

"So how is Mr. Marco?"

"He's fine. In fact, I spoke with him earlier this evening. Right after you called to say that you were in town."

Gerard Brousseau phoned Stephen Rivera. He told Rivera that he would be coming back to New Hampshire on Friday night. Alone.

"You still have the chick?" Brousseau asked. "Or did your 'friend' come back to take her home?"

"She's still here. Branchik's coming back Saturday. Maybe bringing the other one with him. Who knows?"

"Are you sure we *need* him, Branchik? The kid from Maine impresses me."

"Yeah, Jarvis. He came back over after you left Sunday. I comped him a couple bags."

"I think we work him. When he was up here last summer, he had a boner for the strippers, but he had a gleam in his eye for doing some deals. Young man ready to move up."

"I have to talk to my connection in Springfield. If we're gonna get in bed with this kid, we need to know how much he can move, how often. And that he won't get his ass in a sling."

"Strikes me as a get it done kind of guy. No ego. And not as crazy, apparently, as you say your Branchik friend is," Brousseau added.

"We'll go over it when you get here tomorrow."

"I should be there around 10, 10:30."

Thirty One

"It would be good if you could spend a little time with them." Carlos Singleton had spent 5 minutes on the phone recounting a conversation with his sister, Carol.

He sounded stressed. Shortly into our call, after I told him about my day and that I was about to have a meal with an undercover drug cop, he elaborated on earlier phone calls with his sister and brother-in-law. Then he suggested that meeting me might help shore them up, at least for the moment.

"I can do that. They're still in Augusta?"

"Yes. I told Carol I would call again in the morning. If I tell her you can drive over to meet them, it would help. She's really worried about Stan."

"Where are they staying?"

"It's the Senator Inn. Downtown. Close to the state capitol building. I stayed there earlier this week," he said.

"I'm sure I can find it."

"I'll call you in the morning after I talk to Carol."

"Better let me call you. Hard to say where I'll be and if I have coverage."

"OK. Call at 10:00."

"Will do."

Watching the old blue Isuzu turn into the lot, I wondered how many miles he had on it. And if it was his personal vehicle, or some clunker assigned as part of the deception. Fooled me.

Ragsdale saw my Honda and found a space three cars over. He parked front-end in, got out, and walked my way. I climbed out, locked my car, and we headed inside. First thing I noticed was that the undercover guy had apparently showered, shaved, and looked a lot more presentable than in previous encounters.

"So, is that *your* car? Or, government issue?" He smiled at the question.

"It's mine. But I only use it for gigs like this."

The restaurant was nearly full. A young woman was quick to greet us, took two menus from the hostess station, and escorted us to a table halfway to the rear, close to several tables with others already dining.

"Got anything else, something quieter?" Ragsdale asked.

I thought he really did clean up well, especially washing his hair. The clothing selection was only a slight improvement. But, still on the job, he couldn't totally abandon the undercover persona.

The hostess held the menus to her chest, looked around, spotted a table where a couple was preparing to leave.

166

"Would that be all right?" she asked. It was all the way in the back.

"Sure," said Ragsdale.

"Just give us a minute to clear it." We returned to the hostess station.

"How many miles on the Trooper?" I asked.

"Just clicked 300,000 a week ago."

"You're kidding! What *year* is it?"

"Ninety-two. They stopped importing 'em a few years ago. Too bad."

"Original engine?"

"Yeah. Uses a little oil every few thousand miles. Transmission rebuilt twice."

"Amazing."

The hostess again motioned for us to follow and she seated us at a table for two, in a far back corner of *Tony's Italian Ristorante*, Route 302, near Fryeburg, Maine.

The man had the self-satisfied expression of a federal judge.

Fuck. Was he a lawyer? Entirely possible this guy is *Marco's* lawyer. But Marco is in Massachusetts. Or he was. Maybe he's in Maine now.

"You know, I'm sure – Bob, right?" Branchik asked. The man nodded.

"Bob, I'm sure I must've had your name the first time we met. Damned if I remember what it is." Branchik was blanking out.

"Lazelle. Sounds like gazelle. The antelope."

"Yeah. That's what I told the guy at the desk in the lobby."

Branchik wondered if he might slip into a bathroom here. Another snort could get him right. And he felt a *strong need* to get right.

"I meet lots of people. Usually call them by their last name." The man smiled at this, just like a fucking judge would smile. Branchik went on.

"You said Marco's an 'associate'. Whaddaya... guys *do* together?"

"Pretty much whatever we want." The man didn't smile when he uttered this crack.

"Richard and I met shortly after he started his business in Lowell. He needed a financial advisor. That's *part* of what I do for him. Offer suggestions on how and where he might consider making investments."

Branchik felt a slight sense of relief. But the man could still be a lawyer. He'd heard of guys back in Chicago who had MBAs, CPAs *and* practiced law. Bet a few of them did some time, he thought.

"Let me be straight with you, Mr. Branchik."

"Call me Arnie. Nobody calls me mister. That was my ol' man."

"Fine. Let me be straight about *why* I wanted you to drop by." The guy was now giving Branchik eye contact that said "pay attention."

"I've been contemplating, I should say 'we've been contemplating', any geographic feasibility that might permit us to expand some of our enterprises." The man paused. Branchik shifted, took another sip of the vodka.

"When I learned of your, ahh... relatively 'new accessibility' here in Maine, I decided to find out who you are. And if we might collaborate. People I trust, in the Portland area, tell me that you've been around and that you know the score, so to speak."

Is this guy being cute? Playing with me? I fucking don't like *cute*.

"Can I use your bathroom?" Branchik said. "Long drive and I really need to take a leak." The request prompted the man to stand up.

"Let me show you the way."

Thirty Two

"**Jerry West. Sweet!** He's the guy on the NBA logo," said a college-aged kid walking by our table.

West is one of my all-time favorites, so I looked up when I heard the comment. The young man was thumbing through a book as he walked behind a guy who might've been his father. The guy stopped and turned around.

"Shaun, you should've *seen* his jump shot. He really was Mr. Clutch." They went on to the register. The older guy paid for dinner and the college kid was still engrossed with the book on the way out of the restaurant.

When I brought my attention back to our table, Ragsdale was staring at me. Our server, who'd introduced himself as Rod, patiently waited for me to order.

"Sorry. I was trying to see what book that kid was reading. Uh, lemme see." I looked down at the menu again. "I think I'll have the mussels with linguine."

"You won't be sorry," Rod said, writing on his order pad. "The mussels are from PEI. Came in this afternoon." Even I knew he was talking about aquaculture mussels from Prince Edward Island. Rod went off to the kitchen for our food.

"I said this afternoon you must be plugged-in to the Maine State Police. I wasn't being a wiseass. I really need some guidance here."

Ragsdale, now in the clean clothes, neatly trimmed Van Dyke, and hair pulled back in a ponytail, was relaxed in the chair across from me. The smirk, I decided, was more a look of bemusement.

"I guess Merchand's OK with me trying to snoop," I added. "He gave me his home and cell phone numbers." Ragsdale nodded at this as he drank from a glass of water.

"Good guy. Square shooter," Ragsdale commented, putting the glass on the table.

"He'll let you go. See if you find anything. He's not gonna hold you back," he said.

"My conversation with Colonel Hewitt certainly gave me the impression that the state police will handle the murder investigation, while the FBI focuses on the missing girl."

Ragsdale gave a simple nod acknowledging he already knew this.

"One of my hurdles, and I explained this to Singleton, is the feds seem to have launched their effort in Portland. And the girl's family wants me to start up here."

"Don't kid yourself. The feds'll be up here, too. Maybe already are."

I was sure he was right. But I was also sure the FBI had no interest in "citizen participation" from a rookie trying to "help."

"You took a good first step last night. Coming by the Skidder."

"The people I saw there looked pretty harmless," I responded.

"Yeah. For the most part. But of all the places I've found around here, Skidder gets more than its share of fuck-ups."

Rod was back with our food. Ragsdale had ordered spaghetti and meatballs and asked for a second basket of garlic bread. I ordered a half-carafe of the house red to go with the linguine and mussels. When the wine showed up, with two glasses, Ragsdale said he'd have just a little, as he had a long drive home.

"Where's home?" He looked up from his food when I asked this. He touched his mouth with his napkin.

"Need to know basis. Couple hours from here."

Brilliant, Hanlon. You really think a drug undercover cop is going to *tell you* where he lives? Eat your dinner.

After several minutes of mastication and watching other patrons with their food, Ragsdale stopped eating and looked at the phone clipped to his belt. He removed the phone, studied it for a few seconds, then tapped in some words and sent a text message.

"My DH." He put the phone back on his belt.

"As in Designated Hitter?" I asked.

"Yeah. It's his weekend to cover. That's how I get to go home for three days."

Feeling the urge to visit the men's room, I excused myself. Three minutes later when I returned, Ragsdale had finished his meal.

"One thing I discovered this afternoon. Some people seem to know about the condition of the body when it was found." I told him about the guy at the gas station earlier in the day.

"Doesn't surprise me. Small community. Things get out."

"The guy said his daughter knows a sheriff's deputy. You think Merchand has them as part of his investigation?"

"Doubt it. I mean, they know what the state guys are up to. Sheriff's deputies handle mostly judicial matters. Court summons and notices, prisoner transfer, occasional road construction and wide-load escort stuff," he recited.

Ragsdale put a 20 and a 10 on the table and made ready to leave.

"I'm back on Monday. Let's connect then. See what shakes out," he said.

"Unless it's all over by then," I replied.

"You should go back over to The Skidder. Friday night is open mic night," he laughed. "Fucking wouldn't believe what people say when they've had a couple drinks."

"I'm driving over to Augusta tomorrow, I think."

"Saturday night jumps, too. Lot of good ol' boys come in from the woods and bring the 'woman' to Skidder. Park your butt at the bar and just watch. And listen." He was standing and I knew he was eager to take off. I wasn't finished eating.

"Sounds like a plan."

"See if you can spot my guy," he said. The smirk was back.

"You mean your replacement?"

"Yeah. He *really* likes The Skidder."

Thirty Three

She cried and cried and didn't think that she could stop.

Water from the shower began to run cold. The girl slowly turned the selector knob to the off position. The showerhead dripped on the top of her head and she leaned against the wall trying to control the sobbing. She got her breath.

Stepping from the shower to the tile floor, she picked up the large towel and quickly wrapped her body. There were guest towels hanging from two bars in the bathroom and she used one of these to dry her face, neck and shoulders. She combed her wet hair.

Unzipping a clear plastic toiletry travel bag, she removed a toothbrush and toothpaste, stepped to the sink, and looked in the mirror. The thought gripping her at this moment went beyond *where's Marcia?* Watching her own reflection, it went beyond the question of where are *you*?

The voice she played to herself, the voice only she could hear, posed the question in a firm, clear, unflinching tone. The question was directed to her, no one else.

Who... are... you?

She listened for activity outside the bathroom. Where was the man now? What would he do when she came out? When is the other man coming back?

She stepped away from the door and back to the mirror.

Was it her grandmother's voice? Was it the clipped, struggling-with-English voice of her close Russian friend and classmate Viktoriya? Was it her mother's voice?

Who... are... you?

Stephen Rivera and Gerard Brousseau had chemistry.

While both men liked flash – hot automobiles, killer clothing that made them feel *more* than cool, eye-catching jewelry not all men would wear – their easy connection with one another was not grounded in the "flash."

They'd first met as teenagers when Rivera had travelled to Brousseau's native city, Montreal. While his uncle came for the gambling and the strip clubs, Stephen wanted desperately to have a male friend. A few guys in Chicopee were OK and fun to know, but he'd never felt a bond with any of them. That bond was instantaneous with Gerard.

Ramon Rivera loved his nephew like a son. Following the death of his brother, Luis, Ramon protected, nurtured, and educated young Stephen through his formative years. He would teach him about people and business. He would teach him about the streets and about life. And he would cut him loose when he was 25.

It had been up to Stephen to find new territories, new customers. It rested with Stephen to realize the dream his father, Luis Rivera, and his uncle, Ramon, first conceived when they arrived in the states 40 years earlier.

Stephen never doubted his uncle, but now he was old. Stephen needed someone else to confide in, someone to challenge the increasing reticence he felt. Someone to help restore his now shaky self-confidence.

He heard water stop running in the shower. Things needed to change with the girl. Things needed to change with Branchik. Stephen needed to assert himself. He needed Gerard.

Thirty Four

The first English explorers showed up in Augusta, Maine in 1607. Traders from the Plimoth Colony in Massachusetts arrived in 1625 and established a trading post, which they eventually sold to four merchants from Boston. Of course, indigenous peoples had been in the area for thousands of years. All this information came to me from a pamphlet published by The Penobscot Marine Museum.

It was 3:00 Friday afternoon in the lobby of The Senator Inn & Spa. I'd driven to Augusta to see the Turners after Carlos Singleton had arranged the meeting by phone earlier in the day. Now waiting for them to come down from their room, I continued reading about the capital city. Present day population estimated to be 19,326, representing just 1.4% of the state population of more than 1.3 million. Augusta is the third smallest state capital city in the U.S.

Augusta is the eighth largest city in the state, while Portland is the largest, with 66,323 people. In all, there are 16 counties, 23 cities, 433 towns, 34 plantations, and five Indian reservations, including the Aroostook Band of Micmacs; the Houlton band of Malisset Indians; the

Passamaquoddy Indian Township Reservation; the Passamaquoddy Pleasant Point Reservation, and the Penobscot Nation.

Located at the head of tide on the Kennebec River, the city was first incorporated as Hallowell in 1771. The north and middle parishes broke off in 1797 and were known briefly as Harrington. Augusta became the state capital in 1827. Just as I was learning about the state presently experiencing a natural *decrease* in population, according to the U.S. Census Bureau, I spotted Carol and Stanley Turner stepping off an elevator across the lobby.

I went over to introduce myself. We'd exchanged introductory nods at the state police press conference the previous weekend, but hadn't spoken. This was our first meeting.

"Let's go into the restaurant. It'll be quiet in there," Carol Turner said.

I followed them into the restaurant and we took a booth on the side away from the only other couple in the room. Stanley Turner allowed his wife to slide into the booth first; he sat next to her, and I sat across from them. A waitress brought water and asked if we wanted to see menus. Carol Turner asked for a pot of tea to share with her husband, and I ordered coffee.

"Carlos told you about our meeting this morning with the FBI?" she asked.

"Only that the Amtrak video was of no real help. And

apparently no backup security signal from the girls' phones."

"Bunny has a Samsung smartphone. Marcia had an iPhone. No signal registered. And no calls from either phone once they arrived at the train station." Stanley Turner watched his wife relay this information.

"I'm guessing the FBI got right on that with the phone companies," I said.

"It was the state police. Colonel Hewitt said it was one of the first things checked when the girls were reported missing," Mrs. Turner replied. She'd asked me to call her Carol. Even though we were approximately the same age, under the circumstances that seemed too informal.

"The last signal from Bunny's phone was a text from a friend. She received it before they got on the train. Marcia's phone didn't show any activity later than the call to her parents Tuesday afternoon," she added.

"I'm told the technology makes it easier to locate an iPhone," Stanley Turner said. "One of my graduate assistants had his phone stolen last summer. He was able to track it with the built-in security." Now Carol Turner watched her husband while he spoke.

"Bunny is always frustrated with me because I forget to switch on my phone," he continued. "And then I forget to recharge it. So I leave it in my jacket most of the time." He offered the slightest smile with this comment.

"I know Carlos made the case for me to help you. And I suspect he gave you my background as a reporter, *not* as a private investigator." Maybe I was being overly sensitive, but it was important to me that the Turners felt OK with my involvement.

"Yes," Carol Turner replied.

"I'm not afraid to knock on doors when it's appropriate. And try to dig out information when I meet people. But, unlike the police, my approach, or my style if you will, isn't as direct. At least not as stern."

Now both Turners were watching to see where I was going with this.

"Not everyone cares to speak with reporters. And somebody's going to ask where I work. No one around here has any idea of who I am or what I do."

Carol Turner placed her cup of tea on the table and looked directly at me before she responded.

"That makes sense. But if I were someone reading the newspaper, or seeing this on television, and you knocked on *my* door and told me that you were working with the family of a missing person, I believe that I'd be more likely to speak with you." She let that register.

"It's what we all agreed to when Carlos brought up the idea of you trying to help," she concluded. The determined expression on her face hadn't changed. Her husband's expression conveyed some combination of hope and desperation.

Suck it up, Hanlon. These people *do* want your help. Get on with it, for Christ's sake.

"My plan is to make connections with people who live in the Waterford area. No way of knowing where that'll lead or if it will really help in the search for your daughter." I considered telling them about Ragsdale, but decided it would be premature at this point. So I offered only a snippet.

"I've spoken with a couple of people already. One guy seems to know the area and I hope that he'll be able to offer some guidance. Point me to others I can talk to."

"Sounds like you've already started, Mr. Hanlon," Stanley Turner said.

"Carol is correct. We have to be strong. Anything else is going to come from the FBI and the police."

Our meeting concluded with some awkward small talk about Vermont and times they visited friends in years past, about the state's politics, and finally about the weather and skiing. As I was about to leave the hotel lobby, I made sure they knew that I'd be speaking with Carlos Singleton each day while the search continued.

Shortly after 4:30 I was back on Route 117 headed southwest toward Bridgton. For most of the drive in the dark, I thought about finding the body of a young woman 60 miles from where she was last seen alive. I thought about 35,000 plus square miles in the entire state. I thought about what the chances were of finding *another young woman* while she was still alive.

Thirty Five

That was NOT the plan, Branchik thought. Back in the car with the same amount of drugs and cash, but much less certainty than he'd arrived with an hour earlier. Branchik's brain was accelerating to Mach speed.

"Mister Smooth," who'd just provided some good vodka and a quick glance at how others at the top lived, had also provided some good advice on how Branchik could do a lot better by "affiliating" with his old acquaintance from eastern Massachusetts.

Despite the urgent, yet stimulating visit to one of the man's ornate bathrooms, Branchik was still trying to recall his last encounter with the mutual friend, Marco.

Blurred memories of how the connection ended, compounded by "experiences" from his time in prison, as well as events of the past two weeks, all crackled and popped through Branchik's brain at that very moment. It forced him to reconsider the arrangement with the pampered weakling Stephen Rivera.

One thing he knew for certain: he had to go back to Stevo's chalet and deal with the girl. This thought gave him a rush. He removed one of the packets from his coat and there on the front seat of his old Chevy, in front of the high priced-condos, he took another hit. Two minutes later he started his car and pulled into the street.

Robert Lazelle told Richard Marco that he was quite confident. Yes, they could recruit Branchik.

Yes, he was sure they could penetrate the North Country more effectively than they had thus far. And yes, he agreed that it held more promise than some of their long-established routes and increasing competition in southern New England.

Marco trusted Lazelle. The two had been friends and business associates for more than 30 years and shared a penchant for staying low profile in everything they did together.

"He says all product at the moment is coming out of western Mass. That means he's working for the spics in Springfield and Chicopee," Lazelle said into the phone.

"They've become much more ambitious," Marco replied.

"Problem is, they're also very stupid," he added. "Got a bunch of kids getting fucked up and arrested in Vermont and New Hampshire. Teenagers robbing convenience stores, breaking into veterinarians' offices."

"Right after I told him that we were exploring growth opportunities, he asked to use the bathroom. When he came out, it was obvious he tooted up. Looked as though he might launch at any second."

"That could be a problem. If he's become a serious user himself, no telling what he'll do next. Or, if he'll actually *come back* when you send him out on a run." Lazelle absorbed this remark and then countered.

"You're right, it *could* be a problem. But it doesn't have to be a problem if we *take charge* from the outset."

"How'd you leave it with him?"

"I thanked him for offering to sell me some good stuff. Told him I was sure that it was really good, but that I was all set. I think he'd been counting on some quick cash." Lazelle switched the phone to his other ear and took a sip of port.

"I asked him to think about how he might assist us. Told him I was sure that you would want to see him again since it's been a while."

"How'd he react?" Marco asked.

"He said, 'Yeah. I'd like to see Mr. Marco again. Set it up. First I have to deal with another matter.' He wants to wait until next week to meet with you."

"When he calls back, tell him we can meet Monday evening. I'll drive up," Marco said.

"**Come to the lot behind the** American Legion Hall," Rogers told Branchik on the phone. "You might be able to lighten your load and pick up some easy money."

Donnie Rogers was another ex-con Branchik knew. He'd become the contact for selling drugs in southern Maine. A few minutes after the call, they sat in the front seat of Branchik's car. It took less than 10 minutes for the deal to offload the pills, the larger envelope of heroin, and for Branchik to pocket $15,000. At this wholesale rate, it wasn't what Rivera said he could get, but it was cash *now*.

"Call anytime," Rogers said, climbing out of Branchik's Chevy.

When Rogers got back into his car to leave, Branchik decided to go into the Legion Post for a quick drink before finding a place for the night.

Vodka double in hand, watching a news channel on the big-screen TV behind the bar, Branchik froze when he saw the news update on the missing girl. The report included a replay from earlier in the week, the girl's parents offering a $25,000 reward for information leading to the whereabouts of their daughter.

The news anchor came back on and talked about "the Connecticut family of 21-year-old Marcia Farrand, whose body was discovered near a lake in Waterford last weekend." Branchik became deaf to the audio from the TV, to the conversations along the bar, and deaf to all sounds inside the noisy, smoky American Legion hall.

What Branchik heard at that very moment, and the images that accompanied the sounds, came from a week earlier. They came from an all-night, *all-on*, full-bore party at a fancy cabin in the woods of Maine. Arnie Branchik was the only person at that party who was still alive.

Thirty Six

"**Back for the fried shrimp?**" asked the woman behind the bar at *The Skidder*. She nearly shouted this at me above the crowd noise and laughter.

Friday night and the place was packed, no surprise. But I *was* surprised, and maybe a little "puffed-up-in-the-chest" as my grandmother used to say, that she remembered me from a brief visit two nights earlier. Good bartender.

"Sure," I replied. "A basket of the shrimp. And a pint of Baxter IPA."

She smiled, gave me the OK sign with her right hand, went off to the kitchen to place the order and was back 2 minutes later with the beer.

All tables and booths were taken and I took one of only two seats left at the bar. Glancing around the room to get a better sense of the crowd, my eyes were drawn to the stage. A woman dressed in jeans and a yellow cable-knit sweater was at the microphone, telling a story about arguing with her daughter over a pair of boots.

Some in the crowd were laughing, others in conversation and paid no attention to the woman. The storyteller paused, raised her right leg as though she was about to stomp on a bug. She held the leg in midair.

"It took me 35 years to grow to this size," she said, pointing at the raised boot. It was wine-red with fur trim along the top. The woman lowered her leg, held her right hand to shade her eyes and shook her head sideways.

"Cinderella at my house is only 12 and *already* wears these." The laughter picked up and several people applauded. Guess it might've helped to hear the beginning of the story.

The basket of shrimp arrived, with a small paper container of coleslaw, another container of cocktail sauce and a slice of dill pickle. I swiveled my stool around to have dinner. Using the mirror behind the bar, I scanned the others seated to my right.

A man and woman were to my immediate right, talking with the bartender. Then four guys filled out that end of the bar. Two were talking with one another, one guy was facing the stage and drinking his beer and the other guy looked as though he might have been here since 8:00 this morning. Head bowed forward, gripping the glass in front of him with both hands. The stool on my left remained empty.

I dipped a shrimp into the cocktail sauce, ate it, took a drink of beer and thought "bingo." That was easy. Had the bartender come over right then to ask if I'd figured it out, I would've told her.

"Second guy in from the right, wearing the old faded-green Red Sox hat and the camo jacket. The one watching the stage." She then would have announced to the crowd that Mr. Hanlon had won the pool! He'd correctly identified Mr. Ragsdale's DH.

The bartender didn't come over, she didn't ask anything, and there was no talk about any misters. But this had to be the guy. I was tempted to buy him a beer and initiate conversation. It took another 3 seconds for me to determine that was a really dumb idea. So I ate my dinner and said nothing.

Across the room a woman was making her way to the stage. She had long brown hair, brushed straight back. The hair fell nearly to her waist. She was actually wearing a dress, charcoal gray. I did another quick scan around the room and saw only jeans and slacks; no other woman in the place wore a dress. It was Friday night, in a bar, in rural Maine.

The woman stepped to the microphone and tapped it twice. Some patrons turned to watch and listen. It was, as advertised, *Open Mic Night*.

With both hands clasped together and fingers interlaced, she raised her hands to her chin and tilted her head forward, giving the appearance that she was kissing her knuckles. People waited. The woman looked around the room. She took in a deep breath and lowered her hands.

"Most of us here tonight... know that something *terrible...* happened in Waterford last week." She squeezed her hands and rubbed one thumb back and forth over the other thumb.

"The body found at Keoka Lake," she paused. "That young woman was someone's sister. Someone's daughter." The crowd noise dropped considerably as she spoke.

"Someone's friend." She again raised her hands to her chin, now almost like she was praying.

"Could we please observe a moment of silence for that young woman?"

Most of the crowd just went stone silent. There were a few people at a table near the door who hadn't heard what was said from the stage. It took them a beat or two, but they also quieted down and looked a little puzzled. After nearly a minute, the woman on the stage raised her head and stepped back to the microphone.

"Thank you," she said. The silence continued while she left the stage and returned to a booth, where she joined a man and another couple.

During the moment of silence, I tipped my head forward slightly, but kept my eyes open and observed the crowd. Shifting my gaze slightly to others at the bar, the guy in the old Red Sox hat was doing the same.

The girl asked if there was any fruit. Stephen said he didn't think so, but that he would look in the fridge.

"Come sit in the living room," he said. She didn't.

"When your friend is back, will you take me to get Marcia? He knows where she is."

Stephen had other thoughts. *His* plan was for Gerard to take the girl with him, back to Montreal. Or, perhaps across the border to Sherbrooke. But the girl had no ID, so that wouldn't work. Maybe take her to St. Johnsbury, Vermont. Drop her off and keep going. *Somewhere* away from here. Stephen was not prepared to take her himself.

"We have some business to finish when he gets back. Then we'll arrange for you to leave."

He stood in the living room, but she gave no sign of joining him. He went to the kitchen, opened the refrigerator and, after a minute exploring shelves and drawers, returned to the living room.

"No fruit. A lot of cheese," he said.

"I'll take some more cheese. And a bottle of water."

Fresh from the shower, she'd put on a different shirt, long-sleeved, teal-green and with the inscription, *If It Ain't Baroque, Fix It* written in dark-blue script. She wore the same jeans, no shoes, and sat on the bed leaning against the pillows. She pulled her legs up to her chest and wrapped her arms around her knees.

Stephen Rivera brought a plate with several slices of cheese. He placed it and a bottle of water on the bed near her feet. She said nothing. He left the room.

Thirty Seven

Lieutenant R. Merchand got the call at home on Friday night from the Oxford County Sheriff's Department. Deputy Jim McCabe had unpleasant news.

"Pretty gruesome. One of the worst I've ever seen. You'll wanna send somebody over," McCabe said.

"Who found it?" Merchand asked.

"Deputy Mayles was doing property checks. Lost his supper when he went inside a Taj Mahal cottage up in the woods near Long Lake."

McCabe referenced the informal arrangement where absentee property owners requested deputies from the county sheriff's office make periodic visits, sometimes just a drive by, to vacation homes in their area. Routine "property checks."

"Whereabouts on the lake?"

"Pretty far back. Osprey Road. You know that area?"

"Yeah. Come in from the south on Naples a couple miles?"

"That's it," McCabe replied. "Take a right. Up from the lake. There's a sign."

"I'll be there quick as I can. Probably 30 minutes."

"Come all the way to the top of the hill. We have two cars here. Look for stone columns at the driveway. This guy's got big bucks. The ME is on the way," he added.

Like most police cruisers, the sheriff's SUVs had exterior mounted antennae that dramatically increased cell coverage. Up to 90% of a cellular signal is blocked by a vehicle's frame and glass, so a roof-mount antenna is vital to law enforcement in rural areas. McCabe placed his phone back in the holster on his belt, got out of the car and returned to the house.

"Medical examiner from Augusta is on the way. Merchand from state police will be here before the ME. Let me know when he gets here," McCabe said to two deputies.

Deputy Mayles had recovered from the earlier physical reaction to discovering this new crime scene in the woods. He stood with another deputy at the front door of a spacious "cottage." As McCabe went back inside, he turned back to Mayles.

"You said the security system was *not* activated?"

"Two panels," Mayles said. "One by the front door. Another out back at the kitchen door. Both are disarmed."

Standing next to a round, open stone fireplace in the center of a large room, McCabe once again felt a sense of amazement at how much money some people had and how much they *spent* on vacation homes.

The fireplace had a cone-shaped solid-copper chimney that went 10 feet to the ceiling. Circling the edge of the fireplace were hundreds of small colorful mosaic tiles the size of postage stamps. The dark stains from drops of blood on the hardwood floor didn't match any of the tiles.

In the master bedroom, a man's naked body stretched across the bed. The severed head to the body was on the floor next to the bed. The stench was unbearable. McCabe went to the kitchen. More blood, on counters, on a marble-top center island, and on the wall near the door.

He spotted the security system panel. Not touching any surfaces, he stopped himself from opening the kitchen door. Peering through the window to the porch outside, he saw still more blood. There was a long deck that wrapped around the corner of the house. McCabe guessed that it extended to the bedroom he'd just left.

Nearly 40 years in law enforcement and he'd never seen anything like this. Car accidents, hunting accidents, suicides, a double homicide 25 years ago, *never* this much blood splattered in so many different areas.

"My impression is that he's better than you think," I said. It was a little after 9:30 and I was on the phone with Carlos Singleton. He asked what I'd thought about the emotional state of his brother-in-law, Stanley Turner.

"We sat in the restaurant talking for more than an hour. Just before I left, he repeated what you told me your sister had said earlier. The need to be strong, staying positive about Bunny and have faith in what the police and the FBI are doing."

"Good," Singleton replied. "Maybe the shock of all this has started to settle and Stan realizes that everyone is doing *something* to find Bunny."

"Are they planning to stay in Augusta while the search continues?" I asked.

"Oh, I'm sure. Carol won't leave until there's a reason to leave. I know both have made arrangements in New Haven for being away from campus."

We talked a couple of minutes longer. I clicked off and was ready to head back to The Greenway Inn. Before leaving the parking lot at *The Skidder*, I cruised around looking at other parked vehicles. Wasn't sure what I thought I might see, but it felt like the thing to do. Nothing jumped out at me. Cars, trucks, SUVs, and one mini-van. Total count was 21, compared to two nights earlier when there were eight vehicles in the lot.

Just before my turnoff to The Greenway Inn, a state police cruiser passed going in the opposite direction. Blue lights flashing, no siren, the car had to be going 70mph on this secondary road.

It took me approximately one second to decide to turn my car around and follow. The dashboard clock read 9:46PM. Even if I couldn't catch him, I was pretty sure that I could keep his flashing lights in view.

Watching for moose and other animals, and staying

under 60, I thought this guy could be going to a car accident, a fire, or just on his way home. Some of my cynical colleagues *back in the day* used to joke about state troopers speeding on the highway, saying nine times out of 10, the speeding was because it was time for a shift change and they wanted to get home.

Trying to keep the cruiser in sight, I thought about the time when many reporters had police scanners mounted in their cars. Hell, some probably still had them. I didn't miss the constant chatter and frequency checks used by police and fire dispatchers all over North America.

Ten minutes and no animal collisions later, turning off Route 302 onto Naples Road near Long Lake, I could see the cruiser far ahead slow down and make a right-hand turn. The strobe from the blue lights on snow-covered trees had an effect similar to the aurora borealis. The cruiser was climbing a hill before I got to the turnoff. A few seconds later, I spotted a sign that read Osprey Road. I took the same right and started up a long incline.

After probably a mile, I could again see the lights on the cruiser. It had turned left and appeared to have stopped. As I reached the height of land, there were two fieldstone columns on the left side of the road. The columns were about 6 feet high and reminded me of stone cairns on hiking trails in the White Mountains. On top of each column was a black forged-iron lantern. Both lanterns were dark. I turned into the driveway.

On a slight grade at the end of the long driveway was a single-story combination fieldstone and wood house. The contemporary home was long and had a stone terrace across the front with smaller versions of the cairns.

To the left side of the driveway was a building of similar design and materials. When I got closer, I could see this building was a four-bay garage. The state police cruiser had stopped behind two other white police vehicles. One was an SUV, the other a patrol car. Both had SHERIFF Oxford County written on the side in large gold letters.

Going up the steps from the driveway to the house was a Maine State Trooper. It was, or at least from my vantage point appeared to be, Lt. R. Merchand. At the front door he spoke with two other policemen. I presumed they were sheriff's deputies.

Stopping a few feet shy of the parked police cars, I turned my lights down to parking. Engine still running, I thought it might be smart to wait a couple of minutes before approaching the house.

I looked at my cell phone and was surprised to see three bars registering. Had to be the higher elevation. 10:07PM – 29F.

Thirty Eight

Branchik was jacked about as high as he could get.
The effect not quite up to the sex and blood orgy a week
earlier. But still, a full-throttle rush.

Checking into a cheap, no-brand motel away from the
highway was his best play now. It was after 10:30. He
doubted his ability to observe speed limits driving back to
Gorham, New Hampshire. Fuck, he doubted his ability to
avoid eliminating any asshole who came near him. He
needed to think through the next play with Mister Smooth
and his friend Marco.

Branchik had very little interest in confronting law
enforcement of any kind, especially the town cops who
would pull you over for five miles over the speed limit. He
had absolutely *no* interest in spending one more day
behind bars. Too old for that shit. Let the fucking young,
stupid, macho boys take that on.

The middle-aged woman at the motel took his $40
cash and gave him a key. On the registration card, he
filled in phony information on the required blanks – name,
make of auto and license plate. She's not gonna go out
and look, I'll be gone in the morning.

In the motel room, standing at the toilet for what seemed like 10 minutes, Branchik tried to form his thoughts. And his plan.

Stephen Rivera had to become a friend of the past. Stephen had to disappear from everyone's radar. Now. And the girl had to disappear as well.

Branchik turned on the TV with the volume muted, paying no attention to the channel. From his inside coat pocket, he pulled the Sig P220 and placed it on the nightstand next to the bed. He removed his shoes, took the plastic bag with all the cash from the deal with Rogers, and put the bag and the shoes under the bed. Sitting upright on the bed, he leaned against two skimpy pillows and watched TV, keeping the sound off.

His brain was racing and he didn't expect to sleep. Was there a way to get Stevo to get his hands on the reward money? Could he do a deal with Mister Smooth back in Portland? Let him collect the $25,000? No. Who else could he think of who wouldn't bring it all back around to him?

There was a late-night infomercial on TV. It went on forever. The guy making a pitch for something, a juicer, a blender, some fucking thing nobody needed. Branchik studied the screen but kept the volume on mute. The man on TV reminded him of Willard.

Images came to him now from the party at the house in the Maine woods, the house Willard's friend owned. He wasn't going *there* again anytime soon. And Willard was no longer available for "parties." At least Willard would never worry again about going back to prison.

Branchik needed another snort. He got up and reached for his coat.

"How did you get here?" Merchand asked.

For a second I considered answering, "I got here in a Honda CR-V with all-wheel drive." I had the good sense not to say that.

My first mistake was getting out of the car and approaching the house. One of the sheriff's deputies quickly greeted me at the bottom of the steps. When I told him who I was, showed him my driver's license and said that I knew Lt. Merchand, the deputy escorted me back to my car, instructed me to get in and stay in. He would speak with Merchand.

Sitting for another 15 minutes, now with driver's window down and Merchand standing next to the door glaring at me, I resisted the smartass reply about the Honda.

"I followed you here," I said. "You passed me back on 117."

He looked at me without responding. Removing his trooper hat, slowly wiping his left hand over closely cropped hair, he turned his head away from me. I thought I detected a deep breath. He turned back and looked at me dead on.

"This is a crime scene. *Stay* in your vehicle. Do not *move* your vehicle." He paused and looked at the sheriff's deputies on the porch 50 feet away.

"There'll be other law enforcement personnel arriving shortly. They'll check tire tracks, footprints, yellow spots in the snow where someone may have taken a leak, anything. *Do not* get out of your car again."

Lt. R. Merchand walked back to the house and went inside. 10:29PM – 28F.

Carlos Singleton was on the phone with his sister, Carol. He called her every night just before turning in. All their conversations had been centered on Bunny. But this call was different.

"I just can't imagine how the Farrands are coping," she said.

"Back when the girls were teenagers, when I first met Katherine and Nick, I thought she was a fragile person *then*. So protective of Marcia. It was the first time I heard the expression 'helicopter parents'.

"Always hovering," Carlos replied.

"She was. Nick, maybe not so much."

"And that beautiful little boy, Nicky," she went on. Carlos could hear her voice choking.

"He adored his big sister. Bunny used to tell me about when she visited, Nicky wanted to go everywhere with them. Most of the time, Marcia tried to include him. All the girls loved him."

The phone connection was silent for several seconds. Carol Turner was sobbing. Carlos waited.

"I remember hearing an NPR interview once with a man who'd lost his son at a very young age. This was quite a while after the boy's death." Carlos said.

"At the end of the interview, the man said 'The tragedy of losing someone so young never gets better. It just gets different.' I sat in my car for a long time trying to imagine how that man must've felt. How he coped."

Carol Turner let out a big breath. She regained enough composure to finish the conversation.

"I love you, Carlos" she said.

"And you *know* Bunny loves you," she added with a laugh.

Now, Carlos thought that he might lose it. But he didn't.

"We'll find her."

"Goodnight," Carol said.

"Stay warm up there." He put the phone down, removed his reading glasses and rubbed both eyes with the heels of his hands.

Thirty Nine

The girl heard someone coming into the house. She put the magazine down, walked to the door, opened it slightly, and listened. Voices came from the lower level. She couldn't make out what was being said.

It was the man who told her that his name was Stephen. And the voice of another man. The other voice didn't sound like the large man with the shaved head, the man she was convinced had somehow drugged her and brought her to this house.

She cracked the door open another inch or two. They were coming up the stairs now. Quickly closing the door, she went back and sat on the edge of the bed. Earlier, she again refused to come out to the living room. A few minutes after that, he'd brought her some old magazines.

Now, the two men were keeping their voices at a lower than normal conversation level. She still couldn't hear what they were saying.

"I want you to take the girl. Tomorrow, before Branchik gets back." Stephen spoke softly and deliberately, glancing to his right and pointing in the direction of the bedroom across the hall.

Gerard Brousseau stood behind the sofa across from Stephen. Placing his Montreal Canadiens royal-blue duffel on the sofa in front of him, he waited for Stephen to continue.

"The prick went to Portland to sell some coke and pills. Took most of the product I had in the car," Stephen went on. "Said he'd be back late tomorrow or early Sunday. He may bring another girl with him."

"*Another* girl? Not a hooker?" Gerard raised his eyebrows and added, "This girl looks very young."

"I'm not sure she's 18," Stephen responded.

"She won't talk to me. Says her name is Bunny, but I think she's lying," he went on. "And she's hardly eaten since she got here. Some cheese and a little bread."

"You said last weekend she was recovering from being... strung out," Gerard said.

"Branchik brought her the night before you and Vivian came down. She was unconscious when she got here." Stephen stood up and walked to the large windows on his left. He looked out into the darkness, no stars visible.

"I gave her shots of chloral hydrate the first couple days. Branchik has this whole bag full of ready-to-inject syringes of the stuff. Apparently uses them a lot."

"So, he *didn't* meet her in some bar? You think he kidnapped her."

"Yes. Now he has the other one stashed somewhere

else. He knows people over in Maine about an hour from here."

Gerard walked around the end of the sofa and sat down. Drugs and a little cash moving back and forth across the border is one thing. Kidnapping an underage girl is something else entirely. And he believed his friend Stephen wanted no part of this.

And he knew *Jesus Murphy he* wanted no part of it.

"Where do you want me to take her?" Gerard asked. "She can't come to Montreal."

Stephen came back from the window and sat. Gerard had never seen his friend look this beaten, this uncertain. Or, this frightened.

Forty

On CHOM-FM, 97.7 out of Montreal, I was listening to
Amped With the Rockman. Some of the cuts were by
artists I didn't know. Others were classic rock hits. The
commercials were a mix of English and French. A block of
ads finished and went straight to *The Eagles* … "*On a dark
desert highway, cool wind in my hair.*"

Every few minutes, I turned the ignition on and ran
the engine to get some heat, then I shut it off for a bit.
This drill went on for nearly an hour. 11:20PM – 25ºF.

A third Oxford County Sheriff's car arrived, as well as
a van with two people from the medical examiner's office.
The van was white with large blue letters on the side,
indicating Maine State Police and Medical Examiner Unit.
The ME forensic technicians had been inside for over 30
minutes now.

As I started the engine and got the car warmed up
again for maybe the fifth time, I saw Merchand and one of
the sheriff's deputies coming down from the house. They
were heading toward me. Here it comes, I thought. I hit
the button to lower my window.

"I'd like you to join us for a few minutes. Right now.
My car," Merchand said, and he turned

toward his cruiser.

I shut off the engine, got out, and followed him. He held the front passenger door open for me. The deputy got in the back, sitting behind where I'd be seated. I got in and Merchand went around and climbed in behind the wheel. He started the engine and said nothing for a few seconds. The deputy was quiet, too.

"We'll have some heat in a minute," Merchand finally offered, then turned to the back seat.

"Deputy Mayles. This is Michael Hanlon. He's here on special assignment from Ethan Allen and The Green Mountain Boys. Or, is it Howard Dean?" Merchand looked at me when he said this, but there was no smile to match his sarcasm. After the long stretch of music I'd been listening to, I resisted the thought to say that I was on assignment for Grace Potter and The Nocturnals.

Now positioned in the center of the back seat, Deputy Mayles remained silent. He looked to be late 20s, early 30s, about 5' 10", 180 pounds. Either blue or hazel eyes, hard to tell in the dark.

"Expand on what you told me earlier, Deputy. Start with the property checks on vacation homes." Merchand cranked the heater fan to full tilt.

Mayles took his hat off and leaned forward. Before he said a word, Merchand held up his right hand to delay his start.

"Mr. Hanlon. This is for *your benefit* only," Merchand

said. Looking directly at me, he added, "You're *not* going to be sharing this with others. *Not* going to phone or text it to the Associated Press." In the tone of a question, it sounded more like a declaration. He waited for my response. I got it.

"My ears only," I said. He nodded, then put his hand down for Mayles to proceed.

"We have, maybe, up to 20 homes around Long Lake and Crystal Lake that we check on. Mostly between end of October until spring. People from away that normally don't get up here in winter," Mayles said.

"Depending on where the home is and what the owner has set up with the sheriff, maybe we just drive by. See things look OK. Some, we go up and walk around, check the doors and windows."

"How often do you do this?" Merchand said.

"Depends. Sometimes once a week. Others closer in, we might drive by a couple times a week. And there are other deputies doin' the same things in other parts of the county."

"Who pays for this? Surely not taxpayers." Merchand asked.

"No. The non-resident owner makes an arrangement with the sheriff's office. Depends what they want and how often. They pay directly to the county. I think it's part of the operating budget for our department."

"So, when you drove up here earlier tonight. This

property one of those that gets the doors and windows check?" Merchand said.

"Yeah. Guy who owns this place is a stockbroker, or something to do with investing. He told the sheriff some friends were staying at Thanksgiving. But that we should start our visits again first week of December. Tonight was the first time out."

"What time did you come up here this evening?"

"Like I said inside. I did three other properties down by the lake before I drove up here. It was just after 8:00. Dispatcher was finishing frequency checks on the scanner when I pulled in."

"What'd you do when you arrived?"

"There were lights on inside. No big deal, I figured they were on a timer. But when I got up to the terrace to check the front door it was unlocked. I opened it and waited for the alarm. Nothing."

"Aren't most alarms silent in the house, just send a signal to the police?"

"Yeah. But there's a light on the panel by the front door. I watched it and it stayed green. I was ready to call it in if the alarm tripped."

"So, what happened when the alarm *didn't* activate?"

"I knew something was wrong before I started looking around. The smell." Mayles shook his head as though he was shaking off water.

"I yelled 'Hello. Anyone here? Then I see blood by the

fire pit in the middle of the room. When I go down the hall to the big bedroom, it really smells. Blood everywhere. And the body."

"OK. That's a good summary of what you said earlier. Anything else you can think of?" Mayles shook his head. Merchand turned his gaze back to me.

"I think Mr. Hanlon might have a better idea of... " he paused. "Of not stumbling around a situation like this as though he's covering a political convention." Merchand's tone seemed to have softened. Mayles sat there holding his hat and waiting.

"I think we'll go back inside and see how the techs are doing," Merchand added. "Thank you, Deputy Mayles." He nodded when he said this and that prompted Mayles to climb out of the back seat and go back to the house. Merchand dialed down the heater fan.

"That story you covered in Vermont when the state's attorney got blown up. Were you at the scene after it happened?" Merchand said.

"I got there after they took him out of the car and had him in the ambulance. He was dead before they got to the hospital."

"I suspect you've seen some unpleasant things as a reporter. You know what we saw out at the lake Saturday morning. This is worse."

I wasn't sure what Merchand was expecting me to say.

"I'm going to let you come inside, if you want to. This isn't going to make the news before tomorrow. And you told me earlier that you are *not* acting as part of the press corps. Correct?"

"That is correct."

"Only step *where* and when I tell you after we go inside the house." He shut off the engine, opened his door, and got out. I got out and came around to his side of the cruiser.

"Stay out of the way of the ME guys. They don't know and don't care who you are."

"Got it," I said.

"Let's go."

Forty One

Stephen Rivera and Gerard Brousseau were closer to a plan. They'd discussed different options and were now in agreement. The girl would leave in the morning.

"There's a truck stop 10 minutes east of here," Stephen said. "It's on Route 2 after the Bethel exit." He was doodling on a pad.

"Before the ski area," Gerard replied.

"Yes," Stephen said. He stopped, put down the ballpoint pen, swiveled on his stool to face the living room and slowly massaged both temples with his fingers.

"What time should I leave," Gerard asked.

Stephen turned and placed his hands flat on the counter. He looked right at Gerard.

"We'll give her some cash. Then she's on her own. She can call whoever she wants."

"What about the other girl? If Branchik brings her back, then what?"

"His problem," Stephen said, then went on.

"We'll need to cover your license plates. Pull over before you get to the truck stop. We don't want her to see the plates when you leave."

"I only have a rear plate. But what if she tries to get out of the car?" Gerard asked, voice an octave higher. Some anxiety surfaced as they continued talking.

"Before you leave, I'll give her an injection of the chloral hydrate. Half a syringe, enough to make her a little dopey." This seemed to assuage Gerard.

"There's a counter, away from the snacks and cash register. You can help her to a seat. Pretend you're going to the restroom. Then split."

"There must be cameras," Gerard said.

"Probably. You can wear a hat. And one of the ski parkas from downstairs." Stephen's face brightened when he said this.

"Wait," he added. He gripped Gerard's forearm.

"The kid. Jarvis," he looked at Gerard. "He can help you. Take her in *his* car."

Gerard's face relaxed. He smiled for the first time all evening.

"**Put these on,**" Merchand said. He gave me a pair of dark-blue disposable booties to go over my shoes.

Standing just inside the front door, we were in a slate floor entrance hall to the living room. The booties were one size fits all, adjustable elastic around the top and made of a lightweight synthetic fabric. Several pairs were in a plastic bag on the floor.

Pulling the booties over my shoes, I watched as Merchand put his on. He motioned for me to follow him across the living room. We stepped carefully around the edge, avoiding the normal traffic pattern between rooms.

As soon as we turned to a long hallway, the smell hit me. I didn't have to ask. And for a second, thinking back to the body at the lake, I wondered what I was about to see.

Merchand stopped in front of me, took a handkerchief from his pocket and put it over his mouth, tight under his nose. He looked at me and waited. Fortunately, I also had one and did the same. We proceeded a few steps entering a large bedroom.

Dark stains of blood seemed to be everywhere. On the carpet, on the bed, on the wall behind the bed. On the ceiling. We stood to one side of the door, out of the way of the two med technicians working. Both wore disposable protective suits over their clothing, covering on their hair and light blue cone-shaped surgical masks to cover their nose and mouth.

One of the ME guys had his back to us. He was zipping a body bag closed. The other had a camera strapped around his neck. He'd been placing items into plastic bags, putting the sealed plastic bags into an aluminum case on the floor next him. He glanced up when we entered the room.

"We're pretty much finished, Lieutenant," he said. The other tech turned and looked at us. He nodded in agreement.

"You need help with the bag?" Merchand asked, voice slightly muffled under the handkerchief covering his mouth. He looked around, then added, "McCabe still here?"

"He's outside," said the tech next to the body bag. He pointed to a door that exited from the bedroom out to a deck covered in snow. There was an outside light on, but no sign of the deputy.

"We'll get our gear in the van, then come back for the body," the other tech added.

Merchand looked at me and with his right hand, again motioned for me to follow. We stepped behind the tech packing up the evidence bags, crossed the room to where Merchand opened a French door leading outside. I removed the handkerchief I'd been holding over my mouth as soon as we had air. Cold, fresh and a real relief.

Sheriff's Deputy McCabe stood a few feet away from the door, near the edge of the deck. He looked up when the door opened.

"Looks like more blood out here. It's snowed some in the past few days," McCabe said. We stood at the door and didn't step onto the deck.

"Any word on the owner of this place?" Merchand asked.

"Yeah. Guy named George Roland. Lives in Portsmouth, New Hampshire. I don't think that's him," he said. "We think he's in New Zealand. The sheriff's checking."

Listening to this exchange, I tried to recall the time

difference between the eastern US and New Zealand. They're 18 hours ahead, I think. So it was almost six in the evening there.

"Deputy Mayles said your office was informed there'd be people here over Thanksgiving," Merchand said.

"That's right. Tonight was the first property check since then."

"You'll let me know as soon as you speak with the owner?" said Merchand.

"Roger. Sheriff will call you." McCabe had a bright LED flashlight in his left hand. He hadn't moved from his position near steps that led down and back around to the front of the house.

Merchand turned, put the handkerchief over his mouth again. I did the same and followed him back to the entrance hall. We removed the slip-on booties and went out through the front door.

"Let's go to my car," he said.

Five minutes in the front seat of a Maine State Police cruiser and the heater felt good.

"Like the body at the lake, this guy was decapitated," Merchand said.

"Hands and feet?" I asked.

"Still intact. Appeared to be stab wounds. The torso was on the bed, chest down and lots of blood under the body."

Merchand removed his hat and partially unzipped his

216

jacket. He rubbed his forehead in the area where the hat brim normally rested then placed the hat on the seat.

"We won't know until they do the lab work, but the guy probably was sexually assaulted," he said. I looked at him and he caught my expression.

"The position of the body on the bed. I've seen it before," he added. "And the guy was completely naked."

The techs came out of the house wheeling the gurney with the body bag strapped on top. The sheriff's deputy walked in front and opened the rear of the van. We watched as they lifted the gurney, slid it forward, and closed the doors. One of the techs said something to the deputy; he turned to go back to the house and they climbed into the van ready to depart.

Sitting in the relative comfort of the cruiser, hearing his description of the initial discovery of the body, I was glad Merchand delayed allowing me to go into the house.

"You should take off," he said. "Check with me in the morning. We'll know more."

"My inference is that this is too similar not to be connected to the girl's body at the lake," I said. He looked at me but remained silent.

"Call me tomorrow. Late morning," he offered.

Back in my car, I drove slowly behind the ME van down the long driveway, back onto Osprey Road and followed them all the way to Route 302. They turned left and went east; I turned right and headed for The Greenway Inn.

217

Forty Two

"I'm expecting a call from my guy," Jarvis Blevens said to Leon.

"We have enough left now for a few more stops. I know someone who can swing a better deal for us." Jarvis was in the kitchen standing at the sink.

Leon was parked in his recliner watching TV. He picked-up the remote and lowered the sound so he could listen to what his little brother was saying.

"You gas up the Jeep in the morning. I need to leave the Subaru back at the garage for some transmission work," Jarvis went on. "You pick me up and we'll come back here. Then I need to use the Jeep."

Leon nodded in acknowledgement, but his attention was divided between Jarvis and the action on TV. A car flipped twice and exploded.

Jarvis used his fingers to finish eating left over cold potatoes and a greasy slice of ham. He placed the dirty plate in the sink, ran water on it for a second then went off to his bedroom.

While he was getting ready for bed his cell phone rang. He picked the phone up from the nightstand.

The caller ID showed a 514 area code. Gerard Brousseau's cell phone.

Sitting at the computer in his home office, Richard Marco studied the list of contacts. It was after midnight but he was not ready to turn in.

His carefully detailed, organized and much-tweaked spreadsheet showed a breakout of the activity, routes and personnel in Massachusetts. He'd reviewed it numerous times and was convinced that it was solid. He knew there was plenty of competition and that it could change every week. But he anticipated that and dealt with it as necessary. Marco had been at this business for a long time.

He stayed out of Rhode Island and Connecticut completely. The last thing he wanted was to tangle with the crowd from Providence or New York City. The real opportunity was to the north. And now here was a chance to bring back a tough guy who knew the territory, knew the methods, and knew a lot of customers, who would lead to new customers.

He shut down the computer, turned off the lamp on his desk and stood from the chair. The soft light from the desk clock showed that it was now almost 1:00. He'd sleep on it. But he knew the solution to his "field office" personnel problems.

Branchik could be the best investment to pursue. He would find out on Monday.

Pitch black, cold, and very quiet. Branchik stepped from the motel room, got behind the wheel of his Chevy, and started the engine. It was close to four in the morning.

Wired and wide awake for several hours, Branchik knew what he was going to do. What he *had* to do. Deal with Rivera, get the girl back. Get the money.

Although working a plan that would actually produce the $25,000 reward for "information" on the missing girl, *that* was the hurdle. He'd figure that out after he persuaded Rivera how they were going to do this, and when he was back there with the girl. And then Stevo could just go away. That would be an easy fix.

Through the winding, empty back roads of rural Maine and New Hampshire, Branchik drove in darkness in the middle of the night. Stay under the speed limit, don't attract attention.

She felt like she'd been through the wringer. Twice. Sleep came in short intervals. Her body was numb, she couldn't find a way to relax and it had only gotten worse. She thought there couldn't be a teardrop left in her.

Uncertain of how many days had passed or what day it was now, she was able to conclude one thing: this place where they were holding her couldn't be in a city. There were no external noises, things that you'd normally hear if other buildings, or cars, or people were around.

At different times since she'd been alert, only occasionally did she hear what might be traffic sounds. They were barely audible and sounded far away. So wherever this was, it had to be in the country. And while she'd spent most of her life in densely populated southern New England, she knew that the "country" region to the north was relatively wild and unpopulated.

There were no other sounds in the house. Were they asleep? It had to be the middle of the night. Find a clock in one of the other rooms. There must be a clock in the kitchen.

She quietly got off the bed, walked as softly as possible across the carpet, went to the door, and listened.

Forty Three

It was Saturday morning. Jarvis was up early. There were a couple things to handle before his scheduled meeting with Gerard Brousseau at 8:30.

Brousseau had called late the previous night to say that he was back in Gorham and had an urgent business matter that required some help. They agreed to meet for breakfast at the Bethel Truck Stop.

Stepping from the shower, Jarvis brushed his teeth and took a threadbare towel to dry off. He wiped the steam from the mirror and used his father's old electric razor to shave. Rubbing his right hand over his short hair that needed no comb or brush, Jarvis took an extra few seconds to look at his reflection in the mirror.

Back in the tiny bedroom, he took a fresh shirt from the closet and a clean pair of work pants from the dresser that had held his clothes since he was in elementary school. He put on wool socks, boots, and a brown hooded sweatshirt bearing the red silhouette of a rifle across the chest.

Aware of Leon's habit of staying up all night watching TV, Jarvis wouldn't wake him this early. I'll come back after meeting Brousseau. We can take the Subaru to the garage then. He took the keys to the Jeep from a hook on the wall next to the sink.

Nearly 15 years old and with considerable rust, but the engine in the Jeep was sound and the odometer showed only 146,411 miles. Still good for another year or two. It had a great heater.

Light snow was falling when Jarvis pulled out of the plastic-covered carport. He turned onto Route 2 and drove west toward the truck stop. He'd make a phone call and fill up the tank before the meeting with Brousseau.

Branchik turned into the drive leading to Rivera's ski house. As he got closer, he noticed that another vehicle had been there overnight. Snow had fallen around a spot where a car had been parked and was now gone leaving new tire tracks. Rivera's Audi was still there and was covered with an inch of the fresh snow.

It was getting lighter. The clock on the dash of the Chevy showed 6:55. His large-face digital sports watch showed it was actually 6:53:20. He kept the engine running, sat in the car watching the house and thinking about how he would play this.

Deal with Rivera, get the girl back. Get the money.

He checked the magazine for the Sig. It still had eight shells racked, as he hadn't fired it in over a week. He put the gun in his right coat pocket, the twin pouch with extra magazine in his left pocket, shut off the engine and got out of the car.

"It was after midnight when they hauled out," Merchand said. "Don't expect much from the lab before midday."

Col. John K. Hewitt didn't interrupt. He crooked the phone with his left shoulder, put his slippers on, and got up from the bed trying not to disturb his wife. He left the bedroom and went downstairs to his kitchen. It was just after seven in the morning.

Answering on the first ring, he now listened as Merchand continued reporting grisly details from the previous night. Hewitt went to the refrigerator, took out a one- liter bottle of water, and took a big pull.

"I talked to the drug task force guys," Merchand was saying. "The vic found in the house could be 'a person of interest'. Registration on a car found in the garage matches one they've been watching."

"Any signs of drug activity in the house? Somebody manufacturing out in the woods?" Hewitt asked.

"No sign of that. This is an expensive vacation home. Probably a couple mil, easy. No doubt a real view of the lake and mountains from that high up."

"Besides the butchering, other wounds visible?"

"Might've been gun shot *and* stab wounds," Merchand replied. "Lab report will tell us."

"Signs of any other violence being committed there?"

"Deputy McCabe and his guys were doing a full-blown search of the grounds," Merchand continued. "They found the car. Hard to tell from the house. Lot of blood inside. Like I said, all over the place."

Hewitt finished half the bottle of water and would drink the rest before breakfast. He filled the basket of a drip coffeemaker and poured water in while talking on the phone.

"I'm headed in. Should be at the office by 8:15. Anything else comes up, call."

"Will do," Merchand said.

"I'll lean on the lab. They know there could be a connection here," Hewitt added. "You might be in for a long day, Lieutenant."

Gerard Brousseau pulled into the Bethel Truck Stop and parked the Hummer. As soon as he went inside, he saw Jarvis Blevens seated in a booth near the front. He walked over and took a seat across from him.

"I didn't see your car," Brousseau said.

"Driving my brother's Jeep," said Jarvis. "Have to rebuild the transmission on my wagon."

"Well, I'd like you to make a short trip for me. Can you use your brother's car?"

"Yeah. Where's the short trip?"

Forty Four

Stephen Rivera didn't like Branchik's demeanor. What an understatement, he thought.

This man is truly crazy and truly dangerous. Far beyond stealing car parts and dealing drugs, he's looking for the fast lane back to prison, without a doubt. But I need to settle him down.

Branchik sat on the sofa nearest the stairs. He propped his feet on the coffee table and had the Sig P220 lying next to him. Rivera was seated on the opposite sofa.

"No need to panic, Stevo. We can get this done." Branchik held the deadeye stare as he said this.

Rivera had gone to the bathroom when Gerard left. He came out, heard the door downstairs, and assumed Gerard had returned for something before going to meet the Blevens kid. It wasn't Gerard, but Branchik, coming up the stairs with a gun in his right hand.

Now watching each other at less than eight feet apart, Stephen was trying very hard to control both his rage and his fear. His own gun was upstairs in the master bedroom. He knew better than to attempt some excuse to go back up.

Branchik seemed to still be riding something that had him *way out there*. Maybe we can talk this through. Maybe Gerard will see the Chevy when he gets back and know that it's Branchik. *Maybe* it's just money.

"How'd you do with the product I gave you Friday?" Stephen asked. "Had to be worth thirty grand. Not counting the pills." Branchik smiled at this.

"Deal's not complete," he lied. "My guy has to talk to another guy. Lotta people trying to dance here." Branchik deliberately omitted any reference to wholesaling drugs in the parking lot behind the Legion Hall.

"So you're going back to Portland?" Stephen said. "I really don't have any more to give you. The stuff you took was the last I had. No shipments until next week."

"I think we have another..." Branchik paused, turned his head to the right for a second then looked back at Stephen. "There's another way we can go at this."

Stephen was about to feel some optimism until Branchik placed his right hand on the gun. He gave no sign of picking it up, just let his hand rest flat across the butt and the chamber, slowly moving his fingers as though he were petting a cat.

"And what way is that?" Stephen asked, hoping his voice didn't convey the fear.

"Let's talk about the girl," Branchik said, looking toward the bedroom door.

Forty Five

"I'm coming back over this morning. Be there by 8:30," Ragsdale said on my voicemail.

When I came out of the hotel to go to breakfast, I keyed up my phone while the car's engine warmed up. There was enough of a signal to show that I had a new message. I listened to it again before going back inside for my coat.

"Merchand called last night with a heads-up," Ragsdale's voice added. "That body bag you saw at Long Lake. Might be someone we're interested in."

"If it's who I think it is, we've been watching him a few weeks now," he added.

After hearing the message the first time, now again on replay, my mind called up the image of the ME techs wheeling the gurney out, body bag strapped on top, lifting it into the van.

"You might want to be available. Keep your phone on," Ragsdale concluded, then abruptly clicked off. My phone showed the voicemail had come in at 6:32AM.

My watch showed 7:50. I put the phone on the seat, left the engine running and went back to the hotel to get my coat. Two minutes later I was on the road headed for breakfast at Melby's in North Waterford.

Light snow had been falling. If it kept up, the snowplows would be out again. As it was, the driving wasn't a problem yet and I arrived a few minutes later. Both parking lots were full and a couple of cars were parked along the side of the road beyond the gas pumps. Saturday morning, popular place.

Inside, all the tables were occupied but there were three empty seats at the counter. After hanging my coat on a hook at the entrance to the dining area, I sat down.

A young woman working behind the counter quickly placed a mug in front of me. She held a pot of coffee up to attract my attention. The pot had the dark brown plastic spout normally used for regular coffee.

"Yes, please." I said.

Looking over the menu, Acadian Toast sounded good. Freshly baked bread made into French toast, with real maple syrup. "*A Melby's Favorite*", so read the menu. But the delicious aroma of the fresh pastries and cinnamon rolls in the glass case near the register was also very tempting.

I went for the toast. The woman behind the counter, not Charlene from previous visits, took my order and went to the kitchen.

When I swiveled my stool to check the crowd, everyone else in the place was drinking coffee, eating, or talking. One guy, alone at a table near the windows, was reading the paper and eating slowly. A few patrons had finished breakfast but remained at their tables.

Turning back to the counter I realized that my phone was in the pocket of my coat. I retrieved the phone and put it on vibrate only. After the waitress brought my food, sitting there listening while I ate to a couple of guys on my right talk about an auction coming up, I felt a tap on my left shoulder.

Turning, I was struck by the presence of a pretty big guy wearing a woodland-pattern camouflage jacket and an old green Red Sox hat. It took a second to place him as one of the guys from the bar in *The Skidder*. The same guy I guessed as being Ragsdale's DH.

The guy said nothing. Looking at me, he turned his head slightly, flicked his eyes toward the window and with two fingers, motioned for me to come outside. I nodded to him. He turned and went back toward the door.

Two more bites of toast, another sip of coffee, and I looked at my watch. Quarter of nine. I placed two dollar bills next to the plate and walked to the register to pay my tab. I bought a cinnamon roll to go.

Outside I looked across to the parking lot, then to the cars parked along the edge of the road. The guy got out of a white GMC pickup and looked back at me. I walked that way as he got back in behind the wheel and I climbed in the passenger side.

"Jeffereys," he said, extending his right hand across

230

the seat. We shook. I assumed Jeffereys was his last name.

"Michael Hanlon. You must already know that."

"Yeah. Fried shrimp and draft beer," he said, reciting my order at *The Skidder* from last night.

"Do you guys miss *anything*?"

"Not much," he replied. "Louie thought I'd find you here." He pronounced it Lew-ee. "Wants to see you in Bridgton. On his way now to meet Lt. Merchand."

He watched the outside rearview mirror on his truck, seeming to have really nothing else to add. I opened the passenger door.

"Thanks for the alert," I said. "I'll head over."

He gave me a silent nod. As soon as I got out and closed the door, he slipped his truck into gear and pulled away. Real talker. Must be a communications specialist for the Task Force.

Twenty minutes later I pulled into the lot of the Maine State Police sub-station in Bridgton. It was 9:10. Before going inside, I looked around for Ragsdale's old blue Isuzu. It wasn't there. But there was a maroon Honda Ridgeline with a low number Vermont plate – 8303 – parked two spaces over. Two police cruisers were behind the building.

Walking to the front door, thinking I was ahead of Ragsdale and recalling his comment at dinner that his SUV had recently clocked 316,000 miles, I amused myself by thinking "no old Trooper here to see the troopers." Then I thought one could be *arrested* for this kind of humor.

The dispatcher buzzed Lt. R. Merchand who came out to meet me. He looked a little bleary eyed from his long night.

"Hanlon. Come on back," he said, turning toward his small office where I'd visited a few days earlier with Carlos Singleton.

I was surprised to see Ragsdale slouching in a chair when I entered the room. He held a travel mug in his right hand, balancing it on his thigh. He was in cleaned-up mode, wearing an expensive-looking, faded green fatigue sweater and freshly washed jeans. Considerably different attire and appearance from the undercover garb.

"Good morning," I said.

"Maybe not," Merchand replied, taking a seat behind his desk and looking at Ragsdale.

I remained standing. Ragsdale put the travel mug on the floor, stood and stretched, then took his jacket off the back of the chair. It was a retro World War II leather jacket. He put it on.

"We're gonna take a ride," he said to me. "Lieutenant says you know the way to the house out at Long Lake."

"Yeah. Should be easier in the daylight," I said. Merchand was doing something on his laptop and made no effort to participate in this exchange.

"I'll ride with you," Ragsdale added. He stepped in front of me to leave the office.

"The deputies are there. Same as last night, stay out of the way," Merchand said, looking up. "One of our guys went up this morning. He'll take care of you two."

"Got it," I responded, then followed Ragsdale outside.

In the parking lot, Ragsdale went to the Honda Ridgeline and retrieved a small green and gold nylon duffel with a University of Vermont Catamount logo on the side. He locked the Honda and got in the passenger side of my car.

Fastening my seat belt, I started the ignition, made a backward K turn, and prepared to leave the lot. Backing up, glancing at Ragsdale's car, I focused on the Vermont Strong license plate on the front. I sat for a second looking at the plate, then looked at Ragsdale.

"You hoping for a state police escort here?" he said.

I shook my head, put the car in drive, and pulled out.

Forty Six

Jarvis listened, Brousseau talked. There were no other customers dining in the truck stop. Everyone was getting coffee or food to go.

"There's a girl staying at the chalet." When he heard this, Jarvis remained silent.

"She's a serious user. Now she's really mixed up. Thinks Stephen kidnapped her," Brousseau said.

Brousseau raised his hands to his shoulders, palms up, with an exaggerated expression showing surprise and disbelief. Lying about the girl wasn't a problem.

"We want you to take her over to the base lodge at Pinkham Notch. Leave her there." Hearing this, now Jarvis' facial expression indicated a little surprise.

"She comes in and out of being stable. Keeps saying crazy things," he went on. "One minute she can't sit up. Next minute she acts like she'll go out and jump off the deck," he lied.

Brousseau paused for a sip of coffee; Jarvis shifted in the booth and waited to see where the conversation would go. So far, he wasn't thrilled at the idea of taking some girl to Pinkham Notch and dumping her.

"You can help her get inside the lodge. Take her to the women's restroom. Then you're outta there."

"What if someone asks what's going on?" Jarvis asked.

"Tell them you found her wandering on the highway. You don't know who she is." This didn't sound convincing to Jarvis.

"Stephen's going to be sure she has money. She finally gets straightened out, she'll *call* somebody," Broussseau added.

Neither man spoke for a minute. Brousseau appeared anxious; Jarvis appeared skeptical. Jarvis thought they were here to discuss an arrangement to get more drugs, sell more drugs, make more money. *That's* the conversation that started in the Montreal strip club back in August.

"When do you want me to take her to Pinkham?" Jarvis asked.

Gerard Brousseau was relieved this was going *to happen*! Happen just the way he imagined it could when they conceived the idea last night. He looked at his watch.

"I have to go back and help Stephen get her ready to leave. Why don't you come over around 11:30."

"So that back there is a rental car** from the Guildhall airport?" I said to Ragsdale. He laughed.

"I know a guy who actually landed his plane there. *And* took off," he replied.

A tiny little border town in northeastern Vermont, Guildhall is on the Connecticut River, population around 200. The locals pronounce it Gil-hall. It has a bridge that formerly charged a toll, now free, crossing over to New Hampshire. It also has a very small, grass-strip airport.

My curiosity about James Louis Ragsdale ratcheted up a notch when I saw that he apparently was driving a vehicle from Vermont, now parked at the state police lot in Bridgton. He was in no rush to offer further information so we continued toward Long Lake, me driving, him checking the scenery.

Light snow turned to scattered flurries and there was a hint of sun. Osprey Road was coming up, the same right-hand turn I'd taken late last night following the blue lights of the state police cruiser.

At the top of the hill, the same left turn into the long driveway marked by twin fieldstone columns. Fresh tire tracks marked the snow ahead. We parked next to the Oxford County Sheriff's SUV and a Maine State Police car.

"So you live in Vermont?" I said, unable to hold the question any longer. I shut off the engine.

"You think?" he said. The more or less friendly smirk had returned.

"What're you doing undercover in Maine?"

"We work all over," he answered. "Vermont, New Hampshire, Maine. Go where the activity needs attention." My mind recalled his ID – *Northeast* Drug Task Force.

A state trooper came out of the house and was heading our way. He wasn't one that I'd seen previously. We got out of the car; Ragsdale had his UVM duffel bag.

"Morning," the trooper said. "Corporal Wolfe." We gave our names, he shook hands with Ragsdale, then with me. "Lieutenant said you were coming up," he added.

"According to registration at DMV, I think the body was an ex-con we've been watching," Ragsdale said.

The trooper pointed to the building with four garage doors.

"Two cars in there. '65 Mustang under a custom-made cover. Real beauty. Doesn't look like it's been out in a while," Wolfe said.

"Then on the end..." he went on.

"2003 white Cadillac Eldorado," Ragsdale interrupted.

"You got it," Wolfe said.

"That's his car. Won't know if it was him until the lab work is finished." Ragsdale unzipped the duffel and pulled out a digital camera.

"Can we start in the garage?" he asked.

"Sure." Wolfe turned and we followed.

The structure was approximately 70 feet long and at least 20 feet deep, four bays, overhead doors with heavy-duty electric openers. We entered through a solid steel door to a clean, open area. There was a waist-high workbench, a high stool on wheels and two matching tool chests. The chests were four feet high, also on wheels, and each had several drawers.

Once inside, Ragsdale put on latex gloves from his duffel and began examining the Cadillac. He opened all four doors, the glove box, looked under seats, over the visors, in the side pockets, and popped the trunk and the hood, all the while snapping multiple photos.

Corporal Wolfe stood at the rear of the car. I stayed off to one side near the entry door and watched. I resisted asking if we could take a look at the Mustang at the other end of the garage. When he finished, Ragsdale put the camera back in his duffel and looked at Wolfe.

"Inside the house?" Ragsdale said.

Wolfe again turned to leave; we followed. Still wearing the latex gloves, Ragsdale let me walk in front. He pulled the garage door closed and we walked toward the house where I'd accompanied Merchand last night. I wondered how the odor would be this morning.

"*But I didn't shoot no dep you 'tee...*" Ragsdale sang in a low voice. He was walking behind me and gave me a little poke in the ribs.

I turned to look at him; he pointed toward the house. Standing sentry at the front door was an Oxford County Sheriff's deputy in a khaki uniform, dark-brown jacket and Smoky Bear hat. He wasn't the deputy from last night.

Forty Seven

Branchik took his feet off the coffee table and sat forward on the sofa.

"You haven't been watching TV since you been here," he said to Rivera. Stephen shook his head.

"Satellite receiver's screwed up. Watched some DVDs. Haven't looked at TV."

Branchik studied him to be sure he could believe the answer. Rivera studied Branchik to see if he could figure out what the prick was after.

"Turns out the girl," Branchik jerked his head in the direction of the room across the hall, "might give us a little shot at some extra cash."

"How's that?" said Stephen, tilting his head and raising his eyebrows slightly in puzzlement. He shifted on the sofa, then also sat forward.

"She and her friend went missing. The parents are offering 25 grand for information on where she is now."

Stephen wanted to choke the crazy fucker. His conclusion was right. He'd said as much to Gerard last night. Branchik probably grabbed the girl against her will, or drugged her. Now Stephen was convinced Branchik had done both.

"Where's the other girl?"

Branchik didn't answer. He picked up the gun next to him and stood. Stephen watched him.

"Still have the Grey Goose in the freezer?" Branchik said. He took the gun and turned to the kitchen.

She heard them talking, but didn't crack the door open.

The voices weren't as soft as last night, she couldn't hear everything. But she did hear "the girl" and "she and her friend." And she did hear "where's the other girl?"

One of the voices sounded like the bald man with the tattoos who shouted at Stephen early the other morning. The man she knew took Marcia and her from the train station. The man who brought her here.

She stepped back from the door, went to the bed, and sat. The old magazines were on the floor. The light snowfall she'd been watching earlier had stopped. It looked brighter outside now than it had the previous morning. She wondered what day it was.

Reclining against the pillows, she pulled her legs up to her chest, rested her chin on her knees, and closed her eyes.

Were they going to bring Marcia here?

The walk through the house was not as unpleasant as last time. We put on the disposable booties as we entered. Some of the odor lingered and the blood was more noticeable in daylight. But the deputies had let some air in after the techs took the body out the night before.

Areas on the carpet in the living room were taped off, as was the fireplace in the center of the room. There was yellow tape blocking the entrance to the master bedroom, and I could see more tape down the hallway at another room.

After a few minutes gingerly stepping around, Ragsdale turned back to the living room. He didn't take photos inside.

"Nothing really for us to see," he said to Corporal Wolfe. "When all the forensics work is completed, I'd like to know about traces of *any* kind of drugs." Wolfe nodded.

"Sheriff's guys are coordinating with the ME," he said. "Lt. Merchand says a couple FBI guys are coming over later today."

"Yeah. He told me earlier," Ragsdale said. "No reason for me to be here."

"Probably not," Wolfe replied.

"Thanks." Ragsdale pulled off his gloves and threw them into the duffel.

We went back to my car and stood in front of the garage looking off to the west. Below us was the glisten of snow and light ripples on the surface of Long Lake not completely frozen over. A few docks across the lake were pulled onto shore.

Trees all around, but this house was built preserving a near 180° view. And it was a spectacular view, even from this point in the driveway several feet lower in elevation than the house. I could only imagine what it must be like up here on a summer evening. Sunset, lightning storms, any kind of weather would be a real show.

"Can't wait to find out about the owner," I said. Ragsdale shook his head and climbed in the car. I got in behind the wheel. We started back down to the main road.

"So, Eric Clapton had the hit," I said.

"1974. But everybody loves the Bob Marley version," Ragsdale quickly responded. "A year before Clapton. My sister had the album."

"*I shot the sheriff...*" he started again, finished with the "*didn't shoot no dep you 'tee'*" lyric, a fading hum and this white-guy version of a Jamaican reggae moan.

It took just under 15 minutes to get back around the lake to the state police sub-station in Bridgton. During the drive, Ragsdale offered a little information on the murder victim from the night before.

"Classic scumbag. In and out of prison. Sexual assault, stolen property, assault on a police officer, possession with intent to sell, both firearms *and* drugs."

"Must be a few of those types out there," I said.

"You have *no idea*. We're not gonna miss this one."

When I dropped him at his car, he stood with the passenger door open and said he was going to be around the rest of the day.

"I wanna hear results from the lab, talk to Merchand some more. Then I may stay over," he said.

"Can you tell me if Merchand thinks there's a definite connection here?" I said.

"Nothing's definite. Yet. I'd be really surprised if we're *not* looking for the same perp. The girl out at the lake and the grudge whack last night up at the mansion."

"Why do you say grudge?"

"Merchand's speculation, not mine." He picked up his duffel from inside my car.

"I'll call you," he added.

"I should be back at the motel before dark. I'll keep my phone on," I replied.

Ragsdale went into the police station and I turned back onto Route 117 north. 11:14AM – 35F with scattered clouds; partly sunny.

243

Forty Eight

Jarvis Blevens went home to get his Winchester 30-30 carbine, his favorite rifle.

Inside the trailer, no sign of Leon. Jarvis knew his normal routine was up until 2 or 3 in the morning watching TV, stay in bed until noon, unless Jarvis had a special errand for him. On this particular Saturday morning, Jarvis decided it would be better for Leon to stay right here.

He went to the closet in his bedroom for the rifle. It was stored in a canvas case from a week ago when he'd shot a six-point, 170-pound buck. He took extra shells from a surplus metal ammo box. The box, a 30.06 Springfield bolt-action rifle, a Remington pump-action 12-guage shotgun, and other boxes of shells were all hidden in the back of the closet.

Outside, Jarvis placed the rifle on the back seat of the Jeep and the shells in the side compartment of the driver's door. He went back inside to take a leak and was on the road 5 minutes later.

It was starting to look like a pleasant day. No more snow, some clouds around, but more sun than had been visible over the past few days. The drive from Bethel to

Pinkham Notch Base Lodge was about 35 miles and would take less than an hour. Jarvis knew the route.

Much of his time on the road in recent weeks had been after dark. And it had been a while since he'd travelled Route 16. So Jarvis was looking forward to this little run, despite the nature of the trip.

Would Gerard and Stephen have the girl ready when he got there? He wondered how they'd "get her ready," as Gerard had said. He wondered how many winter hikers and other people might be around when he got to the base lodge.

A mile before the driveway to Stephen's ski house, Jarvis pulled over. He got out, walked around the passenger side, and cleaned out the front seat to make room for the girl. Looking at the Winchester on the back seat, he pulled the rifle out and walked to the back of the Jeep and opened the tailgate. He put the rifle in and covered it with the old bloody plastic from the deer kill.

Branchik heard Gerard coming in the door. He waited at the top of the stairs.

But Gerard didn't come up the stairs. He went back outside. Or at least the door opened and closed.

"Let's not get fucking cute here, Stevo," Branchik said.

Holding the Sig flat against his chest, but not pointing it at Rivera, Branchik gave him the crazed, macho glare:

bugged-out eyes, bulging neck carotid artery, tough-guy sneer.

Stephen hadn't moved from the sofa. When he heard Gerard come in downstairs, he was on alert to go to the master bedroom for his own gun. But Branchik didn't give him the opportunity, didn't let him out of his sight. And now Branchik was agitated and walking around with the Sig in his hand.

The downstairs door opened again.

"Stephen. I have to go see Jarvis. I'll be back in an hour," Gerard shouted from the lower level. The door closed.

Branchik walked around to where he could see out the window to the parking area. Brousseau was getting back into the Hummer, preparing to leave.

"Go get him," Branchik shouted. "Now!" This time he waved the gun and started toward Stephen. He grabbed Rivera by the arm and pulled him from the sofa, pointing the gun at him.

"Get that Canuck asshole back in here," he shouted, pushing Stephen toward the stairs.

Stephen ran down to the door, opened it, and shouted at Gerard just as the car started to move. The brake lights came on. He stopped, then backed up.

Stephen motioned for Gerard to come back. He parked the Hummer in its previous spot, shut off the engine, climbed out, and went back inside.

"We need to talk about the girl," Stephen said.

Gerard knew from Stephen's tone that something had changed. Something not good. He looked at Stephen for any sign of what might have transpired while he'd been away for less than 2 hours.

Forty Nine

Carol and Stanley Turner were about to go downstairs for breakfast when they received a call from FBI Agent Gary Guidi. He told them about the discovery of another grisly murder scene at a secluded house not far from where Marcia Farrand's body was found.

Explaining that it was too early to be certain of any connection, but that it in all likelihood, police would establish a link once tests were completed, Guidi added that he was about to drive back to Augusta to meet with state police. He told the Turners he would call again later.

Standing next to his car in the state police headquarters parking lot in Augusta, Guidi pulled his folded suit jacket from the back seat, slipped it on, then reached in for his topcoat. He closed both doors and turned to face Col. John K. Hewitt.

"Two agents are going up this afternoon", Guidi said. Hewitt waited while Guidi finished the phone call and retrieved his coat from the car.

"Let's get some lunch," said Hewitt. "I'm buying."

Guidi studied the state police honcho for a beat. Their

rapport over the past week had been professional, but strained.

"Sure. I'm hungry," Guidi said.

Hewitt pivoted and started back across the lot and Guidi fell in behind. They were walking toward the building's rear entrance on the lower level. Once inside, Hewitt gestured to his right.

"Cafeteria's this way."

So much for having a seafood platter downtown, Guidi thought.

Passing through a long hallway and into an institutional-looking dining hall, each man took a tray, walked along the prepared hot and cold foods, and made their selections. After Hewitt swiped his ID badge at the register, they went to a table in the center of the room. It was a Saturday, and only two other troopers were seated together in the back.

The tile floor was recently buffed, the tables were spotless and the windows were clear like they'd been cleaned that morning. All shipshape. Guidi was impressed and interpreted the appearance of this portion of the building as an extension of "tight management."

"Drug task force rep's been undercover there for over a month," Hewitt said. "He's pretty certain the body last night is a heavy-hitter ex-con who was dealing in everything."

Guidi lifted the top slice of bread off his tuna sandwich, added a generous shake of black pepper, then took a bite. Hewitt ate clam chowder.

"Decapitation look the same as the girl's body?" Guidi asked.

"Hard to say. Merchand went out last night as soon as he got the call." Hewitt added a small package of soup crackers to the chowder.

"There's a lot of blood, all over the place apparently. Like maybe it came from more than just this murder," he added.

"Your lab people good?" Guidi asked.

"We think so," Hewitt answered. "If the same weapon was used to do the cutting on both, they'll know."

"We're running a check on tire tracks," he added. "Gonna be difficult. We've had snow on and off all week."

"The car fender in the security video at the Amtrak station. Looks like an older Chevy or Pontiac," Guidi said.

"We've been checking. More than 20,000 registered in Maine alone. And we're not sure it's from here," Hewitt replied.

Guidi was quiet listening to the state police commander. He ate more of his sandwich while Hewitt worked on the chowder. Hewitt took a sip of black coffee, then continued.

"The two agents you assigned to Bridgton. They part of your search squad or up from Boston? You going to bring them to Portland?" Guidi shook his head.

"My guys will stay over there. Work with Merchand."

"Good idea," said Hewitt. Guidi tried to detect sarcasm, but decided there was none.

"He's not gonna get chickenshit with my men? No petty jurisdictional maneuvering."

"Merchand's a good man. On the level, no bullshit. As professional as you'll ever find *anywhere*. And he likes collaboration," Hewitt responded.

"The radio guy working for the Turners still sniffing around?" Guidi asked.

"Yeah. Merchand corralled the task force undercover agent to keep him in check."

Fifty

"**Against the wall, sucker,**" Branchik said, pointing the gun at Gerard Brousseau's head.

Brousseau looked as though he might faint. Stephen Rivera, standing next to Brousseau at the top of the stairs, wasn't quite as startled as his friend.

Branchik hacked out a sharp laugh.

"I've wanted to say that to somebody for fuckin' ever," Branchik said.

He kept the gun pointed at Brousseau, but relaxed his intensity a bit. Rivera wanted to scream at the childishness of his former associate. What hadn't relaxed was Stephen's growing fear of Branchik.

"Let's have a little talk, boys" Branchik said, waving the gun toward the living room.

Gerard, then Stephen, slowly walked to the room and sat on the opposite sofas they'd sat on so many times before. More than five years of visiting the chalet nearly every weekend during winter months, most evenings ended in this room, sitting where they were at this very moment.

Taking a seat in a leather chair at the head of the room, facing Rivera on his right, Brousseau on the left,

Branchik crossed his legs. With the Sig resting flat on his left thigh, he placed his right hand on top of the gun. On the counter behind him near the kitchen was the empty vodka glass from earlier.

"Which one of you gets to be the hero?" Branchik said.

Visibly nervous, repeatedly twisting a ring on his right hand and not succeeding at controlling his restless left leg, Gerard looked at Stephen, then at Branchik. Stephen had also crossed his legs, leaned back and folded his arms in an attempt to appear calm.

"Who should make the phone call and be the front man?" asked Branchik.

"Somebody has to get in line for the reward," he added, shifting his gaze back and forth between the two of them. Stephen uncrossed his arms and laid them across his lap, clasping his hands together.

"They're not going to hand over $25,000 just on a phone call," Stephen said. "It'll be *weeks* before anybody gets the money. Even if the girl goes home. Wherever that is."

Gerard Brousseau was near frenzy at this exchange. His expression pleaded for some clue of what Branchik was talking about. He looked directly at Stephen.

"The girl's parents are offering a reward. It was on the news," Stephen said.

Hearing this, mouth agape, Gerard continued to stare at him.

"Seems as though she didn't "voluntarily" come along for the ride," added Stephen. He showed remarkable coolness, but fear had a solid grip on his gut.

Branchik's sneer returned and his glare focused on Stephen.

"Here's what I think we'll do," Branchik said. He uncrossed his legs, leaned forward, and held the gun in both hands resting on his knees.

"The French ambassador here," Branchik began, hesitated and laughed. "You actually look like an ambassador," he went on, gesturing with the gun to Brousseau.

"I think *you're* the one to make the call," Branchik said.

Brousseau didn't respond, but his left leg stopped bouncing and he stopped fiddling with his ring. He looked at Branchik.

"I'm guessing you're pretty clean. Good, honest Canadian down for a short visit. They start looking into Stevo, here, who *knows* what they'll find," Branchik said.

Stephen didn't flinch. He sat back, crossed his legs again and rested his hands palms down on in his thighs.

"Let's work on the plan, boys," Branchik said. He stood, went to the refrigerator, and pulled out the bottle of vodka.

Her ear pressed to the door, the girl knew what she had to do.

Her body felt completely numb; her movements had become robotic and she had no energy. Listening first to the shouting that had occurred 30 minutes earlier, and now to the men talking in the living room, a line from a movie came to her. The movie had a woman being held captive somewhere.

What can they do to you?

Only the voice now asking the question wasn't from some movie. It was the voice only she could hear. The same voice she'd heard over the past week.

Who are you?

"You find a place you're gonna buy?" the old man asked. "Look out for them real estate people. That's what my ex son-in-law is. And he's a snake."

"Nah. I'm not looking for any property," I replied. "Just over here trying to get a sense of this part of Maine."

Driving back to Waterford, hoping that I might find Helen MacRae at home, I decided to stop again at the small gas station owned by the talkative old character I'd spoken with two days earlier. He was in top form. How many customers could he have?

"One of my good friends back in Vermont is a realtor, actually" I said. "She's a pretty solid citizen. Don't think they're all slippery." He just looked at me while he pumped the gas.

"Better'n insurance salesmen, maybe," he said. "Or maybe roofin' contractors."

There was no real disdain in his voice. More bemusement. I was unsure of how he might respond to a discussion of the ethics and practices of *any* profession. So I let it go. Paid cash for the gas, thanked the man again, and got back in the car. The light on my phone was blinking.

"Wanna take a drive with me to Bethel?" The message was from Ragsdale. We'd been apart for barely 30 minutes.

"Just had a call that another "person of interest" is out and about this morning," he said. "Call me back."

I hit the green phone icon and redialed his number.

"That was quick," he answered. "Where are you?"

"Just outside Waterford. Stopped for gas."

"Got a guy we've been watching over near Bethel. Somebody saw him with a rifle in the back of his car. Be great if we can get him poaching. You up for more excitement?"

"Yeah, I guess. You think this guy is connected to the murder last night?"

"Don't think anything yet. If this *is* the guy we know about, could be a chance to connect him to drug traffic over the past few months," Ragsdale replied.

"Where d'ya want me to meet you?" I asked.

"There's an intersection at Routes 5 and 35 in North Waterford..." he started to tell me.

"The Crooked River Causeway," I said. "I came over that way on Wednesday."

"Meet me there. Wait. Meet me at Melby's. I'll leave my car there," he said.

"Twenty minutes."

Jarvis Blevens pulled in next to the Hummer. Rivera's silver Audi R8 was there, covered with the recent snow. It had not moved in the past couple of days.

There was also a tan Chevy that looked like an old police car. It had New Hampshire plates. Jarvis knew it was a 1996 Impala SS, because he knew a kid whose dad had bought him the same car a few years back. Only traces of snow on the Chevy, so it must have recently arrived.

Jarvis sat in the Jeep and let the engine idle. He figured that he'd wait for Brousseau to come out and get him when they were ready.

Branchik came back to the living room. He carried the glass of vodka in his left hand, the gun still in his right. He reclaimed his seat in the red leather chair. Neither Rivera nor Brousseau moved during the time Branchik was at the refrigerator.

"You still have her doped up?" Branchik asked Rivera.

"No. I haven't injected her for a week," said Stephen.

"What?" Branchik exclaimed, standing from the chair. "Are you fucking nuts?" Stephen stared at him.

"She's in there right now *listening* to us?"

"Probably."

Branchik looked at the bedroom door, then back at Rivera. Brousseau's left leg began to bounce again.

"Honest to fucking Christ, Stevo. I *really* don't know about you," Branchik said.

Stephen remained calm. On the surface. His stomach got tighter and his brain was starting to gallop at a faster pace.

Branchik sat down again. His eyes flicked back and forth from the bedroom door to the two men. The glass of vodka was on an end table next to his chair and he fondled the gun with both hands. He shook his head.

"All right. Here's what we're gonna do," Branchik said.

"You and I, Stevo, will leave here with the girl. Brousseau, you're going to take a drive and make a phone call."

Stephen didn't respond to this proclamation. Gerard shifted on the sofa, his left leg continuing the uncontrollable twitching.

"A phone call to who?" blurted Gerard.

Branchik reached into his left pants pocket, pulled out a piece of paper, unfolded it, and smoothed it flat on his leg. It was a sheet from a motel note pad with scribbling on it. Watching a repeat news cycle on TV in the middle of the night, Branchik had written down a phone number.

"You get to call the FBI," he said.

Fifty One

Five minutes after I pulled in at Melby's, Ragsdale turned into the lot.

Driving the waxed-up Honda Ridgeline and dressed for success, he certainly made a different impression than a derelict driving the rusty old Isuzu Trooper.

He parked next to me, fetched his green duffel, locked the vehicle, and got in the passenger side of my car.

"We'll reimburse you for the gas," he said. In a few short days, I thought that I'd learned his different inflections, alternating from smartass to dead-on serious. This had the smartass ring to it.

"Good," I replied.

"New Hampshire Fish & Game warden got a call about an hour ago that somebody saw a guy with a rifle next to the road. Along Route 2 just across the line near Gorham," Ragsdale said.

"Deer season's over," he added.

"Even down in the civilized environs of central Vermont we have poachers," I said.

Ragsdale looked at me.

"Environs? You fucking liberals."

"*This* poacher is driving a car I know," Ragsdale went on. "A Jeep Cherokee that belongs to one of two brothers from Bethel. We think they have a lucrative side business."

"Gray Cherokee. A really big guy. Looks a little confused?" I asked.

"*Private Eye*. Very good, Mr. Hanlon. You've been paying attention."

"I saw him right there," I said, pointing at the gas pumps across the street. "First day I came up here. Wednesday."

"Yep. But it was Thursday. You were talking to me, having coffee. I followed him back to the dump where he lives," Ragsdale said.

"In New Hampshire?"

"No. Route 2 in Bethel. Rundown old trailer just off the highway. Let's go," he added, pointing at the road. "It's his little *brother* that we like."

As we drove, Ragsdale explained in a pretty succinct delivery that he and his cohorts on the Joint Northeast Counterdrug Task Force worked with local and state law enforcement and, selectively, kept the locals apprised of "people of interest." Mutual cooperation was important, he said.

"My boss clears us with the state police anytime we move into a new area. Up here, we're working both Maine and New Hampshire. That's why Merchand got the call half an hour ago." I was still puzzled at the explanation.

"The Jeep's got Maine plates. The person who saw it, and the guy with a rifle, spotted it in New Hampshire. So he called the local warden, who works for the state. And the call-in didn't say that it was a big guy driving the Jeep."

We were coming to the intersection with Route 2. A right-hand turn would take us east to Bethel. Turn left and we'd be going west through Gilead, then eventually to Gorham, New Hampshire. We turned left.

"There's a state trooper cruising today over in Gorham. And the game warden. Caller said the Jeep was headed west." Ragsdale pulled out his cell phone and tapped in a number.

While he was speaking I presumed to the game warden, I thought of the earlier crack about liberals. And that thought reinforced my recently arrived-at conclusion, along with the license plates on his personal vehicle, that Ragsdale's *home* must be somewhere in northeastern Vermont.

Outside the region known as the Upper Valley, where I live, not everyone knew of the perceived progressive politics in my home county. The more conservative folk to the north certainly knew. Brilliant, Hanlon.

"No sign of the Jeep," he said, putting the phone down. "He could've gone anywhere."

Fifty Two

Wilhelmina Bonita Turner stepped from the bedroom. Not one of the three men in the living room said a word.

She stood near the door, staring at the man who'd said his name was Stephen, then shifted her gaze briefly to the two other men. She was now certain the bald man sitting in the chair was the same man who'd approached them at the train station. The man was holding a gun.

"Where's Marcia?" she said, looking directly at him.

"Your friend's not here," the bald man said. She didn't flinch.

"Where did you take her?"

The man gave no answer. He stood from the chair, gestured with the gun to Rivera.

"I think you should help her get ready to leave," Branchik said. Stephen didn't move from his place on the sofa.

"I mean help her... *right now*, Stevo."

Stephen got up and stood three feet away from Branchik, looking at him, trying to gauge the man's immediate intent. There was no doubt in Stephen's mind that Branchik was violent and unstable. The look in his eyes when he'd arrived earlier conveyed a volatile mixture of God knows how many drugs, plus the alcohol, and Stephen thought he recognized something else. Branchik was desperate.

Stephen knew Branchik would do *anything* he felt necessary, regardless of past affiliations and understandings. That world was gone. Whatever course played out now, Stephen couldn't envision a future alliance with this man.

Walking slowly toward the girl, Stephen spoke more softly than earlier.

"Give us a few minutes," he said to Branchik. He looked at the girl and lightly clasped his right hand on her right arm.

"Bunny, I need to talk with you."

Jarvis had been waiting in the Jeep for nearly 15 minutes. No sign of Brousseau, or Stephen. Or anyone else.

It was now a few minutes after noon. Jarvis shut the engine off, got out of the Jeep, and walked around the back. He stretched, flipped open the tailgate and put a blanket on top of the plastic covering the rifle.

He got back in the Jeep and waited some more. Seemed like he'd done this before in *this very spot*. Exactly a week ago. It didn't make any sense. And it was annoying. It didn't have the same tingling anticipation of sitting or standing in the woods waiting to spot a deer.

But Jarvis could be patient. At the age of 26, he knew that he wasn't going to die in that trailer. Measured by his father's time on earth, Jarvis had already lived half his life. The ol' man never reached his 51st birthday.

Jarvis needed Gerard Brousseau and Stephen Rivera. They had the contacts, the connection to the drugs from different sources, and they had an interest in Jarvis. Shit, any moron could *sell* drugs. But not everyone could get the backing and the steady supply you needed to keep at it and become successful. And not get arrested.

He believed that Brousseau had thought the plan through before recruiting him to drive the girl to Pinkham Notch. He knew that he could handle it. And if things went the way they discussed this morning, he also knew he'd score big points with Stephen.

Starting the engine again to get some heat, Jarvis would wait as long as it took.

Fifty Three

"Let's pull in at the picnic area up on the left," Ragsdale said. He looked at his phone.

There was a roadside picnic area with a steel grill on a post, a trash barrel, and a table with benches covered in a few inches of snow. Not yet plowed, earlier tracks now covered indicated that people had driven in and out recently.

I put on my turn signal, even though no other cars were visible either way. Swinging in and around the picnic table, I edged the car back toward the highway, stopped a few feet short of the pavement, and shifted to Park.

"Still three bars on my phone," he said. "You go any farther, we'll be in a dead zone and no signal at all."

"The Jeep has Maine plates. If it's our guy, most likely he's coming back this way," Ragsdale added. "The New Hampshire trooper and the warden will make a good sweep around Gorham. They'll BOLO town cops and sheriff's deputies."

Anyone who ever watched a cop show on television, or saw a cop movie, knew BOLO was "Be on the lookout." I kept the engine running and the heater fan turned low.

265

"OK. Your snark about liberals. Where's *that* coming from?" I asked.

He looked at me for a few seconds before responding, then turned his eyes back to the cell phone.

"You live in one of the election hotspots," he said. "Every two years, some statewide race is close. Everybody wants to know if all the Windsor County towns have reported. You and your neighbors have put more than one candidate over the top."

"Yeah, so what? I'm sure the four northeastern counties have a higher registration of, shall we say 'non-liberal' voters."

"That's the problem. They're *registered* all right. But too many don't show up on election day," he replied.

"Maybe you need a good woodchuck consultant to help you get out the vote, *eh*?"

"Maybe not."

We sat without talking for a couple of minutes. I suspected he had a lot of practice doing this. Only a few cars passed, all headed east. No gray Jeep Cherokees anywhere.

"Simon and Garfunkel," Ragsdale finally cracked. "*The Sounds of Silence*, 1965." I had a flash of Paul Simon at a concert in Boston years ago.

Ragsdale's phone vibrated.

"Yes," he answered, holding the phone to his right ear.

He listened for about 30 seconds. I could hear the other voice but not what was being said.

"We're at a roadside pull-off. Route 2," he said.

"Yeah, that's it. Your side of the border," he added. He continued listening for a few seconds more without comment.

"OK. I'll stay here another half hour. I'll call when we're ready to leave." He tapped the end call button and put his phone on the seat between his legs.

"So the reason we're in *my* car is you don't want any 'persons of interest' to see you driving a new $30,000 rig." I said.

"You get quicker every minute," he cracked. "Actually $36,500. It's loaded."

"By the way, Mr. Oldies Guy, wasn't *Private Eye* a hit for Hall & Oates?" I asked.

"That was *Private Eyes*, 1981. The *Olympics* had the hit *Private Eye*. Way-y-y back. Played it on my weekly requests show."

"Where'd you go to school?"

"UMass Amherst," he said.

"The Minutemen."

"And women. School's come a long way since my day."

"How'd you wind up there?"

"My mother encouraged me to pick UMass. A cousin went there and liked it. I applied, got accepted, and didn't think any more about it."

"What's the college radio station?"

"WMUA. Since 1949. Most people listen to the FM online now. Or podcasts"

"What about you?" he asked. "Start in college radio?"

"Nope. I was an out-of-control, really undisciplined guy. Didn't think I could handle the academics. My dad was *sure* that I couldn't handle the partying," I said.

"So, I did the professional trade school route. Some voice and basic on-air training, learned the equipment. Got hooked on news. Found a job at a small station near Harrisburg, PA."

We were watching traffic as we talked. A car every minute or so, most going west. Two tractor-trailers went by, headed east.

"How'd you wind up in law enforcement?" I asked.

"Enlisted in the army after college. Spent a lot of time with the Military K9 Working Dog program. Sent to Iraq in '91, Desert Storm." Ragsdale looked at his phone before continuing.

"Really didn't want to go the career soldier route. Landed a job helping local police departments with K9 training. That led to a job on a state task force. Eventually drug enforcement and surveillance. Last five years with DEA and state police in Maine, New Hampshire and Vermont."

As Ragsdale ticked off his work history, it occurred to me that he must know a lot of the Vermont state police force.

"You know Major Rob Mozingo?" He looked up from his phone and stared at me.

"*How* do you think I got the skinny on you?"

Of course. Mozingo was the guy who led the BCI work on the car bombing I covered. For weeks on end I talked with him almost every day.

"Hanlon, this is not radio. You may have to actually *work* at this a little." Ragsdale was still staring at me. The smartass voice inflection had returned.

Fifty Four

Stephen Rivera was uncertain where this would end.

Or, *when* it would end.

He watched the girl who called herself Bunny go to the bed, sit, and lean back against the pillows. It was the same place and the same way she sat every time he'd been in the room with her. He closed the door, moved her clothes from the chair to the floor, and sat.

"We're going to work this out," he said.

He wasn't clear in his own mind exactly *how* it was going to "work out." But he knew that he needed her cooperation to avoid any violence with Branchik.

Arms folded, she stared directly at him and said nothing. Her eyes and facial expression encouraged him to explain.

"The man with the gun in the living room is the one who brought you here a week ago," Rivera said. "He drugged you, dumped your clothes, and left."

"With Marcia," she said, eyes bulging, hands at her sides and pressed flat on the bed.

"*Where* did he take Marcia?"

"I don't know."

"You're lying. I know you're his friend. I heard you talking out there. And when he was here before. Early in the morning." She turned her gaze away from Rivera.

"He's not my friend. We've had past business dealings. That's over. And I honestly have no idea where he took the other girl."

He did have an idea that wherever Branchik took the other girl, it wasn't a good place. And he suspected she was dead. He wouldn't say that to this girl. Not right now.

"You told me your name is Bunny. You won't tell me anything else."

"He," Stephen continued, pointing at the door, "says it's on the news that your parents are offering a reward."

The girl jerked her head back to face him. Her eyes widened again, but she didn't say anything.

"Gerard, the other man out there, the one with the mustache," he said, "Gerard and I discussed this last night. We were planning to take you away from here today. Make it easier for you to go home."

They heard Branchik shouting in the living room, which frightened the girl. Stephen got up from the chair and opened the door.

"You weasel-y, fucking little frog," Branchik was yelling at Gerard Brousseau. "You fucking *knew*. You were going for the reward money."

Branchik was aiming the Sig at Brousseau, who pushed himself against the back of the sofa. He had both hands up in front of his face.

"Don't," Stephen yelled. "We didn't know."

Branchik wheeled around and looked at Stephen.

"You worthless fucking fags," Branchik said. "Maple leaf here *told me* he was taking her away this afternoon."

Raising his right arm, he took careful aim and pulled the trigger.

The shade on a floor lamp exploded, with the very loud cracking sound from the gun. The shell hit the wood-paneled wall behind Brousseau.

Branchik had deliberately pulled up on the shot. He laughed as Brousseau now tried to curl his entire body onto the sofa.

"Next one's in your fucking ear, weasel," Branchik said. He turned to face Stephen.

"Everybody fucking wants to be cute. Prison guards. Dickheads trying to schmooze you to work for them. Now you and this fucking slime bag."

"We didn't know about the reward," Stephen repeated. "We wanted to get her out of here. That's all."

"Oh, I'm real sure that's all," Branchik said.

He stepped across to the sofa. Still holding the gun in his right hand, he used the open palm of his left hand to slap Brousseau on the side of the head.

"Weasel." He slapped him a second time. Brousseau covered his head and tried to move farther down the length of the sofa.

"You'd be real sweet inside, fucker. All the boys'd make friends with you *day one*."

Jarvis Blevens heard the gun shot inside the chalet. It made him sit bolt upright and open the driver's window halfway.

Subconsciously, Jarvis expected a second shot, often the case when he was hunting. He waited, lowering the window all the way. No second shot. But he could hear muffled shouting inside the house. Next he expected someone to come out the front door. That didn't happen, either.

After a minute, Jarvis got out, walked to the rear of the Jeep, opened the tailgate again, and took out the Winchester. He closed the tailgate, and keeping an eye on the house, walked back to the open door, removed a handful of cartridges from the door pocket, and loaded nine cartridges into the magazine.

He watched and listened. No further activity from the house and no more shouting. Looking around, he wondered if neighbors had also heard the shot. But there were no other houses anywhere close. The drive was at least a half-mile from the highway.

Jarvis climbed back into the driver's seat and placed the rifle across his lap.

Fifty Five

"We're on Route 2 at the New Hampshire border," Ragsdale said into his phone. It was the third call in the hour we'd been out looking for the gray Jeep Cherokee.

"Sure. Set it up. We'll head back in a few minutes." He clicked off the call.

"Two of the FBI field guys just came up from Portland. Merchand wants a meeting," he said. "And the lab results aren't gonna be ready until tomorrow."

"So we're going back to Bridgton?" I asked.

"You got it. Let the game warden chase our guy back across the state line. If they don't get him, I'll just have to nail him another time."

We both got out of the car and walked to some nearby trees to take a leak before driving back. I looked at my watch. 2:10.

Gerard Brousseau shifted nervously. He'd been afraid of Branchik before; now he was certain Branchik would kill him. He was afraid for the girl in the other room and for Stephen. And he was afraid of the idea that *he* would be forced to phone the FBI and talk about the missing girl.

274

Eyes frozen on Rivera, Branchik sat down, cradling the gun in both hands in a relaxed manner, not aiming it at anyone. Stephen turned, closed the door to the bedroom, came out to the living room, and again sat across from Branchik.

No one spoke. Stephen looked at his Canadian friend now seated at the far end of the sofa, as far away from Branchik as he could get. There was a lingering burnt powder smell and after the gunshot the silence was palpable.

Branchik picked up the piece of paper he'd thrown on the coffee table earlier, looked at it, leaned forward, and shoved the paper across to Stephen.

"That's the number from the TV report on the girl," Branchik said. "They ran it across the bottom of the screen while they showed her picture."

Stephen picked up the paper and looked at the number. 1-800-CALL-FBI.

"You know as soon as we make a call, they'll know the number and location within minutes," he said.

"Yeah, I'm sure. But getting back to *my* plan," Branchik responded, "we're going at it from a different direction. *You* are going to go buy a pre-paid phone. That's how we make the call."

Stephen stared at Branchik, then glanced at Gerard, who hadn't made a sound since the pistol shot and exploding lampshade.

"And the cute stuff stops right now," said Branchik. "No fucking calls while you're out there. *No* contact with anybody else. Nothing stupid. Just get the phone and get back here."

Branchik smiled at Stephen.

"They come here looking for the girl, you're gonna have one dead Canuck friend, maybe more. And the FBI, and state police, and even the fucking National Guard, *all* on *your* ass, looking into *your* activities and checking on *your* wandering around New England."

Branchik watched Stephen as he laid all this out for him.

"No 'friends and associates' from Chic-o-pee or chick-o-fila, or anywhere else coming to help you, Stevo. When it's all done, my boys inside will really like to get to know you, too."

Rivera folded the piece of paper, put it in his shirt pocket, and stood from the sofa. Branchik didn't move from the chair, but he raised the gun to a resting position on his lap and casually aimed it at Rivera. Neither man spoke.

"OK," Stephen said. "No reason for..." he looked at Gerard on the other sofa, then went on, "...as you say, for anything stupid. I can drive into Gorham and get a phone at the drugstore."

"Good decision. I think you should do that *right now*." Branchik stood.

"And so we're all clear here and not working at cross purposes, you better leave your phones with me. Both of them." Branchik sneered, pretty sure Rivera thought he didn't suspect that he had another cell phone.

"Let's go upstairs. Get your other phone and your gun before you leave, Stevo?"

Bunny listened as hard as she could, ear pressed to the door. She understood most of what the bald man said, but not all the responses from the man named Stephen, or the other man. The last thing she heard was the bald man saying 'before you leave, Stevo'. Then things were quiet.

She stepped back from the door and looked at the window trying to determine the time of day. It was still light and had been for several hours. Afternoon, she guessed.

All her clothes were still on the floor. The man had moved some things from the chair when he came to talk to her earlier. Almost as though she was on a vacation trip, she'd put her dirty clothes to one side each time she was allowed to shower and change into fresh clothing.

If they take me outside, I'll run.

Fifty Six

Hollywood central casting could have sent these guys. Both FBI agents had short hair, conservative dark-colored suits, white shirts, and dark neckties.

We stood at the door looking at them. Seated, they appeared to be almost the same size and both had dark all-weather trench coats folded across their laps. Lt. R. Merchand got up from his desk and pointed at the door.

"Why don't we step out to the lobby? Little more room there," he said. His office was indeed too small for five people at the same time.

Ragsdale went first. I followed, the two agents behind me and Merchand behind them. The dispatcher looked up as we came into the lobby.

"Don't mind us, Cole. We just need some space," Merchand said to the dispatcher.

Merchand turned to us and made a slow one-on-one appraisal, shifting his gaze from one person to the next.

"This is agent Hollandsworth and agent Yost," Merchand said, gesturing to the FBI guys. Each man nodded.

"Don't let appearances fool you. Ponytail here is Lou

Ragsdale with the Counterdrug Task Force," he went on. Ragsdale gave a little army salute.

"And Mr. Hanlon," Merchand waved his hand my way, "is a private citizen. He's been engaged by the Turner family to keep the rest of us on our toes."

There could be a one-week training section at police academies where they teach sarcasm and wit.

"You fellows need to know that these two," he again pointed to Ragsdale and me, "have the blessing of Col. Hewitt to assist in our efforts. They've already visited the crime scene, where you're headed when you leave here. We have a trooper onsite along with a couple of Oxford County Sheriff's deputies."

The agents said nothing during this monologue. Merchand's tone, except for the slight dig at me, was informal and without pretense or any jurisdictional defensiveness.

"I know you're only here for the afternoon. So when you finish up, why don't we review notes before anyone's boss gets a hard-on about who's doing what?" Merchand looked at the two agents for a response. They nodded in agreement.

"Sounds good," said one agent. Hollandsworth or Yost? I wasn't sure. Merchand looked at his watch.

"Back here around eighteen hundred? That give you enough time?" Both agents looked at their watches.

"Yeah. Couple hours should be fine. We're just here for a look-see," said the same agent who'd spoken before.

They turned to leave the barracks before Merchand stopped them.

"You'll want this," he handed a sheet of paper to the agent who'd done the talking.

"Follow 117 north for six miles, double back to the right onto Route 35, Naples Road. All the way down the lake and watch for Osprey Road." The agent studied the printout.

"It's all there. It'll take you about 30 minutes," Merchand added.

When they were out the door, Merchand motioned for us to go back to his office. We did. Ragsdale slouched in one chair, I sat in the other. Merchand settled behind the desk.

"Hair styles and attitudes..." Ragsdale said. I knew it was a reference to a pop hit from the '80s, but doubted that Lt. Merchand knew.

"Timbuk 3. Moe and Curly, without Larry," Merchand said. Ragsdale made his index finger and thumb like a pistol and tipped it toward Merchand.

After a few minutes explaining what we were doing over on Route 2 at the New Hampshire border, Ragsdale said he'd connect with the Fish & Game warden and the Gorham Police Department to see if the Jeep had turned up.

"They do a vehicle check?" Merchand asked.

"Oh, I *know* who owns the car. Big boy from the

backwoods in Bethel. One Leon Blevens, Jr. We've been keeping an eye on him and his little brother for a couple of weeks now."

"Why special attention today?"

"Somebody spotted the brother taking a rifle out of the back seat earlier this afternoon. Deer season's over. Love to catch him poaching and go check out where they live."

"Well, I need to get some rest. It was a long night and it's been a long day," Merchand said. "I'm going home for a couple hours." He stood, stretched, and yawned. We got up and turned to leave.

"Come join us again, if you like. Be back here to visit with Tweedle Dee and Tweedle Dum," he said.

"Only if you're serving hors d'oeuvres," Ragsdale answered. "Let us know if they have any new spin on the headless horseman up at the estate."

We went back to my car to head back, I presumed, to some form of a stakeout. The sun was dropping in the sky to the west. 3:21PM – 35F.

Brousseau almost wet his pants. There was Jarvis outside sitting in his Jeep.

Branchik ordered Gerard to come stand at the bottom of the steps up to the third floor, while Rivera was ordered to get his cell phone and gun from the bedroom, with Branchik right behind him. Branchik wanted to be able to see Brousseau, while at the same time shadowing Rivera.

Now, standing at the bottom of the stairs, with a view out the kitchen window, Gerard saw the Jeep. With all the yelling Branchik subjected him to, the shot at the lamp instead of at him, getting smacked on the head, then more verbal assaults and intimidation, he *forgot* that Jarvis was coming to get the girl, just as they had discussed earlier. And there he was.

With hands together in front of him, rubbing one thumb nervously back and forth over his other thumb, Gerard anxiously watched for Stephen and Branchik to start back down the stairs. He took a chance.

Turning quickly to the window, he raised his right arm and made a repeated motion as though he was swatting at flies, trying to signal Jarvis to leave.

Upstairs they were still in the bedroom. He could hear Branchik saying something. Gerard pulled a handkerchief from his back pocket, waved it once, then repeated the swatting motion with his right arm. He stole a quick glance out the window, thought Jarvis was looking this way, but the Jeep didn't move.

He turned again to face the stairs, resuming a stationary posture. Stephen came out of his room with Branchik behind him and they came to the top step. As Stephen descended the stairs, he studied Gerard's face.

"Where are your keys, Gagnon?" Branchik asked.

It took Gerard a beat to realize that Branchik was actually addressing him, another snide reference to his French Canadian ancestry.

"Stevo's gonna take your Hummer into town," said Branchik. Stephen was now at the bottom of the steps facing Gerard.

"Be safer if I use your car," Stephen said. "If I get stopped in my car and there's a search, I might have a problem."

"And a little insurance at this end," Branchik chimed in.

"Just in case cops wanna know who owns the sporty R8 out there? Who owns this house? *Who* is running drugs up and down New Hampshire and western Massachusetts?"

Branchik was still holding his gun and had another gun, apparently Stephen's, shoved in the front waistband of his pants.

"Keys are in my coat," Gerard said. He rolled his head toward the steps. "Downstairs."

"Let's go find 'em," Branchik said.

Brousseau turned to go down the steps. His cell phone's ringtone began playing *Rockstar* by the Canadian band Nickelback. He pulled the phone out of his pocket at the same time Branchik was giving him the "cut it" signal, hand across the neck.

"Let your voice mail get it," Branchik said. He held the gun a little higher and glared at Brousseau. Gerard looked at the screen of the phone, then placed it back in his pocket.

"After you, chief," Branchik said to Stephen, waving the pistol toward the lower stairs.

"Get his keys and we'll go outside to the Hummer," he added. Stephen followed Gerard down the steps with Branchik right behind them.

"Hold it," Branchik said as they started out the door. They turned to look at him.

"Dump your pockets on the bench." He gestured with the gun to point at a long wooden bench along the wall under the coats, parkas, scarves, and hats.

Gerard emptied his pockets of a few coins, a small leather wallet, a comb, and his cell phone. He took the car keys and his gloves from his parka. Stephen also had loose change, a gold money clip with a wad of bills, and a ballpoint pen. He put it all on the bench.

"All right. Pick it up. Get your coat, Stevo," Branchik ordered. He waited for Rivera to put on his fleece-lined vest and a parka. Both men put items back in their pockets and all three went outside.

Just as they stepped out the door, taillights braked on a vehicle leaving the far end of the driveway and going downhill toward the highway.

"Who the fuck is that?" Branchik said. Stephen looked puzzled and shrugged.

"How often does your plow guy come," Gerard said.

"Has he been here since you came up last week?" he asked. Stephen turned to look at him. He got the drift, whatever it was.

"Yeah. Could'a been. He normally doesn't plow unless

we have four inches or more. He was here couple days ago."

Branchik looked at the three parked vehicles and saw an extra set of tracks in the snow next to the Hummer. They were wider than his Chevy or the Audi. Might've been a truck. He held the gun up and waved it at Gerard.

"Start it up for us," he said to Brousseau, jerking his head toward the H3.

Fifty Seven

"As I said, some really stupid people are going to jail," stated Richard Marco. He took a sip of his best single-malt scotch and placed the glass on the desk in front of him.

On the phone now for nearly half an hour with his financial guru and partner, Robert Lazelle, Marco rolled his head in a semicircular motion, savoring the taste of the whisky while trying to loosen the muscles in his neck and shoulders.

The conversation focused on *who* was selling *where*, what kind of product they were moving – both in the cities and larger towns, as well as out in the boonies – and how well established the various networks seemed to be. They came back to a topic touched on in a previous phone call, something Marco dreaded and constantly strived to avoid.

"Story in the Globe last week about two kids in Vermont, smokin' up a storm when the cops knock on their motel room door. A guest complained about a strong odor of marijuana in the next room. Desk clerk calls the police. *Hello*? This guy and his girlfriend having a grand ol' time. Cops get a warrant, find packs of heroin, cocaine, stolen electronics, stolen handgun, and ten grand in cash." Marco paused.

"*Not* the personnel one hopes to find," he added. He took another sip of the whisky.

"They have to be free-lancing with one of the newer rapper heads out of Springfield or Chicopee," Lazelle replied.

"But how do you *know* these days? It's harder and harder to hang on to people you can rely on to get it out there, get the cash and keep their mouth shut. You only need one wrong runner who flips," Marco continued.

"Pretty soon somebody is making the best plea bargain they can. And we're getting a visit from DEA."

"Perhaps it's time to reel in. Plenty of opportunity to find safer profits in other ventures," Lazelle commented.

"Maybe you're right. A new year coming on. We're not getting any younger." Both men in their mid 60s.

Marco took a last swallow of the single malt, sat up in his chair, rolled his shoulders and maneuvered his neck again.

"Let's take a better read on Branchik. That might tell us a lot," he said.

Lazelle looked at his watch. Almost 4:00. He'd set the DVR to record an ESPN broadcast of *A History of the America's Cup: Great Moments in Sailing*.

"I expect he'll call this evening. I'll tell him you're coming up on Monday and suggest he might want to join us for a discussion about the future," Lazelle said.

"Yeah. I have to take my grandson to the Museum of

Science tomorrow. I'll leave Boston around 4:30 Monday afternoon," Marco said. "I'll call on the way."

She watched the three men from the window in the kitchen. The bald man was holding a gun, standing next to the man named Stephen. The shorter man with the dark curly hair and mustache was getting into a big SUV. He started the engine and put the wipers on to brush away snow.

Looking around the kitchen and living room, there was no sign of a telephone anywhere. She considered trying to escape. A snow-covered deck was off the living room and appeared to be at least one story above the ground. She turned back to the window to see what was happening in the driveway below.

The short man got out of the SUV and stood next to Stephen. The bald man stepped very close, holding the gun under Stephen's chin. He was saying something and Stephen was leaning his head backward, then he got into the driver's seat, closed the door. He slowly backed up, turned, and drove away while the two other men watched.

She knew they'd be coming back inside.

Before pulling onto Route 2, Jarvis Blevens hesitated, looked both ways, turned right, and headed east back toward Bethel.

Glancing at his phone to be sure that it was on, Jarvis went slower than he would normally drive. Keeping an eye on the rearview mirror he drove a short 5 minutes, then turned into the lot of the Bethel Truck Stop.

Staying clear of the pumps and the main building, he backed in, and angled the Jeep so he'd have a good view of traffic going both ways. He picked up the phone again, checking for messages. Brousseau hadn't called back.

Jarvis wondered what all the frantic hand motions at the window meant. Those two were acting a little strange. First, they tell me to come get this girl and dump her at the Pinkham Notch Base Lodge. Then he's waving me off like he wants me out of there.

Engine running, driver window down a couple of inches, he lifted the rifle and laid it across the back seat. He thought about the Southern guy who'd made the "parts drops" from southern New Hampshire. The guy didn't look any older than Jarvis himself. And the older guy in the BMW who showed up back in the summer. Said his name was Marco. "Like Marco Polo," he'd said, holding a hand to his forehead as though scouting the horizon.

How did he find me? Jarvis spent a few minutes mentally reviewing all the people he saw on a regular basis at the garage. Then last week a phone call from Marco and a second delivery from the same cracker in the big Dodge pickup. *Somebody* is making connections and getting a steady supply of drugs from somewhere.

Then Stephen a week ago acting pretty cool with the idea of Jarvis working with them. Said they'd front him some cash, give him a better cut of everything he moved. Even tossed in the freebie packs last weekend.

Jarvis thought *cash* is good, but not the real concern here. What *is* a concern are people being *unpredictable* and acting strange. And it was getting stranger by the hour.

He'd see what happened next with Gerard and Stephen, then tomorrow place a call to Marco. Talk about "distribution" and "incentives" and perhaps "increased compensation." All that stuff Marco yapped about when he first came to see Jarvis at the end of summer.

Branchik made Gerard play the message received earlier. When he heard a man say, "It's Jarvis. I'm outside in the driveway," he raised the gun and fucking near shot Brousseau on the spot. Instead, he smacked him hard with his open left hand.

Gerard had frantically confessed the earlier plan to have a guy come take the girl to a nearby base lodge and leave her there. Branchik slapped Brousseau again, this time knocking him against the wall.

"Mr. Weasel," yelled Branchik. Gerard rubbed the side of his face, expecting another blow.

"Call him fucking back. NOW!" Branchik shouted. Gerard picked up the phone.

"Tell him to come back later." Branchik looked at his watch. "6:30," he added.

Gerard made the call and got Jarvis on the phone. Branchik shoved the gun against Brousseau's head.

"Our schedule was off. Come back at 6:30," Gerard said into the phone.

The gun felt cold at the side of his neck, pushed tight under his left ear. Struggling to sound normal, he had no doubt that Branchik would kill him.

"The base lodge'll be closed then," Jarvis replied. "You still want me to take the girl?"

"I have to talk to Stephen. We haven't decided where she's going," Gerard lied. Jarvis hesitated before responding.

"Sure. I'll come back," he said. He hit the end-call button. The earlier thought that these two were acting weird was only reinforced by this phone call.

He pulled out of the truck stop and continued east, heading home.

Fifty Eight

"There's your Jeep," I said. Ragsdale sat forward.

It was headed at us from the opposite direction, coming from the New Hampshire border a few miles west. Dusk was coming on.

Five minutes earlier Ragsdale had tilted his head back, reclined the seat, and closed his eyes when I turned onto Route 2. Now he was fully alert, looking through the windshield at the approaching vehicle. The Jeep went by and I glanced to see the driver, a young guy. Ragsdale turned in his seat to watch.

"That's him," he said. I watched the Jeep going away in my outside mirror.

"Pull in at the truck stop," he added, pointing ahead.

I swung into the Bethel Truck Stop and made a full turn, stopping at the edge of the highway. Ragsdale pushed the redial on his phone and I watched the Jeep drive out of sight.

"He just passed us, headed east. Goin' home, I bet," Ragsdale said.

"We'll give him a couple minutes, then do a drive-by. I know where he lives." He was speaking into the phone, now listening. I assumed that it was the NH Game Warden that he'd spoken with earlier.

"Nah, thanks. We'll watch him. I'll let you know how it goes. Call me if you find any signs he actually poached something over your way." Ragsdale hit the end-call button, put the phone on the seat, and again looked at his watch. I looked at the dashboard: 4:17PM – 33F.

The girl stayed at the door. She clearly heard every word this time, including talk about a plan to leave her at "the Pinkham Notch Base Lodge." She was pretty sure that was in New Hampshire, somewhere in the White Mountains.

It was still light outside but the sun had dropped and it would be dark soon. Someone was coming here, at least it sounded that way from this end of the phone conversation. And the man said "I have to talk to Stephen," so he was coming back, too.

The bald man doing all the yelling didn't say anything about Marcia.

Stephen parked near the 24-hour drugstore in Berlin, New Hampshire. Late on a Saturday afternoon, just over two weeks before Christmas, there were only three other cars in the parking lot.

He went inside the store and found it to be surprisingly quiet. Standing for a moment at the front, near a display of wrapping paper and ribbons, he glanced around at shelves running along one wall and the signs above the aisles.

"Can I help you find something?" a young woman asked from behind one of the checkout stations.

He turned in her direction. Late teens, maybe early 20s, he wasn't certain. She wore a red store coat with a nametag: Hannah.

"Prepaid cell phones?" Rivera said.

"Yes. Aisle five, halfway down on the left," she replied. Rivera walked in that direction.

There were at least a half-dozen styles and brands of phones mounted on cardboard and packaged in clear plastic all hanging on pegs at eye level. He selected a simple Trac flip phone that had 100 minutes available.

"Do you have a rewards card?" the young woman asked Rivera at the register. He stared at her for a couple of seconds. She appeared to be about the same age as Bunny.

"Uh, no. I don't," he answered.

"Would you like to apply for one," she handed him a sheet of paper that had the store logo on top and bullet-point information covering the advantages of having a rewards card.

"No thanks," he handed the paper back to the clerk. He gave her cash.

She scanned the SKU code on the package, gave him

change, put the phone and a receipt in a plastic bag, and handed it to him.

"Thank you for shopping at Health Aid," she added.

Back in the Hummer, Stephen read the directions printed on the cardboard that held the phone inside the packaging. He tore open the top of the plastic and pulled the phone out, along with a small wallet-size tri-fold piece of paper, which had more detailed instructions in English, Spanish, and French.

The flip phone was wrapped in another thin layer of plastic. Stephen quickly decided not to remove the peel-off plastic, anticipating that Branchik would go ape shit and accuse him of having already made a call to someone.

He put everything back in the bag, started the Hummer, and resumed the near 30-minute drive back to the chalet.

Jarvis turned off the engine of the Jeep, sat in the carport, and thought. He heard the engine ping from heat in the cold air.

What the hell is this about? The quicker than expected drive back home gave him time to think, but he was really having a hard time making pieces fit in any way that made sense. And Jarvis knew that *he* was not dumb.

Opening the driver's door, he sat for another minute. He kept coming back to the image of Gerard Brousseau at the window with the handkerchief, waving him away. Then the follow-up call telling him to *come back* later.

It just didn't connect with Brousseau's words and behavior at the truck stop this morning. It had been very clear then that he wanted Jarvis to come take the girl away.

Fifty Nine

"OK, go up the road about 6 miles. I'll tell you when we're close," Ragsdale said.

"East. Beyond Bethel?" I replied.

"Yeah. He lives in a trailer just off the highway."

I switched on my headlights and looked at the odometer. Pulling out, I turned right and resumed driving east on Route 2. Ragsdale was checking the signal strength on his phone. After a little more than 5 minutes he pointed.

"There. On the left. Slow down, but keep driving," he said.

I let up on the gas pedal to let the car cruise, quickly dropping below 40mph and at the same time looking to my left. The gray Jeep was pulled under a plastic canopy attached to an old, weather-faded trailer. Lights were on inside the trailer.

"He lives there with his brother. The huge guy you saw at the gas pumps at last week."

I was rubbernecking, still watching when a tractor-trailer blew by me from the other direction. Scared the shit out of me.

"Christ, Hanlon. Don't get us killed before we get the guy," Ragsdale bellowed, a notch above his normal conversation level.

I gripped the wheel and swerved right, but the truck had already passed and we were feeling the wind draft caused by the speed when he went by. It was a narrow stretch of highway without guardrails, but I managed to stay on the road.

"Turn around up here and pull off to the side."

Watching my mirrors now to check if there was other traffic from either direction, I slowed, did a full U-turn, pulled as far off the pavement as I could and stopped.

"Good. Let's just wait for a bit," he said. I let the engine idle and kept my parking lights on.

"He has another car. A green Subaru wagon. I didn't see it back there, did you?"

"Nope. Space next to the Jeep was empty."

"Maybe big brother Haystack is out doing some business."

"You said you've been watching them for a while. So you know they're selling drugs?"

"Without a doubt. We think they're new to it. Somebody down country, for sure, is their connection. But I think now we're gonna have to nail 'em. Sooner rather than later."

"How'd you determine they're dealing?" I asked.

"Like everywhere. Some guy gets busted for something stupid. Wrecking his car, breaking into a house, smacking his girlfriend," Ragsdale went on.

"Local cops find the guy's got some drugs. Didn't get the stuff mail order. So, we watch him to see who he visits, or who visits him."

"And you brought it back to this guy?"

"Pretty much. It's the younger one. Works at a garage a few miles from here. Keeps to himself mostly. I've been watching them both since I got here in October."

"Does the big guy work somewhere?"

"Not a regular job. We've seen him do a few errands and hauling stuff in the Jeep."

Another semi went by, also traveling west. Also pushing the speed limit for a rural highway. I turned the heat up and kept the engine running. Ragsdale pulled a small pair of pocket binoculars from his duffel.

"Too early to be in for the evening," he said, putting the binoculars to his eyes. "Let's stay right here."

Leon Blevens was watching a program about junkyards across America. It was a new show, or at least new to Leon. He looked up when his little brother came inside.

Jarvis went to the sink, turned on the faucet, and let the water run while he got a tall glass from the dish drainer. He filled the glass and drank most of it in one long swallow.

Leaning his butt against the sink, he watched Leon watching television.

"Back early," Leon said, eyes still on the TV.

"Change of plans. I'm headed back out in a few minutes."

Leon lowered the volume, turned to look at Jarvis.

"We got somebody to see tonight?"

"No. Still a little more work with my guy in Gorham," Jarvis replied, filling his glass again from the faucet. He drank the water this time in two long gulps.

"You fuckers keep playing cute and *no one* is leavin' here," Branchik said.

He stood over Brousseau, who was now seated back on the sofa and hoping to avoid more slaps or having the gun pressed against his ear.

"So, do you and Stevo hold hands when nobody's around?" Branchik barked with a laugh as he stepped away from the sofa.

Gerard said nothing. Branchik walked backward to the kitchen, keeping his eyes on Brousseau and holding the pistol at his side. From a cupboard he took out a glass, placed it on the counter, and then went to the refrigerator. He opened the freezer section, pulled out the bottle of vodka. With one hand, he removed the stopper and poured.

Holding the glass just below his chin, not drinking, he took on the menacing stare again. He raised the gun to shoulder level, holding it sideways and aimed directly at Brousseau.

"I don't really like guns. Too fucking loud, too easy to go off by accident. Somebody's always got a better model than you have. Little guys think they're *big* guys when they have a fucking gun."

He took a pull on the vodka, still aiming the pistol and maintaining eye contact with Brousseau.

Sixty

A vision of his father flashed through his mind. It was during the winter holiday season and they were coming out of a department store in Holyoke.

Stephen was only 6 years old. His father spotted a man walking in front of them. They stopped and his father knelt next to Stephen.

"Stay here. Don't move," he said.

His father stood, took a few quick steps, and grabbed the man by the elbow. Stephen recalled his father getting very close to the man's face as he spoke to him. The exchange was brief; the other man turned pale and said nothing.

His father turned away, came back to Stephen, taking his hand, and they continued out of the mall to the parking garage. His father didn't talk on the short ride home. A week later, his father was dead. It was three days before Christmas. Three days before Stephen Rivera's 7th birthday.

Now, 35 years later, driving on a dark, quiet road with few other cars out, Stephen was experiencing a strange sensation. Looking at the interior of this vehicle built for military use, now popular with some in the SUV crowd, he gazed at the mirror on the windshield in front of him. His face didn't reflect how he felt. A real fear for his life gripped him like the onset of a nasty cold. His throat was dry and scratchy. He coughed twice and wasn't sure he could speak.

The mirror showed his dark brown, almost black eyes as calm and natural as they always were, a feature that had helped him more than once in his life. Since his teenage years he'd been aware of his ability to convey to others a self-confidence and steadiness that didn't match how he really felt.

Alone in the car at this particular moment, the eyes in the mirror looked as though they belonged to someone else. He was also conscious of an unwillingness or inability to embrace the cold, mean, detached violence he often saw in others. He never had the stomach for it.

On the seat next to him was the bag with the new cell phone. He'd be at the chalet in a few minutes and would again be face to face with a real psychopath. If he knew anything, he knew that Branchick would kill Gerard and kill him, and eventually kill the girl.

Jarvis was yet again behind the wheel of the Jeep and thought about what he would do when he got back to the ski chalet. He started the engine but hesitated before backing out. He thought for a few seconds about what he was getting into.

The Winchester was now lying against the side of the passenger seat next to him, barrel resting on the center console between the two seats and aimed at the back seat. He opened the glove box on the dash and saw Leon's old Smith & Wesson target pistol was there, under some papers and highway maps. It was a small .22 caliber, but might come in handy. He took the gun and a half-empty box of shells and placed them on the seat next to the rifle.

Jarvis put the Jeep in reverse and backed out of his driveway onto the road.

"**Here we go. Kill your lights.** Junior's gonna take us somewhere," Ragsdale said.

The small guy had come out of the trailer, climbed into the Jeep, started it, then sat there for a minute. Now he was backing onto the highway. The tail end of the Jeep backed in our direction. When he was out of the driveway, he proceeded east, back in the direction of the New Hampshire border 15 miles away.

"Wait," Ragsdale put his left hand on my arm before I put the Honda in gear. "Let him get around the curve before you pull out," he added.

I waited. When the taillights disappeared a couple of hundred yards in front of us, I checked my outside mirror, switched on the headlights and my left turn signal, then slowly pulled back out onto the road to follow the "likely-sometimes-poacher, without-a-doubt drug dealer."

"When you see him, adjust your speed to his and keep a good distance between us," Ragsdale directed.

"Got it. Just like on TV."

"You don't see a lot of 4-cylinder CR-Vs on any cop shows that *I've* ever watched."

"Just a matter of time. Hell, they'll be driving hybrids all over the place before you retire."

She felt like she was going to vomit again. It had happened during the past couple of days, but she now had a real sense of why people said "I have butterflies in my stomach." Deciding that it was because she had eaten so little for what must be more than a week, she breathed deep gulps of air and hoped that she would *not* get sick.

The men in the other room had gone quiet. Bunny was paralyzed with fear.

She didn't hear Stephen come back into the house. She didn't hear the bald man force the other man to go downstairs. She didn't hear the voice that spoke to her earlier, asking her *who are you*. She didn't hear her mother, sitting alone, also in a strange room not a hundred miles away, sobbing, trying to hold on to her strength and hope for her missing daughter.

Sixty One

"Ragsdale's got the radio guy with him. The FBI twins are still out there. And the early results from the ME confirm what we suspected," Merchand said.

On the phone with his boss, State Police Commander "Jake" Hewitt, Merchand had just arrived home. It was three minutes before six. Two hours of additional sleep would be wonderful. His cell phone buzzed as soon as he stepped inside the house, before he could get to the bedroom.

"Give me the highlights," Hewitt responded.

"Exact time of death's not fixed yet. Lab says the body was there more than a week, maybe late on the 29th or 30th . They'll be more precise in the writeup. The guy was sodomized. Fifteen separate stab wounds; the slashed throat finished him," Merchand added.

"Some really sick people out there." Hewitt paused, then added, "Doesn't seem to be getting any better, does it?"

"No, it doesn't. When we get this kind of activity, gives you a better perspective on what they're dealing with in the big cities."

No response, but Merchand could hear Hewitt taking a breath at the other end.

Jarvis slowed as he approached the driveway. The winding dirt track was on the opposite side of the road. It led almost a half mile up to the ski chalet.

He turned in, stopped, and looked down at the phone on the seat next to him. It showed signal strength of three bars, no indication of new voice mail. His watch read 6:10. A very light snow had started again. He turned the headlights to park.

As he was about to continue up the driveway, the Hummer pulled in next to him and stopped. The driver lowered the passenger side window and Jarvis saw that it wasn't Brousseau but Stephen Rivera behind the wheel. He rolled his window down so they could talk.

"**Drive past them,**" Ragsdale said.

The Jeep sat at the bottom of a dirt road just off the highway and a dark-colored SUV pulled in next to it. It was higher off the ground than most. Ragsdale got a better look at it.

"Go a bit farther and turn around. Pull over and kill your lights."

I checked the rearview and outside mirrors for other traffic. Once out of sight of the two parked cars, I made another slow U-turn as I had 20 minutes earlier, switched off my headlights, and drove back along the shoulder until I could see the taillights of both vehicles. They were more than 100 yards up the road from where I'd stopped.

"If he's doing a deal, stay with the Jeep. Don't let him see you pull out," Ragsdale said.

The cars in the driveway ahead didn't move. Ragsdale tapped numbers on his phone and stayed focused on the parked vehicles. He put the cell phone to his ear and hit the button to lower his window a few inches.

"Hey. We're out watching the little brother in Bethel. I think he's about to make some cash. Where are you?" he said. I could hear a voice but not the reply on the phone.

"No. He's by himself, driving the big boy's Jeep. Pulled over talking to somebody in a Hummer. Have you seen that rig before?" More talk from the other end.

"They're pulled in on a dirt road off the highway. I'm with Hanlon, the guy from Vermont. We're in New Hampshire, maybe a mile into Shelburne." Ragsdale glanced at me as he spoke and continued listening to the person on his phone.

"OK. If I need you, I'll call back." He clicked off.

"Jeffereys. He's at The Skidder watching the parking lot," Ragsdale said, as he put his phone into a coat pocket.

Up ahead, the Hummer was moving forward, going up the dirt road. The Jeep stayed put.

Branchik looked at his watch, then took another swallow of the vodka. He was leaning against the wall at the top of the stairs, alternating his gaze from Brousseau, seated on the sofa, and the kitchen window that looked out over the driveway. No sign of Stevo's return in the Hummer.

Rivera had been gone for more than an hour. It was approximately 30 miles round-trip to Berlin and the drugstore. He should've been back by now.

And there he was, the SUV cresting the top of the driveway. A light snow had started again, scattered flakes falling in the path of the headlights.

Sixty Two

Rivera parked in the same spot in front of the chalet. Looking up at the center window on the second floor, he caught a glimpse of Branchik.

Pushing off the wall where he'd been standing, Branchick walked to the window. He watched as Rivera came to a stop next to the Audi, letting his engine idle for a minute before shutting it off and getting out of the car.

The light snow was picking up. The flakes were larger and melted as soon as they hit the warm hood of the Hummer. Stephen watched for a second, then took the plastic bag with the new phone, climbed out of the car, and went inside. Stamping his feet to remove snow, he placed the bag on a bench, removed his parka and vest, and hung them on the wall next to the other winter garments.

"We're still here, Stevo. Come on back to the party," Branchik said in his smart-guy tone.

Now at the bottom of the steps, gun in his right hand, glass in his left, Branchik sidestepped and motioned with the gun for Rivera to go upstairs in front of him. Gerard was standing near the steps waiting.

"Have a seat, ladies," Branchik said.

Brousseau went to the far sofa. He looked as tense as someone attending mass for the first time in 40 years. Stephen remained standing, trying to give off a vibe of reassurance. He didn't know how well it might work this time.

"Sit," Branchik said, pointing the gun at Rivera. "We'll go over the plan."

Stephen looked at him, hesitated, then went to the other sofa and sat across from Brousseau.

"I have a better idea for your young guest in there," Branchik said, waving the gun toward the room where Bunny Singleton had been held against her will. "She'll be leaving with us," he added.

"Where are we going?" Stephen said, in a voice calmer than he might've imagined under the circumstances.

"You and the girl will go with me. In the Chevy. Gagnon here will drive his Quebecois assault vehicle and go ahead of us. We're going to Connecticut."

"I have to... be back at work.. Monday," Gerard Brousseau stammered.

"You can phone it in, sweetheart. You may need a few extra days," Branchik said, glaring at Brousseau.

"Where in Connecticut?" Stephen asked.

"I have some friends. Private little farm near Hartford," replied Branchik. "Too much activity up here to wait it out."

"What about my car? Can't we take -   " Stephen began to ask before Branchik cut him off.

"Somebody will fucking bring you back to get it later. This is *your* house. We need to deal with the girl *first*."

Stephen didn't respond. Gerard remained silent as well.

"When we get to the Vermont/Mass border below Brattleboro, we make the call to the feds. Start the process," Branchik said. He looked directly at Brousseau.

"You'll stay in front of us all the way. I mean no more than two car lengths. I see any stupid moves, you're gonna be wearing a lot of glass from the back window. And a couple of fucking slugs in the back of your head."

The Jeep backed up and turned around. It hadn't moved after the SUV pulled out earlier, now it was back on Route 2 and headed east toward Bethel.

Five seconds later, I eased onto the highway. When the Jeep gained distance ahead of me, I put my lights on and picked up some speed. Ragsdale was back on the phone.

"Yeah. Looks like we had a sale. We're gonna follow him back to Maine. I'll let Merchand know, but you're closer. Can you come over?" he said. I presumed he was talking with Jeffreys again.

"We'll wait at the Bethel Truck Stop," Ragsdale said.

"Hop to it, kid. I'd really like to get back home

tonight," he added, as he hit the end-call button and held the phone in his lap.

I let the Jeep get farther ahead of us and within a minute put on my turn signal, pulled into the truck stop for a second time, and parked in the same area where we'd parked earlier.

"He'll be here pretty quick," Ragsdale said. "Drives a white GMC pickup."

"Yeah, I saw it when he came to fetch me at Melby's this morning," I said.

"I'll go with him. We'll go pay a visit to Junior and his brother at the trailer."

"You going to arrest them?"

"Nah. Just put a little fright into them. See what they do. Bust won't happen for a day or two, that's when we bring the state guys in. They love it."

"You want me to follow you?"

"No, when Jeffereys shows up, you drive back over and cruise up that dirt road. See where it goes. See if you spot the Hummer somewhere. We'll meet back here."

"**Come back when Gerard calls you.** Maybe a couple hours". Jarvis now had new directions, this time straight from Stephen Rivera, who was driving Brousseau's Hummer.

The conversation was brief and Rivera pulled away and headed for the chalet. Jarvis was now headed home to wait, again. The annoyance at being jerked around was escalating by the minute. *Not* the kind of treatment he'd put up with much longer.

Driving, he thought about Marco and, in contrast, his straightforward "this is a good business and we all can make some money" approach. While he wasn't crazy about the cracker Marco sent as a courier, he thought he *could* put up with him. Only have to deal with him briefly every few weeks. And the guy might not be around forever.

Parking next to the trailer once more, Jarvis put the target pistol and shells back in the glove box, and got out. He reached in for the rifle and placed it in the rear, behind the back seat. They might be going out again later. On occasion, customers spent a few minutes sitting in the Jeep when the exchange took place. When that happened, it was Leon up front and Jarvis riding in back. Jarvis always led the conversation and controlled the transaction.

Jarvis was rapidly losing interest with characters who didn't know what they were doing. He would not hold his breath waiting for a phone call from two guys trying to unload a girl that was giving them problems.

Sixty Three

The door opened abruptly and the girl didn't move. She heard them come back up the steps and talk in the living room. Now the two men came into the room and the bald man stood behind them.

"Time to leave, Bunny rabbit," said the bald man. He seemed to be under the influence of alcohol.

His tone was harsh and frightening. He was holding a gun in one hand and a glass in the other. He reminded her of a loud, obnoxious guy she'd seen at a party at school.

She looked at them, focusing on the one who told her that his name was Stephen, the same man who'd offered her food, brought her bottled water, and allowed her to shower. He stared back, but said nothing. The other man, the one she thought was a friend of Stephen's, looked frightened.

"Little road trip, then you may get to go home to mummy and daddy," said the bald man. He laughed and added, "Right, Stevo?"

Stephen Rivera looked at him, then turned back to Bunny.

"We're going to leave together. It'll be OK." She didn't reply. And she didn't believe him.

Paul Jefferys really wanted to go home, too. A soon-to-retire municipal police sergeant – only 46, but with 25 years of service on a small town department in southern New Hampshire – he was now "on loan" to the Joint Northeast Counterdrug Task Force. The assignments and the hours were often unpredictable. Like now.

Jefferys was staying in a hunting camp owned by a friend for this particular deployment. When he got back from The Skidder later, he planned to spend time on his bird carving. But after two quick phone calls a few minutes apart, he was instead likely to spend the evening with Louie Ragsdale and others. The bird carving would wait.

The drive to the Bethel Truck Stop took 15 minutes. He pulled in, cruised slowly, and spotted Ragsdale getting out of a Honda CR-V on the other side of the lot. He drove over and stopped next to the Honda. He put his window down.

"Hey. Thanks for comin' out," Ragsdale said. "This shouldn't take long."

"Whatever," Jefferys said.

"I think he did a deal back up the road. Just across the line in New Hampshire."

"You said that on the phone."

"Yeah. So, you and me go knock on the door. Goose 'em a little. See which one gets nervous first," Ragsdale added.

"You said it was the little brother. Big guy wasn't with him?"

"Nope. By himself," said Ragsdale.

Jeffereys looked at the Honda. The radio guy was sitting behind the wheel.

"We gonna let him tag along?"

"Nah. He's going on a scouting expedition. Take a drive up the road where we saw the Hummer."

"See the plates on the Hummer?" Jeffereys asked.

"No. He left before we pulled out to follow the Jeep."

"Pretty expensive rig for this neck of the woods. Gotta be somebody from away," Jeffereys said. "Or one of the kids over at the prep school."

"I'm sure that's it," Ragsdale cracked. "Let me talk to Hanlon for a minute, then we'll take off." He turned and got back in the Honda.

"Bring her out here," Branchik said. He backed into the living room and waved the gun at Brousseau to follow, glaring at Rivera and the girl.

"We're talking *today*, Stevo. Like this very fucking minute!"

Stephen went to the side of the bed where Bunny sat. He hesitated, then unlike earlier, he firmly took her arm and forced her to stand. She resisted, but didn't lash out or put up a real fight.

"It'll be OK," he repeated, almost a whisper. "This will be over soon and you can go home."

He now held her right arm, placed his other hand on

her back, and forced her forward into the living room. She kept her eyes on the bald man.

Brousseau was in front of Branchik at the top of the stairs. Branchik put his empty glass on the coffee table. He grabbed Brousseau by the elbow.

"Wait. Let your sweetheart take the girl down first," said Branchik. "Get her a coat," he added, looking at Rivera and the girl as they crossed the room.

Stephen nudged the girl along in front of him and they passed within inches of where Branchik and Brousseau stood. As they went by, the alcohol fumes from Branchik were like a barroom that had missed its last round of disinfectant spray.

Downstairs, Stephen got a parka from one of the hooks along the wall. It was red, and like his own parka, the hood was trimmed with fur. The two other men had followed them down the steps and were standing next to the door.

"Wear this. It's cold," he said. He helped her put the coat on. He looked at her feet, turned, and got a pair of black over-the-ankle boots from a large wooden box next to the door.

"Put these on." She hesitated, then took the boots, sat on the bench, and pulled them on. They were a little snug.

Branchik watched. Gerard Brousseau didn't move a muscle.

Sixty Four

Jarvis came inside the trailer. The smell of pizza hit him as soon as he opened the door. He placed his phone on the kitchen counter next to the sink.

Leon was watching NASCAR highlights. He had a folding table, permanently in an unfolded, upright position, situated directly in front of him, four feet from the TV. On the table was a round tray holding half of a pizza. He held a partially eaten slice in his hands when Jarvis came in from the car.

"There's more pizza in the freezer," Leon said, not taking his eyes off the television.

Jarvis didn't respond. He took his coat off, placed it on a hook near the door, and then went to the refrigerator. Taking out some bologna and cheese, he got two slices of bread from a plastic breadbox on the counter, and put them into the toaster.

The TV program ended and a series of loud commercials came on. Leon got up from his chair in a process not unlike an elephant getting up from the ground. Jarvis watched him.

"How much do you weigh now?" Jarvis asked.

"More than anybody playin' in the NFL," Leon answered, big grin on his face. He brought the empty tray back to the kitchen, placed it in the sink, and got a liter bottle of Mountain Dew from the refrigerator.

"We're not goin' out, you said."

"Right. Not for a while. Still waiting for a call," Jarvis answered.

"What're you doin' in Gorham?"

"The guy from Montreal and his friend that owns the ski house. They need me to give somebody a ride."

The bread in the toaster popped up. Jarvis removed the slices, put them on a plate, and went back to the refrigerator. He got a jar of mustard and some pickles, then began putting together his sandwich.

Back in his chair Leon started surfing through channels, pausing for a few seconds at each stop. The variety of sounds and dialogue became a streaming jumble of noise that always irritated Jarvis, but he said nothing.

As he was about to sit down at the kitchen table with his sandwich, there was a loud knock at the door. Leon didn't seem to hear it. Jarvis went to the door.

A guy holding a pistol in one hand and a badge ID case in his other hand, looked right at Jarvis. There was a second guy standing off to the side of the door, also holding a pistol.

"Police," the first guy said, pushing his way past Jarvis into the trailer. Leon turned in his chair when he heard the word "police." The guy flashed the badge at him, not aiming the pistol at anyone, but holding it close to his hip. Another guy with a gun came in behind the first guy. No uniforms; neither of them looked like a policeman.

"Stay right there, big fella," Ragsdale said to Leon. He looked back to the kitchen where Jeffereys was in position standing close to Jarvis, who hadn't moved a foot since he'd opened the door.

Ragsdale did a slow scan of the interior of the trailer. It was a dark, cramped, unpleasant place to be. Worn, threadbare furniture, stacks of magazines, a pile of DVDs scattered in one corner near the huge screen TV, a lamp on a table, and two different folding tables in a small living room. And the very large guy in the recliner staring at him.

Both men kept their guns at their sides. Ragsdale moved into the living room and stood near Leon in the chair. Jarvis paid no attention to his sandwich, he was staring at Jeffereys.

"We'd like to have a little chat, fellows," Ragsdale said.

I turned the Honda and headed west again on Route 2. As Ragsdale instructed, I headed back to where we'd observed the drug deal earlier.

He wanted me to go to the spot where the Hummer drove away, just across the line in New Hampshire, follow the turn-off and see where it went. Then come back to the truck stop and wait. The road was coming up on my left. No traffic in either direction; I slowed and turned in.

It was a gradual ascent, curving up the side of an embankment away from a brook, a solid-packed road covered in fresh snow. Within a half-mile there was another road on the left, a driveway. Much farther along I could see distant lights, maybe a farm.

I kept going up the hill and would check the driveway on the way back down.

Waving with the pistol forward, Branchik paraded everyone outside. He popped the trunk on his Chevy.

Not taking his eyes off the other three, he reached into a sport duffel inside the trunk, removed something, and placed it in his pocket. He stood, closed the lid, and stepped closer to Rivera and the girl. Brousseau was standing next to the Hummer.

"Ride in the back," Branchik said to the girl. "It's gonna be a long trip."

Turning her gaze back to Stephen, she didn't move. He gently pulled her arm toward the car and opened the rear door. The snow fell off as he opened it.

As she bent forward to get in, Branchik stepped close to the girl and jabbed her in the right thigh with a syringe. She gave a startled yelp, began to turn, then collapsed with Stephen catching her before she hit the ground.

"Get her on the back seat," Branchik said.

Rivera pulled Bunny up so he could lay her across the seat. He positioned her on her side, folded her feet into the car, and stood up.

"Start it up. Get the heat going," Branchik said, handing the keys to Rivera.

Stephen got behind the wheel of the Chevy and turned the ignition. He pushed the heat lever to max, got out of the car and closed the driver's door.

Branchik gave a quick jerk with his head in the direction of Brousseau, who was standing next to the Hummer. Stephen walked that way.

"How much room in the back?" Branchik asked.

Gerard looked at him, shrugged, and said nothing.

"Open the tailgate. Let's have a look." Gerard walked to the rear of the SUV, hit the button on his key fob and opened the rear hatch.

"Lots of room," Branchik said, stepping close behind him to get a better look.

Branchik raised the gun and shot Brousseau point blank in the base of the skull. The shot made Gerard jerk upward. Then his body began to slump.

With a demonic grin on his face, Branchik pushed Brousseau's body against the spare tire on the tailgate. He raised his right leg and pressed his foot against the dead man's back to keep the body from falling over.

Stephen started to lunge toward Branchik after the shot, but stopped short when Branchik raised the gun and aimed it directly at his face.

"Don't wanna be stupid, Stevo." Branchik made a half-rolling motion with the gun.

"Let's get him into the car."

Sixty Five

"**You two get around a lot, huh?** Tell us about your travels," Ragsdale said, turning his attention to Jarvis.

"What were you doing up the road pulled over with the Hummer?"

Jarvis stared at him, but offered no reply. Ragsdale stared back. And waited.

Leon used the remote to mute the TV and started to get out of the chair, pushing on the arm rests to raise himself up.

"Sit down," Ragsdale said. "We're OK here. I'll tell you when you get to move."

"I gotta whiz," Leon said.

"Hold it. You can piss later."

Leon shifted, then settled back in the chair. Jeffereys came in from the kitchen and sat on a folding chair close to Leon. He gave him a hand signal to stay put, the same gesture he'd use with his dog to signal "stay."

No one spoke – Jarvis and Ragsdale staring at each other, Leon looking uncomfortable, and Jeffereys watching all 300+ pounds of him squirming in the recliner.

After a minute, Ragsdale stepped back into the

kitchen. His height and bulk gave him the advantage of physical intimidation.

"It's really pretty simple," Ragsdale said, standing over Jarvis by a good six inches. He put his gun back in the holster under his jacket and glanced at Jeffereys, who kept his gun in front of him and visible for all to see.

"We want to know who you're working with," Ragsdale continued. Jarvis edged back against the sink.

"*Somebody*, and there is a whole shitload of possible candidates, somebody is making sure that the Blevens brothers of Bethel, Maine are picking up a lot of unreported cash," Ragsdale cracked.

"And running a distribution system that the US Surgeon General would *not* be pleased to learn about," he added.

Ragsdale took the wiseass approach. He'd dealt with his share of young and dumb yahoos who thought they were way smarter than the average bear. He wanted to see how the clever younger brother would play this.

Jarvis stared some more, then finally spoke.

"He's not involved," Jarvis said, gesturing with his chin toward Leon.

"Stop right there, pardner. We've been shadowing *both* of you for a few weeks now." Ragsdale turned to look at the big guy sitting in the chair. He actually felt a flash of sympathy for Leon.

"Bubba may be your chauffeur, but trust me, he's involved," Ragsdale added.

Jarvis closed and opened his fists a couple of times, tilted his head forward and rubbed both eyes like he was just waking up. Ragsdale waited.

"It's a man from Massachusetts," Leon blurted. "Drives a fancy car. One a them Mercedes."

Jarvis raised his head and shot a look at Leon.

"Really?" Ragsdale said. "Probably has onboard navigation, built-in bluetooth phone. Maybe a fuckin' microwave oven."

"It's a BMW," Jarvis said. "*Not* a Mercedes."

"Oh. That's better," Ragsdale quipped, looking at Jeffereys before continuing.

"We need to know a little more about him. And like I said a few minutes ago, who's driving the Hummer you were noodling with up the road half an hour ago?"

A large white house, faded shutters, sagging front porch. Bit of a sag to the barn roof as well. Definitely an old farm.

Lights on inside the house and a mercury-vapor light over the barn. No sign of livestock outside, but the appearance of recent cattle shuffling in the snow inside a fenced area next to the barn. There was a dark blue Chevy pickup next to the house. A larger, older red Ford truck and a really old looking Case tractor, both parked off to one side in the barn.

I turned full arc near the barn and proceeded slowly,

watching the farmhouse in my rearview mirror. No one came out after I turned around.

6:38PM - 26°F, said my dashboard. I studied it for a second and thought about a web designer friend who explained the term "dashboard" in his work, used for management of information systems. Made sense.

Now headed back down the same road, I calculated that I could check the other driveway, see where it led, and be back at the Bethel Truck Stop in 15 minutes or less.

Stephen Rivera almost lost it as he lifted his friend's body into the back of the SUV. He thought he might still be alive, but checking the artery under his right ear lobe, the pulse was gone. Branchik watched him check the carotid.

Standing very close and keeping his gun hand free, Branchik pushed the dead man's legs into the rear compartment of the Hummer as Stephen lifted the body. They got him in and closed the tailgate.

"You drive," Branchik said, pointing the gun at the Hummer.

Stephen looked at him, then at the Chevy with the girl in the back seat.

"What about her?"

"She's not going anywhere. Shut it off. We'll unload the body and come back for her."

Hesitating, Stephen then stepped around the Chevy, opened the driver's door, and shut off the engine. He looked at the girl, she was still out. He pulled the keys from the ignition and closed the door.

"Let's go," Branchik motioned with the gun.

Stephen walked to the Hummer and got behind the wheel. Branchik climbed in the passenger seat.

Sixty Six

"Go ahead," Ragsdale replied with an exasperated sigh.

The big guy worked his way up from the recliner and started for the bathroom, which was off a very narrow hallway on the other side of the kitchen. Jeffereys stood up and followed. He waited outside the bathroom door.

Ragsdale took a couple of steps back and leaned against the wall to give Jarvis a little breathing room. Every place inside the trailer was cramped.

"Hot shots with flashy cars and lots of cash all over the place these days," Ragsdale said. "Tell me about the guy from Massachusetts." Jarvis said nothing.

Ragsdale raised his left hand and with his little finger, scratched the inside of his left ear and waited. Mr. We Have All Day Here.

"Look," he said, finally. "This fucking guy's gonna have more lawyers than you have friends. And *you* are gonna have shit. And *you* are going to jail. Don't be dumb. You help us, it might go a smidge easier when Bubba and you get in front of a judge."

Jarvis turned to look Ragsdale in the eye. Ragsdale

had the good sense to shut up. Maybe the kid would see the light.

"Leon's not part of this," Jarvis said. Ragsdale let him go on.

"I'm gonna help you, I need to be sure Leon doesn't have to go to jail."

"We'll work on it. No promises," Ragsdale said.

Jarvis did the eye-rubbing maneuver again, this time seeming to take a deep breath when he finished. He put his hands palm down against the kitchen counter, tilted his head back and stretched his neck.

"The man says his name is Marco. Like Marco Polo. He came here last summer. Stopped at the garage where I work, then called me a few days later."

Ragsdale waited for more.

"Said he needed someone reliable up here. Told me how to get the word out to people who needed some stuff. Said that I could make a lot of cash."

The toilet flushed and a few seconds later Leon was coming back to the kitchen with Jeffereys close behind.

"Let's sit and talk about this for a bit," Ragsdale said.

Jarvis looked at Leon, nodded, and the four men crowded into the living room for what Ragsdale hoped would be an enlightening conversation.

Stephen started the engine but didn't move the vehicle. He waited for the next command from Branchik.

"Up the road at the end of the driveway," Branchik said.

Stephen shifted into drive and moved forward slowly. Down a slight dip and at the end of his driveway he turned left. As he started up to the Campbell Farm, headlights of another vehicle were coming down the hill toward him.

Jarvis repeated and expanded the story about the man from Massachusetts, adding some snippets of phone conversations he'd had. He gave up the phone number he used to make contact. Ragsdale wrote down the number in a small spiral-bound note pad.

Telling about a delivery of drugs a week ago from a younger guy in a big-tire, shiny new pickup, Jarvis said it was the second time that guy had made a delivery. He did *not* say that Leon had been the one who received and *paid for* the last shipment.

Then Jarvis started to bargain.

"There are others trying to work this area. Not just Marco," Jarvis stated.

"I'm sure," Ragsdale said. "You know who they are? Maybe have a name or phone number?"

Jarvis looked at him before responding. He looked again at Leon, with only a passing glance at Ragsdale's partner Jeffereys, who was now standing against the wall and still holding a gun in his right hand.

"What can you do about the judge giving Leon, uh... some probation?"

"We don't know what all the charges will be. It's not going to be a slap on the wrist. For sure, *you* have been selling drugs. No way out of that one. You're gonna do some time."

Jarvis listened; Ragsdale went on.

"The more cooperation we get, the more likely the public defender, unless you know a lawyer, the more likely they can have some influence with the court. No promises. We're not authorized to make a deal."

Another car came out of the road below me and was headed up the hill. It would be a tight passage. Ten seconds later, I moved over to the right and geared down to first.

It was the Hummer. No front license plate. Looked like two people in the car. The driver turned his head my way as we passed, but too dark to get a good look at his face. I braked and slowed even more, letting them get farther along.

When the Hummer reached the top of the road behind me, I turned to the right, into the road he'd left a minute earlier.

Another short ascent up what appeared to be a driveway. It led to a large, flat, open area in front of a three-story, Swiss-style ski house with a small balcony on the upper level. Some lights were on inside. Two cars parked in front: an older, cream-colored four-door Chevy

Impala with New Hampshire plates, and a sporty looking, two-door silver Audi with Mass. vanity plates. It was low to the ground, had wide tires and alloy wheels. Both cars were parked facing the house and were 10 feet apart.

They were partially covered with the recent snowfall. Another car had been parked between them and tire tracks backed out, turned, and led down the driveway. The Hummer.

Slowly circling, I noticed a lot of fresh footprints in the snow. Most of the prints were in the area where the now-absent car had been parked. There were prints around the Chevy, as well. I pulled up closer to the Audi, stopped, and watched the house for any signs of someone looking out. Nothing.

I made a note of the license plate – CARPE D – then climbed out, let my car idle, and walked closer to the sports car. I was able to see through the top portion of the driver's window over the snow. Using the flashlight app on my phone, I could see two leather seats, earbuds, and a magazine on the passenger seat. The flashing red pinpoint light of the anti-theft alarm blinked on the dash.

Looking across the roof of the Audi at the other car, it was apparent that it had arrived more recently. While the Audi was covered with maybe 4" of snow, the Chevy had only a couple of inches. The snow had been brushed off the driver's door and the door behind it.

Still no sign from the house. I walked behind the Audi and over to the Chevy.

Sixty Seven

"**Stop. Who lives here?**" Branchik asked. Stephen braked the SUV.

"An old farm couple. The Campbells."

"How old?"

"Eighties. The old man might be ninety," Stephen replied.

They sat in the Hummer, blue lights from the gauges and the screen monitor glowing in the center of the console. Silent intermittent wipers brushing away the falling snow. Stephen watched Branchik, who was looking at the farmhouse 200 feet away.

"Drive over to the barn," Branchik said.

Stephen began to move forward slowly. When they were in front of the barn, Branchik held up his left hand to signal stop again. There was a tractor and an old truck backed inside the open section of the barn. It looked like some other farm implement was stored behind the truck.

"Let's give 'em a thrill," Branchik said.

Stephen looked at the barn, then back at Branchik trying to figure out what the monster was going to do.

"C'mon," Branchik said, opening the door to get out. "We're gonna put Frenchy in that truck."

Both men got out of the Hummer and walked to the back of the rig. Branchik still had the gun out. Stephen stood back from the tailgate.

Branchik's original idea, not shared with Stephen, was to cut off the head and hands, then position the body in the driver's seat. But his tactical military knife was in the trunk of the Chevy. So much for that thrill.

"We're gonna lift him to the back of that truck," Branchik said. Stephen stared at him in disbelief.

"They'll find him. I live less than a mile from here. He was my friend. Then... they'll find *me*. "

"You don't live here. You *visit* here. To ski. But you never fucking ski!"

"They'll connect the body to me." Branchik waved the gun in a dismissive manner.

"That's a fucking hay truck. It ain't comin out 'til next spring."

They stared at each other, then Branchik motioned to the tailgate.

"Let's do it."

They pulled the body out, Stephen holding his dead friend under the armpits. Gun still in his right hand, Branchik took the body under the knees. They lugged it to the back of the truck and lifted it up, almost five feet off the ground.

At the other end of the barn were cows, maybe eight or 10 of them. They were in milking stalls. Two cows watched; the others had their heads down munching hay.

Branchik looked around the inside of the barn. He spotted some old, faded canvas tarps rolled up and stored in the rafters.

"Pull one of those down," he said, pointing with the gun.

Stephen found a wooden sawhorse, pulled it over, and got one of the tarps. They unrolled it in the back of the truck, rolled Brousseau's body onto the tarp and continued forward as though they were rolling carpet. When they'd finished, the body was snugged up against the back of the truck cab. For extra measure, Branchik instructed Rivera to throw some loose hay on top of the tarp.

"**How many customers you line up around here?**" Ragsdale asked.

Jarvis didn't answer immediately, but he seemed to be calculating in his head. Ragsdale waited. Leon continued to shift in the chair again. Jeffereys gave the impression that he was at a prayer meeting, except perhaps for the gun in his hand.

"The Hummer. One of your regulars?" said Ragsdale.

"No.

"You were talking about football scores? Maybe some good spots to poach deer?"

"I don't poach," Jarvis said, a tinge of anger in his voice.

"Good. That'd add a problem to future discussions,"

Ragsdale retorted. "So, the Hummer. What were you doing there?"

Jarvis hesitated. This was, he believed, a bargaining chip. He wasn't sure yet how to play it. He looked at Ragsdale a few seconds longer. Neither of these two looked like real cops.

"Can you show me your badge again?" Jarvis asked.

Ragsdale was slightly amused, but pulled out the thin leather case with his Task Force photo ID and badge.

"We're the real deal, Junior. This isn't some hustle," Ragsdale said.

Jarvis took the ID and studied it, then handed it back. Ragsdale returned it to his shirt pocket.

"It's a different guy. He's trying to line up someone to sell drugs for him. Nothing to do with Marco," Jarvis offered. Ragsdale glanced at Jeffreys standing against the wall and Jeffereys gave an almost imperceptible nod.

Just before Thanksgiving, Ragsdale had speculated with Jeffereys and their boss at the Task Force that more than one group was trying to get a foothold on drug trafficking in the more rural sections of Maine and New Hampshire.

"Where's *this* guy from?" Ragsdale said.

"There are two of them. One from Canada, the other guy has Massachusetts plates on his car."

"The Hummer?"

"No. That belongs to Gerard. He's from Montreal."

337

Sixty Eight

I knew it was Bunny Turner as soon as I looked in the back seat. At least that was the *thought* and instant electric jolt that my brain felt.

Standing next to the Chevy pressing my cellphone light to the window, the body was right there, not moving. I stared for a couple of seconds before opening the door. Then I did open it, put my left leg inside, braced the back of the driver's seat and stretched my right hand to feel for a pulse.

Placing two fingers against her neck behind the left ear, looking at the side of her face resting on the seat, I felt a strong, steady pulse. She was alive. Her skin felt warm, despite the temperature outside.

I backed out, closed the car door, and looked at the house to see if anyone had noticed me. There were lights on in the house, but no activity I could see. I hit the recent calls list on my phone, found Ragsdale's number and pressed the tiny green phone icon to make the call.

"Yes," he snapped, answering on the second ring.

"It's Hanlon. I found her."

"WHAT? Where?"

"She's in the back of a car. Up the road from where we saw the Jeep and the Hummer parked."

"Is she alive?"

"Yes."

"Is she OK?"

"I don't know. She's unconscious, but breathing."

"Get her into your car. I'm on my way." He clicked off.

Ragsdale put the phone back in his coat pocket. He motioned for Jeffereys to step into the kitchen with him. They moved away into the hall close to the bathroom. Jarvis had watched and listened when he took the call a minute earlier.

"Hanlon found the girl. Not far from here." Ragsdale's eyes shifted toward Jarvis.

"Close to where we saw Junior talking to someone earlier," he went on, voice just loud enough so only Jeffereys heard what he was saying.

"You need to stay here," he added. "I'll take your truck and go to where Hanlon is." He looked back at Jarvis and Leon in the living room.

"I'll call Merchand on the way. Get one of his guys over here to give these boys a ride to the state police barracks."

Jeffereys nodded, pulled the keys to his pickup from his jacket, and handed them to Ragsdale, who was out the door without another word.

Turning back to Jarvis, Jeffereys walked over, placed a hand on his shoulder, and firmly pushed him toward the living room.

"Let's watch some TV," he said. He kept his gun pointing down at his side.

"You didn't need to kill Gerard," Stephen said, as soon as they were back in the cab of the Hummer. Branchik was looking at the barn.

"Of course I did, Stevo. He was a pansy. He woulda been with the cops the minute he got back to Montreal." Stephen looked back at the truck in the barn.

"Probably would've called 'em soon as he got through customs," Branchik went on. "He was a fucking weasel."

Stephen was all too familiar with Branchik's name-calling and crude descriptions of virtually everyone he came in contact with. His demeanor had amused others, but it was something that made Stephen uncomfortable from the day they'd first met.

Branchik waved the gun at the steering wheel as he held Rivera's gaze.

"Time to get the girl. Let's go," he said.

Stephen looked back at the farmhouse to see if anyone was aware of their presence on the property. No sign. He started up the Hummer, put it in gear, slowly moving through the snow, out to the road that would take them to Bunny Singleton in the back of the Chevy.

Sixty Nine

Ragsdale was driving well over the speed limit. The truck had good tires, he was a good driver, and he wasn't concerned about the wet, snowy conditions. The highway hadn't yet been plowed.

When his call went straight to voicemail on Merchand's phone, he tried the Maine State Police, requested a trooper be sent to the Blevens' trailer off Route 2 in Bethel, and asked the dispatcher to have Merchand call him just as soon as he checked in.

Wipers going, the soft, steady snow in big flakes still coming down, Ragsdale was 20 minutes away from the turnoff where they'd seen the Hummer.

I backed my car closer to the Chevy, positioning it so I could get Bunny into my front seat. I got out, walked around to the passenger side of my car, and reclined the seat slightly, leaving the door open.

It occurred to me that it would be easier to pull her from the back seat of the Chevy, then lift her into my car. And it was. Once I got her upright, resting against my left shoulder, I was able to lift and move her into the front seat. She opened her eyes for a second, rolled her head, and was out again.

Reclining the seat another notch, I positioned her so the back of her head rested on the seat support. I pulled the seat belt out, reached across her and fastened it. As I closed the rear door on the Chevy and got back behind the wheel of my car, headlights were coming up the driveway toward me.

It was the Hummer.

Pulling up next to me, nose to tail, the driver's window went down. The man behind the wheel looked at me, but said nothing. Hard to get a fix on his features; he looked to be in his late 30s, maybe 40. There was another person in the passenger seat I couldn't make out.

"Wrong place. Sorry. I was looking for a friend's house," I said, putting the car in gear.

The driver continued to stare at me. His passenger said something that made him turn away and look at him.

I pulled out and started down the driveway, back to Route 2.

"Is this the car we saw leave earlier?" Branchik asked. Rivera looked at him without answering.

"*Earlier*," he repeated. "The Canuck said it was the snowplow guy."

"I don't know this guy," Rivera answered. The Honda had pulled away from them.

Branchik jumped out of the Hummer and went to the

Chevy. Gun in his right hand, he yanked the rear door open with his left. The girl was gone.

"The fucker has the girl," he shouted, jumping back into the Hummer. Stephen's mouth opened slightly as though he were about to say something, but nothing came out.

"Get the asshole!" Branchik shouted louder, waving the gun in the direction of the departing vehicle. Beyond them, the Honda was beginning to descend the driveway.

Stephen turned the Hummer wide around the Chevy, accelerated back the other way, and saw the taillights go out of sight.

"Don't lose the motherfucker," Branchik yelled, leaning forward in his seat.

"**Jesus Christ and Pope Francis**," I muttered to myself. "And all the help you can send." The Hummer was coming after me.

The driveway descended nearly a quarter mile to the other road. Then it was about a mile back out to Route 2. The snow was wet and maybe three inches deep. I hadn't seen a snowplow anywhere.

I shifted down to second gear and accelerated as I turned onto the road I'd driven 15 minutes earlier. The lights from the Hummer were coming over the rise behind me in the driveway.

By the time I reached Route 2, they were closing the distance. I looked at Bunny Singleton in the seat next to me. Her head was tilted away as though she was looking out the window. I was pretty sure that she was still unconscious.

Taking my phone from the tray between the seats, I hit the redial on Ragsdale's number and pushed the speaker-phone icon. I put the phone back on the tray and kept both hands on the wheel. I turned right, heading east, back in the direction of Bethel.

"Where are you?" Ragsdale was saying on my phone.

"Just pulled onto Route 2. The Hummer is coming after me. They showed up just when I got Bunny into the car."

"Head for the truck stop. I'm 5 minutes away."

The Hummer was turning onto the highway not 50 yards behind me.

Seventy

The shot sounded like a distant crack of lightning. It apparently hit the back of the car near the top of the rear window, but the glass was still in place.

I goosed the Honda and was up over 60. The Hummer closed on my bumper, less than a car length between us. Then he pulled out to go around.

Holy shit. He's gonna force me off the road.

When they got right beside me, the passenger window was down and a bald guy was pointing a gun at me. I swerved to the right but didn't leave the highway. This isn't going to last.

Just ahead was a commercial log yard on the right. There were industrial lights on poles scattered around the yard. There was room to turn in and *maybe* get turned around. If I did it right, the Hummer would go past the entrance before he could turn.

It didn't work. The Hummer stopped abruptly as I went into the log yard.

Instead of turning around to face him head on, I drove through the log yard. 10 feet high stacks of tree-length, mill-ready logs were spaced all around the place. I went left toward the far end of the yard. Out on the highway, the Hummer backed up and was coming for me.

Ragsdale saw two sets of headlights down the road, maybe a half-mile away. Then they were gone, as though both vehicles had turned off their lights. He pressed the gas pedal and watched for cars behind him.

Now he could see it; both cars had turned off. The sign read *Petrosemolo Lumber and Log Yard*, Gilead, ME. It was a large open area just off the highway.

Jerking the steering wheel to the left and sliding as he turned, Ragsdale had the driver window down when he heard the shots. He grabbed the phone when it slid into the corner of the dashboard in front of him.

"Hanlon," he yelled.

I turned, the car fishtailed. In the seat next to me, Bunny's body shifted but she didn't wake up.

When I turned into the slide, the car fishtailed again the other way. Weaving and trying to maneuver in and around the logs, my left front fender clipped the corner of a log and that stack began to roll out in front of me.

"Shit!" I jammed the brake pedal and stopped inches from the logs now spreading out like a box of giant toothpicks spilling onto the floor.

Backing up to go in the opposite direction, the Hummer was right there blocking the way out. It stopped in front of me and the guy with the gun jumped out. He left his door open and immediately shot both my front tires. The front end dropped on one side, then the other.

"Hanlon." I heard Ragsdale's voice. He was still on my phone there between the seats.

"Are you still with me?" Ragsdale was asking.

"They just shot my tires. We're in a log yard," I shouted, not sure he could hear me.

"I'm right behind you. Stay in the car," he yelled back.

Branchik looked in at Rivera behind the wheel of the Hummer.

"Open the tailgate," he barked, crouching to keep cover behind the passenger door while watching the front end of the Honda. Nothing appeared to be happening with the driver in the Honda. He didn't get out.

"OK, asshole. Step out *real slow*," Branchik yelled. "Keep your fucking hands in the air."

Nothing. The guy still didn't leave the car.

Branchik raised his gun and rested it on the open window of the door. He aimed at the driver's side of the windshield in the Honda.

"Five seconds, dickhead," Branchik said. "We want the girl. Now. And maybe you can get out of here alive."

Nothing.

Then the sound of another car somewhere behind

him. Branchik looked away over his right shoulder. He saw the glow of headlights above the logs. The lights were moving toward him.

I looked at Bunny Turner on the seat next to me. She was still out. I thought about her parents in that coffee shop at the hotel in Augusta. I could see her father's smile when he talked about Bunny getting after him for not keeping his cell phone on.

The vision of Carol Turner's face was clear to me as she'd stood at the press conference a week ago. I could hear her voice.

"We want to know that our daughter is safe." The reporters hadn't made a sound when she spoke to them.

The guy with the gun yelled that I had 5 seconds to get out of the car. I knew he would shoot the windshield. Maybe *not* a good time to stay in the car. Duck? He'd come around the side.

Opening the door slowly, raising my hands as I got out, I stood next to the car.

"Smart move, asshole," the guy said. "Step in front of the car."

Seventy One

"Get the girl," Branchik shouted.

Rivera climbed out of the driver's side of the Hummer and went to the other side of the Honda. The dome light was on and the seat was tilted back. The girl was there, still unconscious. But the door wouldn't open. The guy watched him and said nothing.

"The door's locked," Rivera said. He looked at the guy who'd been driving, now standing there with his hands in the air.

"Cute," Branchik said. "Unlock the fucking car." He stepped forward and kept the gun raised. "Real slow," he added.

The guy reached in with his right hand and hit a button on the driver's door. The locks clicked.

Ragsdale stopped the truck, pulled his gun from his holster, and got out. The glow of the car lights shone in a high arc behind a stack of logs. They were probably 100 feet away from him on the other side. Along with the reflection from lights on the poles, the snowflakes appeared to be the largest he'd ever seen.

The stacks of logs 30 feet apart went in all directions. The car lights were on the other side of a stack ahead of him on the left. He heard a voice and moved in that direction.

"Put her in the Hummer," the bald guy said. He took another step closer to me, holding his arm straight at shoulder height. The gun was aimed at my head.

The other guy walked around my car, opened the door, and started to unsnap the seat belt.

"Police. Drop the gun. Do it. NOW!"

I looked to my left and Ragsdale was on top of the logs.

The guy wheeled around and fired a shot. He jumped back behind the door of the Hummer and fired again. Then a shot from Ragsdale hit the front end of the vehicle. The guy scrambled to the back and went to the driver's side and got in.

The other guy ducked behind the passenger side of the Honda. I squatted to a crouch, ran around the tailgate and came at him from the rear.

It was like high school football practice and a 200-pound tackling bag. I went into him hard with my right shoulder and wrapped both arms around him. The force took both of us into the snow and we slid forward.

Another shot was fired and the Hummer backed up to turn around. The guy under me was squirming and pulling at my arms, but not with a lot of strength. I released the bear hug and raised myself to one knee, then hit him twice as hard as I could. The first punch caught his left ear, the second hit him square in the nose.

The guy grabbed his face. A lot of blood, real fast.

When I pushed myself up, Ragsdale was coming down off the logs. The Hummer was moving away. I got to my feet and looked at the open car door. Bunny Singleton was still unconscious.

Ragsdale stood over the guy on the ground. He gave him a little kick in the ass, then knelt down to frisk the guy for a weapon and found nothing.

"Don't fucking move, pardner," he said. The guy was still down, holding his nose with blood seeping between his fingers.

"Sit on him," he said to me. He turned to go after the Hummer.

I didn't sit on him, but rested my butt against the hood of the Honda with its flat front tires. If the guy made a move to get up, I was ready to go at it again.

"Call 911. Get Merchand," Ragsdale yelled as he ran around a stack of logs chasing after the Hummer.

I went to the back of the car, opened the tailgate, and pulled a towel from my soccer gear bag. When I took the towel and threw it to the guy for his busted nose, he accepted it without a word.

"Do what my friend says and we'll be OK here. Don't move," I said. The guy bunched the towel in his right hand and placed it over his nose.

"Keep your head back. Might help."

When I got my phone from the car, it showed the call in progress connected to Ragsdale's phone had been going for 14:03. I broke the connection and punched in 911. Bunny Singleton had her eyes open. She looked really groggy, like a person coming out of anesthesia after an operation.

I told the woman at the other end that we had an unconscious kidnap victim and some other injuries. I told her where we were. I knew that Gorham was the closest town with an ambulance only a few miles away. Then I found Lt. R. Merchand in my contacts and pressed the call button again. It was ringing.

On the other side of the log yard I heard a shot. Then a second shot.

The distinct throaty sound of the Hummer's engine accelerating is what I heard next. It was going away from us.

Then I heard nothing.

Seventy Two

Merchand answered the call and said that he was headed out the door. The dispatcher had called him a few minutes earlier and another trooper had been sent to where Ragsdale's partner Jeffreys was babysitting the Blevens brothers at the trailer.

He asked where I'd found the Turner girl and I told him. I told him about the guys chasing me, the shoot-out in the log yard, and that I was pretty sure the shooter had escaped in the Hummer.

"Stay with the girl," Merchand ordered.

On the ground in front of me the guy with the bloody nose was now leaning against a log, ass in the snow and head tilted back. He had the towel to his nose and gave no indication that he wanted to get up.

As soon as I clicked off with Merchand, I went over to Bunny Turner. Her eyes were closed again. I took her right hand and held it in both my hands.

"You'll be OK. We're here to take you home."

She opened her eyes, looked at me for a few long seconds, said nothing, and closed her eyes again.

Branchik took less than 5 minutes to get back to Rivera's ski chalet. He wouldn't take the time to check for more drugs and cash in the house. He needed to get away from here *now*.

He parked the Hummer, but kept the keys. Then he got into his Chevy, started the engine. Using the sleeve of his coat, he brushed snow off the windshield and rear window enough to see. A light crust of ice remained on the glass. The snow had stopped.

Two minutes later he was on Route 2 driving toward Gorham. An emergency transport van with lights flashing passed him headed in the other direction. Then a New Hampshire State Police cruiser with light bar flashing and another police car following it went by.

Branchik stayed under the speed limit all the way through town. He would pick up Route 3 and go south.

Col. Jake Hewitt got the call from Merchand, then placed his own call to Special Agent Guidi, who told him that the two field agents were still in the area. They would be sent to the log yard east of Bethel.

Guidi said that he would call Bunny Turner's parents and would send an agent to bring them to the hospital in Berlin.

"We've started a search for a dark colored Hummer," Hewitt said. "Shooter got away a few minutes ago."

"**Total fucking scumbag,**" Ragsdale said as he came walking around a stack of logs.

"Shot the tires on Jeffereys' truck," he added.

I was certain Ragsdale had been shot by the guy in the Hummer.

He walked over to the guy sitting in the snow and gave him a good kick in the leg.

"OK, dipshit. Stand up." Ragsdale still had his gun out. He was reaching around the back of his jacket as he stood over the guy. The guy was looking up, still holding the towel to his face.

"Get up. Now." The guy put a hand on the ground and pushed himself up. He was taller than Ragsdale, thin build, probably just over 6'.

"Put your hands behind your back. Turn around real slow." The guy did as he was told, dropping the towel to the ground. The bleeding had stopped, but his was nose was really swollen and showed traces of blood.

Ragsdale managed to pull plastic flex cuffs from his back pocket, shifted the gun to his left hand, put the cuffs on the guy and, using only his thumb and index finger, quickly pulled the plastic strip to tighten the cuffs.

"Stand right here. Two steps and I'll shoot you in the head before you take a third," Ragsdale said. The guy didn't move.

My phone vibrated and chirped at the same time. I looked at the screen. 911 Emergency Services. The same female voice I'd spoken with a few minutes earlier was now telling me the ambulance was approaching the log yard. She would patch me though directly so I could give directions.

While she was connecting us, I heard the siren and saw lights flashing out at the highway. I told the EMTs to follow the car tracks in the snow around the stacks of logs at the back end of the yard.

"You'll see a Honda CR-V. We're next to it," I said. "You should see the lights."

Ragsdale was now at the car door standing next to Bunny. I heard him talking to her but couldn't hear if she responded.

Seventy Three

Within 20 minutes, there were five police vehicles on the scene. Two cars from the New Hampshire State Police, a Coos County Sheriff's SUV, a squad car from the Town of Gorham out at Route 2 at the entrance to the log yard, and Merchand's cruiser from Maine, which had just pulled up in front of us.

The EMTs placed Bunny Turner on an ambulance stretcher, moved her to the back of the van, hooked up some monitors, and departed for the Androscoggin Valley Hospital in Berlin, approximately 10 miles to the north. I called Carlos Singleton to tell him that Bunny was safe and on her way to the hospital.

"My God," he said in a soft voice, then went silent. He was clearly choked up.

Briefly I described where we were and what had happened. He wanted to call his sister and brother-in-law.

Before the ambulance left, Ragsdale had one of the EMTs take a look at our guy in handcuffs. He gave him some aspirin and water, then placed a gauze pack in his nostrils. The guy was in the back of one of the police cruisers with a trooper standing guard.

Merchand, Ragsdale, one of the other New Hampshire state cops, and I were all gathered next to the cruiser Merchand was driving. Ragsdale was talking.

"The rig had a blue and white Quebec license plate - X14 237." He was repeating information he'd given earlier on the phone with the NH state police. I presumed there were other cops out looking for the Hummer.

"The guy is stocky, maybe 5' 10", bald, wearing a dark jacket and jeans. Headed back toward Gorham when he took off," he added.

"What's this guy have to say?" Merchand asked, looking at bloody nose over in the NH cruiser.

"Nada," said Ragsdale. Merchand looked at me.

"Say anything to you when you were rolling around in the snow?"

"Nope. Didn't put up much of a fight," I replied. "Went passive on me and hasn't said a word."

Merchand looked at the NH trooper and the sheriff, then back at the cruiser. He took his hat off, rubbed a hand across his short hair in one swipe, and put the hat back on.

"Take him to your barracks," he said to the NH trooper. "The feds will be all over him in an hour anyway."

After a little more discussion, it was decided Ragsdale and I would ride with Merchand. Two of the NH troopers were taking the prisoner in their car. The other NH trooper was stretching yellow tape around. I knew forensics people would be there soon to look for the slugs from the gun and anything else they thought important.

"Take a look at the rear window on the Honda," I said to the trooper. "He shot at me before we came into the yard."

The sheriff's deputy was staying behind to coordinate two different tow trucks coming for my car and Jeffreys' pick-up.

"Show me where you found the girl," Merchand said when we pulled onto the highway.

"Up ahead a mile or so. Road on the left. No sign," I said.

Branchik did his convenience store routine. This time in the town of Jackson, New Hampshire, at the foot of Mt. Washington.

He bought a large coffee, an apple pie snack in a small box, paid, and left them on the counter while he used the restroom. He needed a good hit before starting the drive south.

Three minutes later he was back at the car, trunk lid open and checking the cash he'd stowed from the Portland deal. It was still there along with his "other" supplies in an old beat-up athletic bag. He closed the trunk lid and got back behind the wheel.

The snowplow had made a recent pass on Route 16 and the road was good. Branchik took his time. It was always a strange sensation, jacked up on coke and still being able to drive like an old lady her first time out in a new car. He always had to be careful not to go *too slow* that it would draw attention to his driving.

Up ahead a man was walking at the side of the road. He was on Branchik's side, walking with traffic and not facing oncoming cars the way most pedestrians did. As he drove past him, Branchik could see that the man staggered, and appeared to be drunk. He pulled over ahead of him and got out of the car.

"How you makin' it there, pop?" Branchik yelled. The guy tried to pick up his pace a little, happy to get a ride.

"Where you headed?" Branchik asked when the man was closer to the car.

"Jes' down the road a ways," the old guy said. He reached to open the door, but it was locked.

"Really bad night to be out," Branchik said. He raised the Sig, rested it on the roof of the car and shot the guy in the center of his forehead. The old man fell backward into the snowbank.

Branchik got in behind the wheel of the Chevy and left the door open. He sat and let the release ripple through his body. Slowly he pulled the door closed and put the car in gear.

Branchik laughed as he glanced in the rearview mirror pulling away from the body.

"Dumb old fuck."

Seventy Four

We couldn't believe the Hummer was right there, parked next to the snow-covered Audi. But the other car, the one where I found Bunny Turner, was gone.

The lights were still on inside the house, no sign of life. Ragsdale got out of the car first, gun in hand. Merchand got out and pulled his gun from the holster. I got out and followed.

Walking around the Hummer, Ragsdale opened the passenger door and held his gun up. Nothing.

"You said the other car was a Chevy?" Merchand asked.

"Yeah. Tan-colored Impala four door. Hadn't been here long," I answered.

"Plates?"

Shit. Once I saw Bunny in the back seat, I didn't look closely at the license plates.

"New Hampshire plates. I didn't get the number." Merchand looked at me.

"The girl was in the back seat. I thought she was dead. When I realized she *wasn't*, I called Lou. Then I got her into my car."

It was exactly what I'd already told him. Merchand watched me and nodded as I offered the explanation again. He kept his gun at his side.

Ragsdale was moving toward the house.

Carol Turner was sobbing. She held onto her husband's embrace and they didn't speak for a long minute.

Stanley Turner pushed back from his wife, removed his glasses, and placed them in the left pocket of his jacket. He sat on the edge of the bed and put his head in his hands. He began to weep.

"We have to go, Stan. I'll just be a minute."

She went into the bathroom of their hotel room. She'd get her composure back and be ready when the FBI agent arrived to take them to New Hampshire. Bunny was safe.

"We'll make the announcement together," Col. Hewitt said. He was on the phone with Agent Guidi.

"As soon as the parents arrive at the hospital, you give me the signal," he added. "Brief statement issued to the media tonight. Press conference at noon tomorrow."

"OK by me," Guidi responded. "Any more on the guy who got away?"

"Cops all over New England looking for a light-colored Chevy Impala. We *think* it has New Hampshire plates, didn't get the number. The sports car belongs to the guy they brought in."

362

"Rivera. We have a prelim on him already," Guidi said. "The New Hampshire state guys called me. Home address listed in Chicopee, Mass. Appears as though he's had previous interest from both city and state cops down there. What about the SUV from Quebec?" he added.

"Dealer plates. Registered to a company with dealerships all over eastern Canada. Still checking."

They talked for a couple of minutes about Merchand's phoned-in report of the log yard confrontation and shoot-out. They agreed that it was fortunate nobody was killed.

"Could've been a lot worse," Guidi said.

"Then there's the Farrand girl. And the body at the vacation house up in the woods," Hewitt said.

"Still, by any standard, pretty gruesome business," he added. Guidi did not disagree.

Bunny Turner was being attended by a nurse and a physician's assistant in the emergency room. She was awake, less groggy than before, but remained subdued.

Appearing to be physically unharmed, the nurse and on-duty ER doctor had examined her within minutes of her arrival. She now had an intravenous drip tapped into a vein in her right arm. They told her that her parents were on the way to the hospital.

"What about Marcia?" Bunny asked.

The nurse replied that she didn't know about her friend and that the state troopers would be back when her parents arrived. In fact, a New Hampshire trooper was posted outside the emergency room at that very moment.

Branchik was now in North Conway. He would follow the secondary roads through the Lakes Region of New Hampshire, take his time, and could still be in Massachusetts at daybreak.

Of course, there was the very real chance that a description of his Impala was out there and that other law-enforcement agencies along the way could be a problem. On the rear seat was a 12-gauge pump shotgun.

The plastic zip bag containing cash from the drug sales was now under the front seat. The military-style tactical knife with 3.6″ blade was in a leather case once again strapped to the calf of his right leg. The Sig, with a fresh clip of eight shells, was on the front seat next to his phone.

He was pretty sure he could deal with a traffic stop if it came to that.

Seventy Five

We were in the state police offices in Berlin, New Hampshire. Ragsdale leaned against a window frame, I sat at a desk, and Merchand was walking around talking on his phone.

Once we determined there was no one else inside the ski chalet and Bunny Turner's clothes were found in a bedroom, it was obvious she'd been held there. Merchand declared the feds would handle the inside out, down to the dirt in the carpet investigation of the house. Clearly their jurisdiction in the kidnapping.

And it was in New Hampshire, not Maine. At this point, all Merchand could do was keep communications going.

The guy with the busted nose was identified as Stephen Rivera, age 42, from Chicopee, Massachusetts. Ragsdale said it was one of several cities in the western part of the state known to be a base for drug dealers. The proximity to I-91 made it easier for runs up and down northern New England.

And Rivera was talking. During the initial questioning, according to Ragsdale, who participated with a New

365

Hampshire state cop, Rivera identified the shooter who took off in the Hummer as Arnie Branchik, someone he'd known for several years.

Branchik had arrived unexpectedly over a week ago, he said, and dumped the girl at his house. He said there was another girl in the car when Branchik left that same night. He *claimed* that he knew nothing in advance about the abduction.

Then Rivera told about Branchik shooting his friend, Gerard Brousseau.

He revealed that Branchik forced him to help get rid of the body. Another state police trooper was dispatched to the farm to check on the story about Brousseau's body. I figured, all told, there must be a dozen police cars from two states out on a snowy night working this remote area.

Counterdrug Task Force member Paul Jeffereys was happy to be relieved of his babysitting duty with the Blevens brothers. They were now en route to Augusta, shackled in the back seat of a cruiser, with two Maine state policemen as their escort.

When told about the shoot-out and events in the log yard and that his truck was being towed, Jeffereys reclined on a chair and stretched his legs. He'd wait at the Bridgton barracks for Ragsdale to return. It did annoy him slightly that Ragsdale's vehicle, recently detailed and prepped for winter, was still out front, locked up and with four good tires.

366

The black Chevrolet Suburban with tinted windows, flashing lights mounted on the dashboard and on the tailgate, came roaring north on Route 16. It slowed abruptly and entered the parking lot of the Androscoggin Valley Hospital. It was a few minutes after 11:00.

The driver pulled close to the Emergency Room entrance, got out, and opened the rear passenger door, allowing Carol and Stanley Turner to climb out and enter the hospital. Stanley Turner thanked the FBI agent who'd brought them from Augusta. A minute later, a nurse's assistant was leading them past the New Hampshire state trooper and into the room where their daughter was resting.

Bunny turned her head when the door opened and her parents entered the room. Tears she didn't think were there welled up in her eyes. She held both hands to her mouth and found it difficult to breathe.

Carol Turner rushed to the bed and took her daughter in her arms. The sobs came in jerks and Bunny's upper body shook. Her mother didn't say a word and they held their embrace.

Stanley Turner stood behind his wife. He put a hand on her shoulder and found Bunny's hand, giving it a tight squeeze. The state trooper closed the door. Both he and the nurse's assistant gave the Turners privacy.

Nearly 200 miles to the south, four hours away, Carlos Singleton packed a bag in preparation for an early-morning drive to northern New Hampshire.

Since the phone call informing him that his niece was safe, Singleton had shifted into an almost Zen state of going through physical activities in a deliberate silence that would have surprised even his most ardent admirers. The calm that overtook him was matched with a mixture of joy, relief, and aching sadness.

Earlier in the day, Carlos and his sister, in a phone conversation, had again discussed the incredible grief that had swallowed the Farrand family. Singleton knew they'd find an unspeakable bittersweet flood of emotions in the news about Bunny.

Marcia Farrand's life had been stolen. Her family, her friends, and people who never knew Marcia, all were cheated of promise and the gifts the world would now have to look to others to provide.

Seventy Six

By mid-morning on Sunday, we learned about the body of a man murdered in Jackson, New Hampshire. Video, as well as a description from an employee at a nearby convenience store, implicated the same man Rivera had identified as Branchik.

The "Be on the Lookout," with Branchik's most recent arrest photo, was sent to every police department on the East Coast and would go national within the hour.

The car registered to him was identified as a 1996 Chevy Impala, tan, four-door. It had been purchased at a government auction and was, in fact, a former unmarked police car. The man who'd bought it at the auction then sold it to Branchik a year ago, not long after he was released from prison.

Gerard Brousseau's body was retrieved from the barn where Rivera said it would be found. The old farm couple there seemed oblivious to things that had occurred the night before. Police in Montreal were to contact relatives of Brousseau.

The FBI, with assistance from both New Hampshire State Police and municipal police from Gorham, were doing a thorough search at Rivera's house. Both the Hummer and Rivera's Audi were about to be hauled to an FBI impoundment facility outside Boston.

My car, with a badly cracked rear window and two flat tires, was hauled to a service station in Gorham. Jeffereys' pickup already had new tires and was back in his possession.

"There will be additional information forthcoming. Count on it," said Col. Jake Hewitt, as he finished reading a 2-minute description of events and arrests.

FBI Agent-in-Charge Gary Guidi, in a crisp white shirt, dark-green necktie, and dark-brown pin-striped suit, nodded in agreement. He declined Hewitt's invitation to further address the media.

Twenty-seven people from newspapers, TV stations, the Associated Press, and three radio stations crowded the conference room at the Maine State Police headquarters in Augusta. They jockeyed for the best camera angles and closer proximity to the podium.

Hewitt suspected that before the day was over, more reporters would be nosing around the log yard and other areas in the Bethel, Maine/Gorham, New Hampshire region.

"Will we be able to talk with the Turners?" a young woman reporter asked. Hewitt looked at her, then responded.

"I believe that *someone* from the family will be available to speak to you later. Perhaps this afternoon, or tomorrow," he said.

The reporters jumped on that and they began talking over one another, several questions coming at the same time. Hewitt held up a hand to signal a halt to the chatter.

"We'll be in touch. As soon as *we* know it, and when it's appropriate to this ongoing investigation, *you* will know it." He turned away from the reporters and he and Guidi went back to his office.

Turned out the service station didn't have tires to fit my car. But they'd have them later in the day and would send the car to a glass repair shop for the rear window. As far as the badly dented front fender and seriously cracked headlight lens, I figured that would be a couple of thousand bucks more when I got back home, mostly for the headlight.

Ragsdale had gone back to Bridgton to get his rig, and said he'd give me a ride to the motel where I was staying. It had been a long night. A lot of coffee this morning, three donuts, and some orange juice, but I was still hungry. When he arrived, we decided to stop at Melby's for a real lunch.

"I need to tell you something important here, Casey Kasem," Ragsdale said as I climbed into the passenger seat.

"Yeah. What's that?" I fastened my seatbelt.

He stared at me and let the engine idle. We were parked in front of Cloukey's Sunoco waiting to pull onto Main Street in Gorham.

"You need to learn... *how... to... use... a... gun.*"

"I'm not so crazy about guns," I said.

"There's an enlightened attitude. You keep doing this 'Radio Rick' private-eye stuff, you can always throw your phone at the bad guy." He held the look.

"Maybe take that little digital camera and bash in some windows on your own."

Even with the smirk, his tone was a notch above being a wise guy. Now I gave him the stare. No traffic on the street, but he wasn't pulling out yet.

"I'm serious," he went on. "You *see* what's going on in the world. There are a lot of *nasty people* who are not impressed with charm and persistence."

Looking up and down the street, he eased out and we headed east on Route 2.

Seventy Seven

Wilhelmina Bonita Turner left the hospital with her parents. It was early afternoon, bright sunshine and blue sky after the snowfall the night before.

The same FBI vehicle that delivered Carol and Stanley Turner to the hospital the previous night was now taking the family back to Augusta. The agent driving the SUV was now followed by two fellow agents who'd arrived earlier. The agents had video-recorded a brief, preliminary interview with Bunny in the hospital room. Guidi and others would wait until tomorrow for the full debriefing.

Before releasing Bunny, and after consultation with a colleague, the ER doctor had suggested an herbal antidepressant anxiety medication. She said that it was quite mild and less likely to be addictive, but that it had proven to be effective. There was concern and a lot of talk about the residue of chloral hydrate in Bunny's bloodstream. And that she was still undernourished from a week without proper nutrition.

Earlier in the day, when her parents told her about Marcia's death, but not all the details, Bunny had wept inconsolably. Now, three abreast in the back seat of the SUV, she rested her head on her father's shoulder while her mother held her hand.

The drive east to Augusta would take 2 hours.

After lunch, made shorter by little conversation, mostly Ragsdale commenting on various songs coming from the speakers in the cafe, he took me back to the motel.

Waiting in the car he read a magazine while I had a quick shower, and put on a clean shirt and socks. A few minutes later we made the return trip to get my car.

"Whaddaya gonna do with the money?" he asked. I sensed another wisecrack coming.

As a kid, I'd often heard my grandfather asking people what they did with the money. "What money?" "The money they gave you for singing lessons, because you sure spent it on something else," etc.

"The *reward*," Ragsdale said. "They hired you. You found her," he added.

"Uh… I'm not sure it's going to work out that way," I answered.

"Hey. They had the FBI hotshot right on camera saying 25 big ones for 'information and the safe return of their daughter'. She's safe."

"I know that. But I *believe* that was an effort to engage the public. It was a couple of days after Marcia Farrand's body was found. They were scared out of their wits."

"Yeah. And *who* found the body?" Ragsdale was enjoying this little taunt, but there was a touch of playful seriousness in the question. I didn't respond.

He kept tapping the seek button on his radio, not leaving it set for more than a few seconds on any one station. A few minutes later, we pulled into the service station and my CR-V was parked out front. The NH state trooper at the log yard had told us earlier that the shot hit right at the top of the window and ricocheted somewhere into a snowbank. So I now had four new tires *and* a new rear window.

"Part of the money can pay for your tires," he said, pointing at my car.

I got out, went inside, and settled up with the young guy on duty. They had my credit card information and the total came to $987. While he processed the payment, I wondered for a few seconds how the insurance company would view all this and if I might get stuck with the entire bill. Would my policy consider this work-related activity?

When I got into my car, Ragsdale waited while I started the ignition. I left the driver's door open and walked back to his car. He put the window down.

"Don't forget, Private Eye," he said.

"Don't forget what?"

"Olympics, 1959. California R & B group. Look 'em up."

I let that vital information soak in for a couple of seconds while I studied his expression.

375

"I'm guessing that you probably did *not* have a lot of dates when you worked in radio."

"Not true," Ragsdale responded. "That's when I met my wife."

"Thanks for the ride. And the lunch," I said.

"We'll talk again, I'm sure." He put his window up and pulled back onto the street.

I needed sleep , so I went back to the motel. My body was absorbing the adrenaline from the past 24 hours and I felt like I'd been hit by a truck. Coat on the chair and shoes on the floor next to the bed, I was asleep in a matter of seconds.

When I woke up, I had to think about where I was. It was dark and the clock next to the bed showed that it was 5:38. I got up, went to the bathroom, then opened the door to look outside. The first light before dawn was showing on the hills to the east.

Fiddling with the coffeemaker in the room, I figured that I'd slept for nearly 12 hours.

Seventy Eight

Early Monday afternoon I was back in Vermont. Phone calls first with Carlos Singleton, then Lt. R. Merchand of the Maine State Police and I was up to date with all that was going on back there, including the news that Bunny Turner had not been sexually assaulted.

Carlos said she was "better than one might imagine" considering the circumstances, but that she was truly distraught over the news of her friend Marcia.

"How do you ever recover from something like that?" he said.

We didn't speak for a few seconds before he went on to say that we should plan to meet later in the week, probably in New Haven with Bunny and her parents. He would work out details and let me know.

A phone conversation with Ragsdale was longer than the other two. More information matching the brief summary Merchand had offered in his call, most notably that police in southern New Hampshire had discovered the abandoned Chevy Impala in a parking lot near the Rockingham Park race track.

"This fucker is really bad news," Ragsdale said. "Rap sheet goes back over 30 years and it's been getting progressively worse."

He was describing one Arnost Waclaw Branchik, born in 1970, grew up on the lower west side of Chicago. And in trouble with the law from a very young age.

"Early arrests for predictable juvenile stuff, then robberies, a couple assaults, a rape charge he beat. Came east 10 years ago, busted for assault again in Connecticut. More recently he did 3 years in Berlin as part of a chop-shop ring. They really had quite a spree through New Hampshire before state and local cops broke it up and five guys went to jail."

"What about the Rivera guy?" I asked.

"We're pretty sure he had his own drug operation in western Mass. Never seems to have been nailed in the past, but his luck just ran out. Still claims he knew nothing about the kidnapping. Says Branchik just showed up with the girls."

"What's Branchik's connection to Rivera?"

"That's what we're working on. Drug Task Force guys in Boston are working with the FBI. They'll have something before the day is over. Rivera will take a deal."

We were on the phone for another 10 minutes, with Ragsdale doing most of the talking. He ended with an invitation.

"Listen. You did OK. I know I yanked your chain a lot,

but you *really* need to learn something about firearms." I didn't respond. He continued.

"If you *never* do another gig like this in your life, you're still gonna be better off knowing how to protect yourself." I laughed and went for the bait.

"C'mon, Louie. That sounds like a standard NRA recruitment pitch. Do I get a jacket patch, too?"

"Maybe. But I'm tellin' ya, it's for your own good. I can take you to a shooting range and a top instructor less than an hour from your house," he added.

We agreed to drop it and "explore" the idea over lunch sometime during the holidays.

Seventy Nine

Branchik broke the shotgun down and stashed it in the woods near the shopping mall. He stuffed the plastic bag of cash into his pants and walked across the parking lot. There was a thrift store on the other side of the street.

It was early and the woman behind the counter was startled by his entrance. She had just unlocked the front door a minute earlier. He saw her jump and place a hand on the counter.

"Sorry," he said. "I just need to get some good clothes. Got a job interview this morning."

The woman relaxed and showed him the racks where men's used clothing was displayed. It took 5 minutes to find a clean, dark-gray suit, size 44, with two-button jacket, a white long-sleeve shirt, socks, a belt, and a decent pair of shoes.

"Can I use the dressing room?" he asked.

"Behind one of those curtains," she said, pointing to the rear of the store.

He came back to the checkout wearing the new clothes, carrying the worn athletic bag with his old duds and the cash. He found a newer leather athletic equipment bag and a tweed hat, took them to the counter, and gave the woman $40 for everything.

At 9:45 on a bright, cold morning in Salem, New Hampshire, Branchik went across the shopping mall lot into the woods, retrieved the shotgun, and placed it in the bag with his cash. He put his phone in the pocket of the new suit jacket, threw the old clothes and bag into a dumpster. He kept the Sig 220 in the back of his waistband.

There was a convenience store just a half-block from the thrift shop. He would get what he needed, visit the restroom, go find another car, and confirm his meeting with Marco and Mr. Smooth.

Branchik would change more than just his clothes. He needed to become a different person.

There was unfinished business.

Acknowledgements

- *Two Lanes of Freedom* - Tim McGraw (2/13 – Big Machine)
- *Antalogia* – Shakira (10/95 – Sony Music/Columbia)
- *WHYY* in Philadelphia went on the air in 1954 and was a Charter member of National Public Radio in 1970.
- *American Pie* - Don McLean (11/71 – United Artists)
- *Gotta Serve Somebody* – Bob Dylan (8/79 – Columbia)
- *Scenes From An Italian Restaurant* – Billy Joel (11/77 – Columbia)
- *CHOM* in Montreal, on air 1963 as CKGM, changed call letters in 1971.
- *Hotel California* – The Eagles (12/76 – Asylum)
- *I Shot The Sheriff* – Eric Clapton (7/74 – RSO; written and also recorded by Bob Marley)
- *The Sounds of Silence* – Simon and Garfunkel (9/65 – Columbia)
- *Private Eyes* – Hall & Oates (1/81 – RCA)
- *Private Eye* - The Olympics (9/59 – Arvee)
- *Hairstyles and Attitudes* – Timbuk 3 (10/86 – I.R.S.)

Thank you for the music.

- Town of Waterford, ME (Neat place, cool website.)
- Peyton Place - Orford, NH (One of a kind.)
- C & A Pizza – Hanover, NH (My favorite pizza.)
- *Melby's* MARKET & EATERY – Waterford, ME (Great food!)
- The Senator Inn & Spa – Augusta, ME (Good place to stay.)

Unfortunately, *The Skidder* and *Tony's Italian Ristorante* (at least in Bridgton) do not exist. If they did, I would go for Open Mic Night *and* the mussels with linguine.

The author is a former broadcaster who lives in Vermont. He began his career as a reporter covering state and local events, government meetings, and political campaigns. And the real abduction and murder of two young women. But, you perhaps should again read the first paragraph on page 7. This is a work of fiction.

Excerpts from *A Quiet Evening in CONNECTICUT* – to be published spring 2015 – appear on the next two pages.

One

A pleasant breeze off the water, the sun dropping to the horizon beyond the city, and you might have believed that it was early June. In fact, it was a lovely, warm *April* Sunday evening in New London, Connecticut.

Easter Sunday. And despite the whistle of the Acela Northeast Amtrak train that had passed through a few minutes earlier, all the cars and trucks lining up in the parking lanes of the Cross Sound Ferry terminal, and the chatter of people in and out of the ticket office, there was a relative quiet to the evening.

No horns or car alarms, nobody yelling at kids, dogs that didn't bark or yip when owners took them for a quick walk just before boarding the ferry. It was as though some studio engineer had cranked the master volume control right down to that notch above zero.

That's when I realized that I still had my foam earplugs in and was just coming back from a nice restful nap.

Reclining in the Adirondack-style chair in front of the deli and snack stand next to the terminal, my back to the parking area and traffic, I'd fallen asleep 10 minutes earlier. I sat up now, earplugs still in, and watched an elderly man getting coffee at the takeout window. He was putting change in his pocket and turned to walk my way.

The man froze in place and dropped the cup. Coffee splashed on the sidewalk in front of him, onto his shoes and pant legs. His mouth was open, both hands stopped in mid-air, his eyes showing surprise. Or fear.

That's when I heard the shots somewhere behind me.

Eleven

She said it had to be them. No one else knew about the date and time when he would come over from New York. No one else knew who was going to meet him at the ferry.

It was our second phone call in 24 hours. I waited for her to say more, but she went quiet again.

"OK. If the police are ignoring you, if they don't believe this, what next?" I said.

Twenty Six

"They all know what's going on here," Ragsdale said. I wasn't so sure.

"Maybe. But my impression is that it's more *fear* than indifference."

"Guess we'll find out pretty quick," he replied.

Going back to Montauk and chasing an early run of striped bass was not likely at this point.

Forty

"How many chart hits did they have?" Ragsdale demanded. I had to think for a minute.

"Is this going to cost me money? *You're* the oldies guy. I don't wager with hustlers."

"Christ, Hanlon. Did you just *read* the news? Did you never *listen* to the music?"

He put a $5 bill on the table for a tip, stood up, and gave me his "I can't believe you don't know this" smirk.

Michael Perry Casey Hanlon and Louis James Ragsdale, out of Maine, out of Vermont and back for yet another spin with *A Quiet Evening in CONNECTICUT* – to be published spring 2015.

Made in the USA
Lexington, KY
03 October 2018